Never Have an Outlaw's Baby

Deadly Pistols MC Romance

Nicole Snow

Description

WHEN HE FINDS OUT ABOUT OUR BABY...OH, GOD.

SUMMER

I didn't have an outlaw's baby. Honest.

I didn't run, didn't hide our son, didn't suffer alone. There's *not* a bastard with a gun to my head, sending me running to the bad boy I left behind. Making me lie to everyone.

Yeah, I'm full of it.

Here's the truth – I'm frozen because I'm finally face-to-face with the wild, gorgeous man with the icy stare who lit me on fire three summers ago. Joker rocked me to my core, left me with a kid, and it's just a matter of time until he discovers everything.

Never have an outlaw's baby. They're cute, but they come with serious strings attached.

Like Joker's kiss. I can already taste it, the growl rising in his throat. Coming for my lips, coming for the truth, coming for *me*.

JOKER

Pure hell tore my heart out one night three years ago. There ain't room in that hole for Summer, a lyin' spitfire I swore I'd never see again.

I screamed, I shoved, I told her to get out, and stay out. Made myself numb so I'd forget about those lips I used to own, or having her between the sheets.

Worked like a charm 'til...the kid.

I know he's mine. Know something evil isn't adding up. Know he's the first light I've had in the darkness for years, and Summer's the second.

If she hates me, I don't give a damn. This baby changes *everything*.

She ain't running anymore. Neither am I.

I'll put my name on her sweet skin. Hear her beg the way she used to. Remind her that a woman never has an outlaw's kid without sharing his bed, his bike, his brand. Always.

The Outlaw Love books are stand alone romance novels featuring unique lovers and happy endings. No cliffhangers, no cheating, and a secret baby surprise! This is Joker and Summer's story in the Deadly Pistols MC series.

I: Times Gone By (Summer)

A real man leaves his shadow hanging over you, even after he's gone.

Three years to the day since he left, and I was still blinded by his.

Go ahead, judge me.

I wasn't stupid, or weak. God, I'd shed those words long ago after everything I'd been through since Jackson Taylor.

Illusions could sometimes fog up my heart, but they didn't get to my head. I knew who he was, what he was, and why he'd left his big, bad impression stamped on my heart.

And I knew the future, too – clear as fucking crystal.

The bastard was gone. He wasn't coming back.

That's what I told myself every single day, ringing up customers at the Jiffy Hen, hoping I'd lose another day without having to think much at all.

Didn't always work out that way. Hell, maybe never.

A girl has plenty of time to think about right and wrong when she's trying to pass the time. The past reaches up, takes her by the throat, and doesn't let go until she's shaking, cursing herself.

I thought about Jackson constantly, and I hated it. Day in, day out.

The passion, the loss, the empty hole he'd carved in my chest, the void that wouldn't heal, no matter how much time passed.

My body missed him too. My nipples still turned to pebbles every time I thought about that night, our last night together. That was the night he'd taken me the hardest, over and over, leaving a piece of himself behind forever.

I lived in his shadow then, except it was a whole lot more real.

His shadow crawled all over me like a furious demon that night, clinging to his body over mine. Jackson slammed every ounce of strength he had between my legs while his hand jerked my hair around like reigns.

He'd owned me.

I'd let him.

I'd loved it.

I cried out when he tensed and exploded, filling me, bringing me off so hard I scratched his back raw.

He might've been an absolute rat bastard, but the boy could sure fuck.

I had living proof of it waiting for me at home. The fact that he left me wet and wanting after all these years said something about the black magic he had in every kiss, every movement, every single time he shoved me under him and shook me to my core.

Of course, I hated it. I hated everything about it – the memory, the want, the prison of this life without him.

I even hated that I hated it. It wasn't fair.

God. God fucking damn it!

My eyes always pinched shut at the worst times, when it became too much, fighting back the tears.

I'd battled them ten thousand times by now. I lost more often than I wanted to admit, feeling the hot tears rushing out when I was alone in the backroom on my breaks, or in my car, or changing another diaper alone.

The memories chased me like wolves, night and day.

Relentlessly, hounding me, straight into the dark hollow I called my life.

I remembered him every time a loud motorcycle roared by on the busted up street.

The worst were the sticky summer nights, listening to the bugs humming in the trees through my crappy apartment window. We were entering the thickest nights now, here in Georgia, as alive with life and noise as they were long.

Those were the nights when I sat in my PJs after dinner, bad TV yammering in the background, fighting for distractions.

Those nights, I broke out the whiskey, toasting the times gone by before they put me in tears again.

Never more than a shot or two. I had to work early most days, after all. I was an adult now.

I stopped short of that sweet, ultimate buzz that would've laid me down, and let me forget. Not for my own sake, or because I wanted to make another helpless attempt to run away from the past, and the boy who'd left me in this lonely hell.

I had to do it for him. *Alex.*

Leaning over his crib, I reached down and stroked my son's brow. Nighttime helped hide how much he looked like the face I wished I could bleach from my head forever.

He'd just had his second birthday a couple months ago. Since the day he was born, I'd told myself I'd keep going, however hard it got. I'd live and die by my baby boy, and to hell with the old times wanting to get in the way of that.

Sure, days like this took the damned cake.

But they didn't stop me. Nothing ever would.

Not even when I remembered the short-lived forbidden romance, the fiery kisses, the passion that created the little miracle sleeping in the corner.

That was then. This sleeping, innocent baby was my now.

Alex trembled, yawned, and rolled over in his sleep.

I smiled, planting a long, desperate kiss on his forehead. "It's okay, baby boy. Long as it's just you and me, we can take on the world. You're going to be ten times the person I've been someday. A hundred times the man your father is, too."

I caught myself near the end, pulling away in a whisper. Had to be more careful soon. I couldn't keep talking like that unless I wanted some *very* hard questions ripping open old wounds.

In just a few more years, he'd be talking up a storm and going to school. A few years after that, he'd be thinking about life and big dreams, not to mention where he came from, wondering why he didn't have a father.

I didn't have an answer. Not even a noble lie to feed him, until he was old enough to understand.

And that made me want to break down all over again. I stood up, pulling my bottoms tighter, hugging myself as I stood next to the dark window, staring out at the lights in the parking lot through the blinds.

A drunken neighbor staggered through the darkness. He dropped a bottle, making a loud clang in the night, swearing to himself as he tumbled down to pick it up.

Fuck my life.

Fuck. Everything.

I'd put myself here because I'd gotten involved with the wrong man. Maybe I deserved it, misery as punishment, but the baby sleeping behind me sure didn't.

The longer I stared through the dusty glass, watching other tenants come and go, revving their old cars long into the night, the more it caught up with me.

Half an hour later, I buried my face in my hands.

I remembered everything. I hurt and bled over it, too. The harder and better I fought, the worse it caught up with me in the end, and tonight was one of *those* evil nights.

Oh, God. The times gone by swallowed me alive.

* * * *

Six Years Earlier

I was working at my Uncle Robby's bar after school when they came in. Two loud, hollering groups of frat boys, passing by for spring break, tearing through Seddon on the way to Atlanta, or maybe the beaches further south.

It didn't take them five minutes for the first one to grab my ass. The smug, shiny eyed asshole pinched it – hard – and eyeballed me a hundred times harder than the menu I'd just handed him.

"Yeah, I think I want the special," he said, shooting me a savage look. "How much for a quickie?"

He pulled his hand away to slap the table while his fellow assholes jeered, high-fiving themselves.

"Fuck, man, you looked so serious!" one of them said, roaring. "Keep it up and you'll have her panties off by sundown. These bitches love that shit."

Without missing a step, I retreated, fighting the urge to shoot him a dirty look over my shoulder. Past experiences taught me fighting back would only invite more trouble. I could still hear them by the bar.

"Have her bring us another pitcher, boys! We'll fuckin' save some for her when she gets off her shift. These bitches around here are all dirt poor trailer trash. They'll slobber your knob like their life depends on it for a couple drinks!"

Bastards. I swore underneath my breath, angrily punching the keys on the bar's old computer for the order.

Worst of all, the place was empty except for the dozen college boys, and maybe one or two drunken regulars over in the corner, staring sadly into their beers. Uncle Robby made a tidy profit from managing this place since I'd been a little girl – but he did it on the backs of the biggest losers and worst tourist chumps around.

Seddon attracted scum like a stagnant pond.

I served them, day in and day out, the last I could do to pay my uncle back for taking me in, now that mama was so sick.

I needed the money bad, too. Scrimping for bad tips here was better than nothing. I'd need every dime I could get with summer coming up, and no good future in sight.

Homework hadn't been going so well. I'd be lucky to graduate if I couldn't get my grades up.

College wasn't even on the radar. Not that I had any shame.

Walking away with a GED or a high school diploma was a big win in this town, and I'd at least manage that. The rest could wait.

If I could buy time, I'd lock down hope with it.

I'd just turned eighteen a couple weeks ago, after all. Time was on my side, ready to help me kick ass and take names.

There wasn't anything to worry about, except surviving yet another rowdy night, praying the pricks at the table wouldn't stiff me too badly on tips.

I tried not to laugh out loud because I already knew they would.

Half an hour drifted by. Scrambling to keep the tables supplied with cold beer and peanuts, I ran back and forth between the kitchen and diner, wondering why there was such a holdup with the round of burgers.

Uncle Robby was hitting the bottle again, which always meant he made mistakes as the bar's substitute cook.

Charlie, our one and only true chef, was out today.

I busted through the double doors and looked around, covering my mouth. The strong scent of burning meat hit me the second I was in, and I looked at the empty grill. My Uncle wasn't manning it anymore because he'd burned himself along with the beef.

I ran over, watching him nursing his hand, swearing up a storm as he halfheartedly ran it under water.

"Here, let me have a look," I said softly, pushing my way to the small sink. Several puffy red blisters were already rising on his skin.

"Oh, hell!" I let out a whistle and shook my head. "Ouch! Looks bad, Uncle Robby! You should take off and get it looked at."

"Shit, no, Summer. Can't be taking time away. Who the hell's gonna cook up the orders? I'm the only man here who knows how to make this shit when Charlie ain't here."

I looked around desperately, anxiety weighing in my stomach. Ugh, I couldn't argue with that.

Lately, I'd been paying more attention to the kitchen. I'd seen Charlie back here making sandwiches. Sometimes, I helped him with the prep work, slicing bread and veggies while he worked the grill.

"Fuck!" Uncle Robby tried to grip the spatula. He instantly dropped it from the pain, letting it clatter into the sink.

"Don't do this to yourself! I can take it from here, Uncle. I've watched you and Charlie cook *tons* of times! Go get it looked at. Trust me."

Wincing, he stared at me, his wrinkled face crinkling up before he let out a long sigh. "Okay, dammit. We'll try. Hurts like I picked up a fucking wasp's nest. You know where the meat and all the fixings are?"

I nodded. He hesitated for a minute longer before he finally headed for the door, stopping one more time and looking back at me. I was already pulling apart the frozen patties, ready to start cooking.

"You run into any trouble with the work or the money, you tell Tina, okay? She's in charge 'til I get back."

"Got it!" I hollered after him, breathing a sigh of relief when the door slammed shut.

I worked like a fiend in the kitchen. In no time, I had half the order ready, only stumbling a little bit when I plunged the fries into oil.

It all smelled heavenly. My stomach growled, and I smiled, glad that I'd finally had a chance to do something right today.

The small victories meant a lot. I couldn't do much to help mama with her bills or the sickness eating her up. I'd never be a grade A student. But, damn, if I couldn't cook like my life depended on it.

I was so busy prepping all the food I didn't hear the heavy double doors open.

"Yo, where the fuck's our eats?" a voice said behind me.

I spun around and came face-to-face with the same bleary eyed idiot who'd grabbed me before. My hands shot up, and motioned to the plates with burgers off to the side.

"Just a few more minutes! I'm sorry about the wait, sir,

we're a little short handed." Calling him anything besides *asshole* caught in my throat, but a little southern hospitality went a long way toward smoothing things over, especially in crisis situations like this.

"What the fuck?" He looked around. "There's only six plates here. Food's gonna be cold by the time you're done half-assing it! Let me help."

Help?! He couldn't be serious.

Before I could say anything, he lunged for the frozen patties next to me, haphazardly slapping them on the grill.

"Hey, hey! Stop! You need to go back to your seat. You're not allowed back here. I already told you, it's coming –"

"Bullshit." He shoved me to the side, grabbing the spatula out of my hand." Move over, doll, and let a man show you how the job's done. You can thank me later with those pretty little lips."

Great. Now, I'd have to scream for Tina, hoping she could hear me out in the bar. I couldn't leave the idiot here. If he started a fire, or burned himself…the bar couldn't take that kind of damage.

Besides, there was already some kind of commotion out there, judging by the shouts behind the door.

"God, just…I'm trying to be nice. Give me the spatula already, you dick!" I spat, reaching for his hand, losing my control.

Professional hadn't gotten me anywhere so far. It was time to fight for it, and hope he'd give up, stumble away from the kitchen.

He stopped, burning the burgers. Holding the metal

spatula away from me, he slammed it against the cook top. "What'd you say to me, bitch? Did you just call me a 'dick?'"

The asshole heard me loud and clear. He didn't ask again, just lunged for me, pulling me into his arms. I spun, careful not to fall face first into the sizzling grill, clawing at his neck.

"Stupid ass trashy slut! Why don't you forget about the food? Me and my buddies would rather have a piece of something else."

I froze, beating feebly against his back. His hands moved swiftly, defiantly, rummaging up my back, reaching for my bra.

This. Can't. Be. Happening.

Oh, but it was.

The bad day I'd tried to turn around was about to get a whole lot worse. I didn't have any hope of fighting off this drunken animal.

Time to scream. I opened my mouth and screamed bloody murder, until it seemed like my lungs would rip in two.

"Ah, fuck! You'll bust my fucking eardrums. Shut up!" He clumsily stuffed a hand over my mouth.

My vision blurred, and time seemed to slow down. He pushed me against the counter, holding me down, running his filthy tongue along his lips while the meat sizzled behind him.

I was too stunned, too terrified, to hear the freight train barreling toward us. The door burst open, and a split second later, they were on us.

Two big men clad in leather slammed into the frat boy so hard I nearly went flying to the ground with him. I caught the edge of the counter, screaming, and watched as two of the meanest looking twins I'd ever seen laid into the drunk.

I didn't need to see their faces a second time to know my would-be monster had just gotten himself into a universe of hurt.

The Taylor boys were *bad* news. The worst, actually, ever since they'd both joined the Deadly Pistols MC, a biker gang just over the border in Tennessee.

Rubbing my eyes in disbelief, I took a hard, long look at the killer angels in front of me.

I saw double. They were identical, except for the wild ink going up their muscular arms.

Twice the savage energy, twice the grief, twice the primal beauty.

Ruggedly smooth, chiseled as the Blue Ridge Mountains. Both boys were bigger than life. Just walking, talking, ass-kicking contradictions who swept in like a hurricane and left legends in their wake.

Seddon didn't have superheroes, and too many petty villains to count. But we did have the Taylor brothers, Jackson and Freddy. For this little town, they were enough, a two man freight train who left shattered bottles, blood, and desperate women wherever they went.

They'd come into the bar before, and barely said a word. Sometimes with their grandpa, Don. I'd served them once or twice, losing my usual pleasantries in sheepish whispers.

They usually found a quiet corner and talked among themselves, asking for beers and shots of whiskey, sometimes a burger or two on the side.

It wasn't my first time seeing them. But never like *this*.

Seeing Jackson give me the evil eye, sizing me up, before his face smoothed back into stoic calm…that was new. So was destroying a man in front me. The cold efficiency in every blow they pounded into the frat boy made me gasp.

It all happened so fast. They'd saved me, but I had to remember, these weren't good men.

Supposedly, they'd done all kinds of terrible things. I believed the legends, sure, but I also knew they tipped well.

Like, *really* well.

My best day ever working here was the last time I'd waited their table. I'd feared the worst, tip-toeing around with their orders, triple checking to make sure everything that came out on my tray was picture perfect.

There hadn't been a single complaint. Instead, I'd found a tip for the same amount as their tab waiting for me after they left, leaving my jaw dragging on the floor.

Now, they finished laying into the devil rolling on the ground, begging for his life before each brother delivered a couple more kicks to his ribs. Frat boy couldn't breathe, much less whine anymore.

I backed away slowly into the corner, wondering if they were about to kill this kid in my kitchen.

Jackson and Freddy weren't much older than the college boy, come to think of it, but they carried themselves like men in every way. They seemed older, darker, somehow wiser.

If it wasn't for their patches, I wouldn't have been able to tell them apart. They were both as big and beautiful as they were dangerous, two hazel-eyed, dark haired brutes packed with muscle.

Jesus, how was I supposed to talk to them if I couldn't remember them by name? *Think, Summer, think.*

Once, Uncle Robby spelled it out. He told me Freddy had the dagger on his leather cut, underneath his name patch. Jackson wore the smoking pistol, and he'd recently added two more, blood red patches underneath his name. Both skulls.

They'd taken road names since joining the Pistols. Anybody who didn't address them properly was begging for trouble.

JOKER, Jackson's patch said. Freddy's said PIECE.

Two ridiculous, weird biker names that should've left an ordinary person rolling their eyes. But there was no laughing, no doubt, no derision while they brutally knocked some sense into the jackass on the floor.

"That's enough, brother. We don't wanna lay him out. Can't have this little cocksucker bleeding all over the fuckin' kitchen back here," Piece growled, pulling back his twin brother.

Joker wanted to keep going. He stepped away reluctantly, his clenched teeth showing in a rough smile. He looked at me, stepping out of his brother's hold, extending a hand.

"You all right? We both came running, soon as we heard the scream."

My lips trembled. *I'm fine*, I wanted to say. Just brush it off like it was no big deal, but my eighteen year old brain cracked.

"No!" I squeaked, tumbling forward into his grip.

He held me. That shocked me to hell and back.

Jackson "Joker" Taylor was the last man in the world who should've swept a crying, down-on-her-luck teenager into his arms. But he did, swallowing me up in a bear hug as big as the world, holding me as all the crap I'd suffered for the last year or two came pouring out.

"Piece, drag the kid to the door and throw him the fuck out. His posse'll follow as soon as they see him hit the pavement. We've busted him up enough. They'll shit their pants when they see. Make sure they pay Tina, too."

"No, no, it isn't right. I didn't even get a chance to finish their order," I whined, too sad to see how little sense that made just then.

"Babe, don't you fuckin' worry about it. We got it taken care of. Everything. We'll make sure none of these shitheads ever show their rat faces anywhere around here again."

Frat boy groaned as Piece scooped him up. I listened to Joker's twin start humming a country tune as he pulled him out through the kitchen, no different than dragging out the trash.

Tina came rushing in a second later. Her eyes bugged out when she saw me wrapped up in Joker's arms.

"Holy Lord and Moses, Summer! What's going on back here? Should I get the police?"

"Fuck no," Joker growled, turning his head to face her,

without pushing me from his arms. "It's all under control, Miss Tina. Run along. I'll help the girl find her way home."

"You, Jackson? But her shift's not over 'til…"

"It's okay, Tina." Sniffing to clear my sinuses, I looked up, hating myself for being such a mess. "I'm going to stand by for a few more evening orders and then I'll go. Don't know when Uncle Robby will be back. He burned his hand real bad. I'll find a way home."

"Jackson, she doesn't get on that motorcycle unless you have a helmet for her," Tina said sharply, folding her arms.

"Dammit, Tina, it's Joker now. *Joker.* You use that Jackson shit again, we're gonna have a problem. Piece and me just did the bar a favor, unloading those motherfuckers. Make sure they're paid up when you check the counter."

Sighing, Tina threw up her hands. "Okay, whatever. I don't have a clue what this is about. You just…learn to keep your distance. Summer's a good girl. Her mama, Christine, don't need more problems, worrying about her daughter coming home with a guy like you. She's too sick for that crap."

Joker gave her an icy stare on her way out. His muscles hardened around me, and for the first time, I noticed how huge he really was.

He could've hoisted me up without breaking a sweat. Probably could've broken rocks all day long, just like the old timers talked about, back when the mines boomed.

He must've been two hundred pounds of perfect muscle. Maybe more.

Just a tall, dark, and dangerously handsome twenty-something year old man. Walking, talking, killing steel stuffed into human skin and slathered with scary tattoos.

I looked up, slowly easing myself out of his arms. God, why was it so hard to leave?

"Thanks for the help," I said softly, having a hard time keeping my eyes on his.

Those dark, hazel gems in his face had a grip even stronger than his hands. Every time I met them, I fell in.

I wanted to keep staring, sinking, defying every warning I'd ever heard about these men.

"Don't bother," he said, running a hand through his short, but thick hair. "This'll all be our territory someday, babe. We'd be fools not to lay down the law. We already own the fuck outta Tennessee. Gonna have Georgia, too, and the least my brother and I can do is start keeping order in our own damned town."

"You really grew up here?" I asked, walking over to the grill to push the badly burned burgers off it. "I mean, I already know you did. It's just hard to believe. This town makes too many boring men."

He chuckled, a rich, throaty sound that tempted me to get up close and personal. "Born and raised. Still come back every week or two to see our grandpa. Owe that man my left nut, and maybe the right one, too."

Crude. I smiled anyway, eyeing him over my shoulder while he realized how rough he was talking, muttering an apology.

"Shit, let's pretend you didn't hear that. How long 'til the end of your shift?" he asked.

"Maybe another hour. I just need to cover for Tina a little longer in case anybody wants food. Sounds like the crowd is clearing out after the rumble back here..."

"Yeah, my brother's out there, playing peacemaker. Don't worry. We'll make sure those fuckers gave your boss every cent she was owed. We'll leave some extra for the mess from our own pockets on top of it." His lips twitched, and he looked down at the blood drying near his boot.

"You don't owe us anything else," I said nervously. "You and Freddy have already been a big help. Really."

"Babe, his name's Piece. Mine's Joker. Get it straight." He looked at me sharply, and I nodded. Then he cocked his head. "Say, what the fuck was yours again?"

"Summer," I said, feeling my cheeks turn beet red. "Summer Olivers."

"Ah, yeah, grandpa used to see your ma to hash out his VA shit at the bank. Christine, right?"

I nodded. Talking about mama reminded me I really needed to check in with her soon, just in case she needed anything on my way home.

She was stocked up on prescriptions. The days when she'd ask me for snacks or water were becoming less and less, the nausea catching up with her a little more by the day.

I tried not to think about it.

"You don't have to hang around if you have somewhere else to be," I said. "Really, Joker. I can clean up and find my way home."

"Fuck that. You're going for a ride, whether you want to

or not. Trust me, babe, it'll do you some good to get the wind in your hair for a few minutes after the shit that went down back here."

"Okay, well...fine." I looked at him and smiled, instantly dropping my eyes when he returned the glance. "I'll wrap up as soon as I can."

"Whatever. You let me know when you're ready to go. I've got a beer to finish out in the bar. Say the word and I'll help you mop this shit up before we go." His boot tapped the bloody smear where they'd wiped frat boy's face on the floor, after they'd finished kicking the hell out of him.

I watched Joker turn smartly and disappear through the swinging doors.

Then I doubled over, propping myself up on the counter next to the grill. Waves of confusion washed over me.

Christ. What the hell was wrong with me?

A hundred knots twisted my stomach. It wasn't just all the recent shock. The tension tugged a little lower, tingling, kicking up a heatwave that made me sweat and flush.

It wasn't just because the man standing in front of me was a crazy, unpredictable thug.

Honestly, my eyes couldn't see it every time I looked at him.

They saw the rugged, muscular beast who'd narrowly saved me from a nightmare.

They only saw power, forced me to imagine how easily the same big, strong arms that sheltered me against his chest could throw me around, undress me, roam every inch of me...

This man punched, kicked, and swore without any apologies. Would he kiss the same way?

Closing my eyes, I stumbled through the rest of my shift, trying to ignore crazy emotions slashing through me like comets.

I called mama to check in with her just before I wrapped up. She asked me if everything was fine, and I lied through my teeth.

She couldn't know about what went down today. If she heard about the frat boy, it would kill her. So would finding out that I was about to ride home with one of the two biggest, meanest bastards in Seddon.

Whatever happened next was private. Between me, Jackson Taylor, and God.

Oh, crap.

* * * *

"You've never ridden before? Bullshit. Looks like you were made for it," Joker said, cupping my chin and pulling on the straps, making sure my helmet was secured tight. I watched him climb onto the bike in front of me.

My pulse quickened when I realized how little space there was between us on his motorcycle.

"Ain't no mystery when it comes to riding. Put your little hands around me and hold the fuck on, woman. That's all there is to it. I'll have you home in five or ten."

He didn't ask me twice. My hands softly curled around his stomach.

No surprise, his abs were as rock hard as the rest of him. Joker put his hands over mine, adding pressure to my fingers, urging me to hold him tighter.

I did, clenching my jaw the entire time. Then, in another heartbeat, his engine growled to life and we were off.

Lurching from the sudden speed, I let out a little yelp, hugging him for dear life. His abs rippled underneath my fingers, perfect and happy, his chuckle drowned out by the engine's rumble.

We rode through the hills leading into town. Every bump where I didn't fall off the bike gave me a little more confidence. Slowly, I eased up straight, edging my grip on his muscles until I finally had my bearings.

The bike must've scared the hell out of me for at least a solid minute. But by the time I realized I wasn't clinging to him like I scared cat, I also had the smile pulling at my lips, one he saw in his mirrors.

"Shit, little girl, you sure you've never ridden before? You're doing fuckin' fantastic. Looks like you belong back there."

My face lit up. I leaned into him a little more, relishing the cool southern breeze, catching a whiff of something rolling off him that warmed my blood.

He smelled…amazing.

Oil and pine mingled with leather, a tinge of tobacco, and a bold masculine musk that sent shockwaves rippling through me.

It'd been too long since I'd had a crush. I'd been a late

bloomer, and carried a few extra pounds from too many late night dinners in Uncle Robby's bar.

New excitement tightened my core like a lasso, every time I inhaled the oxygen alive with Jackson, Joker, this raging ghost who'd torn through my life and saved me from one more tragedy.

"I like this," I whispered softly. "It's smoother than I expected out here, I mean. Can't imagine what it must be like on the highways."

"Babe, it's smooth as fuckin' hawk's tail. Ain't nothing like riding. Everything else in this world can get fucked. When you're out here on the road, you find peace. Some folks find themselves. Same thing sailors and pilots are after when they're gliding along, free as the day they were born."

I blinked, surprised that his words were so poetic, between all the crude curses. How many layers were there to Joker and his twin?

Everybody talked about them like they were the last devils you'd ever want to run into at night on an abandoned road or in a broken down back alley. Maybe that was true.

But if these boys were demons, then they were the slickest, fittest bastards who'd ever crawled out of hell.

They were the fairest, the realist, the most tragic. Because in another time and place, they might've been heroes, not part of an outlaw biker gang with skulls and guns all over their bodies.

Too bad this was Seddon, and this town didn't forgive. Joker probably had more mercy in his deadly makeup than this God-forsaken place.

That scared me. Turned my blood to bitter ice, or it would've, if only holding onto him didn't make me thaw.

Joker felt warm. Strong. Like the fire in his blood burbled to the surface, brightening the world around it, the only flame shielding me from the greater darkness.

Several minutes on his bike, and I never wanted it to end.

Of course, it did, and soon we were coming down my street, rounding our way down the long unpaved road to mama's house.

"No lights on. Your ma most go to bed early, yeah?" he asked, killing his engine before we crept too close to her car, and jerking off his helmet. He turned around.

Those bright, hazel eyes glowed like a mountain lion's in the moonlight. I lowered my eyes, unable to hold his gaze for more than a second.

"Yeah. She hasn't been doing too well lately. The doctors don't know what it is."

Or if they know, she isn't telling me, I thought bleakly. Mama hated when I suffered or worried about her, so she hid the hurt. Just kept it to herself, except for the nights when the breakdown in her body became so overwhelming she cried in her sleep.

Joker stood up, extended a hand, and locked his fingers perfectly in mine. The helmet slid off my head. He helped me up, tucking a loose lock of hair back behind my ear.

"It's been one fuck of a night. Go crash, Summer. Sleep it off 'til you can't remember that prick I knocked to hell back there. He ain't worth your time. Bastard'll be too fuckin' busy getting his face rebuilt to worry about giving you any more trouble. Promise. Tomorrow's gonna be better than this shit."

"It hasn't been all bad," I said shyly, dragging one foot on the ground.

God. I was like a cartoon schoolgirl with my heart beating out of my chest every time I tried to speak to him.

Stupid.

Outrageous.

Irresistible.

"Yeah?" he said, reaching into his pocket for a cigarette, then giving it a flame. "Can't say I see the glass half full when it's full of mud, but I ain't blaming you for looking on the sunny side. Keep that shit up. You'll go places, little Summer."

Little? Jesus, he couldn't be more than five or ten years older than me. My heart sank, flaming the whole way down, hating the fact that he just saw me as some dumb girl he'd pulled from the fire.

Hated it even more that I couldn't assert myself, couldn't even meet his eyes when he gave me those slow, smooth glances in between staring out at the stars overhead.

"You oughta get in so I can take off," he said, taking a long pull off his cig. "No need for your ma to stumble out here and see me hanging around."

"It doesn't have to be this way," I said, stepping up to him. "It doesn't have to be a bad night. I never got a chance to thank you for what you did back there, you and Freddy."

It took every ounce of strength I had to throw my hands

around his neck. I did it quick, clumsy, but God help me, I *did.*

Joker's eyes narrowed. Slowly, he reached up and pulled the cigarette from his mouth, blowing a last strand of smoke out the side of his lips.

The cig hit the ground and crunched loudly under his boot as he rubbed it out. Then, his hands were on me, jerking me in so fast I slammed into his chest.

Crap, crap, crap. My heart couldn't keep up with my head spinning a thousand miles an hour.

One rough, huge hand cupped my face, stroked my loose black hair back, and pulled me into him. Our lips touched like lightning splintering the sky.

For a split second, there was a sweet hesitation, a tease so hot I whimpered. He silenced me by bringing it home.

His lips crushed down on mine. My mouth opened, perfectly unlocked for his tongue. Trembling, I let it happen, let him push his tongue against mine. Twining, lashing, owning it in the first kiss I'd ever had that truly took my breath away.

This wasn't even in the same universe as the clueless boys I'd made out with before. This was a man's kiss, a kiss that would've brought me to my knees if he hadn't tightened his hold, keeping me against him.

This kiss pulled me under the storming sea named Jackson Taylor, stripped me bare, and refused to let go.

Suddenly, he tore his lips away from mine, leaving me to gasp for sorely needed air.

"That what you wanted?" he asked, a smug quirk pulling at his lips.

I still couldn't speak. So, I just nodded dumbly, moving my hands over his neck. A second later, he gently pushed me away, heading for his bike.

"We're done here," he said, words that dashed my feverish lush like gun smoke.

"Hey, wait!" I whined, running after him. I caught up with him just as he was fixing his helmet.

He looked at me, pushed his hand against my face, holding a finger over his lips. "Don't give me any bullshit, babe. That's all you get, and it's a lot more than you deserve."

Deserve? What?! I stopped cold in my tracks, shot through the chest by his words, wondering where the hell I'd screwed up.

"You look goddamned beautiful under this moonlight. Don't ever let a man tell you less." He paused, straddling his bike, ready to start it anytime. "Trouble is, I ain't a fuckin' fool. You're barely on the right side of being jailbait, and I'm not biting, Summertime. You're too fuckin' young, babe. Too new. You deserve better. You're looking for more than skin and sweat when you kiss. I can't give you that."

"Why?" I whispered, so hoarse it was painful.

He smiled. "I *fuck,* babe. Skin and sweat – that's all I know. Never take it any further than that. Never fuckin' will. The girls who hitch their hearts to this patch, they get fucked and they get wrecked. You and me? Hell, we're not even hitching a damned thing. I'm letting you off easy."

My lips trembled. I wanted to curse him, plead with him, reach out and slap him all at once.

What the hell was wrong with me? What was it about him? Why, why, why did I feel more alive with this rage and confusion?

"You think I'm a bastard. Go ahead, girl. You're right. I'm a dyed in the wool son of a fuck, but I ain't a monster. You're a sweet girl, Summertime. Ain't breaking your heart by popping your cherry and taking off."

Joker turned, reaching in his pocket for another cigarette. He started his bike, keeping his eyes trained on me while he held up his lighter.

"Promise me you'll be try to be good, try to find a man who gives a fuck. Hope to hell it happens, but if it doesn't...if you don't find him, if I come back to this town and you're down to get dirty, look me up. We'll finish what we started tonight, babe. I'll fuck you and fuck you and fuck you 'til you're hoarse from screaming my name. Then you'll wake up the next mornin', and I'll be gone."

"Asshole!" I screamed, finally caving. "Forget it! What kind of girl do you think I am?"

He rolled his eyes. "Fuckin' finally. I was wondering how many damned buttons I'd have to push to see. Listen, I know what kinda girl you are – you're a good girl. Too fuckin' good for me, or any other bastard wearing this patch. You keep your fuckin' distance, Summertime. Find yourself a boy who'll bring you heels and roses. It sure as shit ain't me, babe, and that's awesome. That's called me doing you a favor."

I shook my head, totally blasted, trying to understand what the hell he was getting at.

"Don't fuckin' look at me like I just stood you up at prom. I did you a solid tonight, saving you from a greedy pick who wanted your body, and nothing else. Those ratfucks go down easy. Just takes a blow to the ribs to drop 'em. The boys who try to charm your pussy wet – they're the ones you really gotta watch out for. Only one of those motherfuckers I can save you from is me." He paused, looking me up and down, one final tease before he left me in the dust. "You're young, you're good, and I hope to fuck you'll stay that way. Next time you get hot when you hear a bike humming or see a brother with this patch, you ignore that shit. You run."

He thumped the skull with the blazing guns going up the side of his leather vest. As if I *needed* a fucking reminder.

Then he took off, cutting way too close to our old storage shed. Just the perfect angle for making his motorcycle's steel glow on his way out.

My knees collapsed. I dropped to the ground and cried, utterly humiliated, knowing deep down I should be thanking him that he hadn't taken advantage of me.

The bastard was right, more right than he had any business being with his teasing, his arrogance, his good for nothing good looks.

Lord, I fucking hated it.

I told myself if I didn't see Jackson, or Joker, or whatever the hell he wanted to call himself ever again, I'd live my life happy.

But life never goes according to plan.

II: Another Night (Joker)

Three Years Earlier

Piece had my back. My brother by blood and patch was always with me, every single trip we made to this dirty little town.

We rode in, heading for the bar before we hit grandpa's house, the only place that ever felt like home outside the clubhouse in Knoxville.

Seddon had gotten its fucking skull caved in by the economy taking a dump. It showed in every tumbleweed blowing through the abandoned streets, in front of the boarded up buildings. Some desperate fucks had broken the windows outta the old pharmacy – desperate ass junkies looking for their next fix.

We'd stopped hauling that shit around a couple years ago, when Early met a bloody end and passed the gavel to his son, Dust.

New Prez didn't want a damned thing to do with drugs, no different than the rest of us. So he'd sent us here on a different kind of club business.

'Course, we came for pleasure, too.

There was always somebody hanging around, waiting to get their ass kicked. The bar brawls out here were easy. They were fun. The motherfuckers on the receiving end always deserved it.

Tina and Robby Olivers appreciated the regular cleanings we brought to their watering hole, knocking out the riffraff who threatened to chase away the drunks and the softer types passing through town.

Piece killed his engine and stepped off his bike first. I followed him, heading into the bar. My brother pushed straight through the old timey saloon doors without noticing the pink slip taped to the window.

It hit me like a ton of bricks when I stopped and read it. "Fucking shit," I growled, taking it in.

GOING OUT OF BUSINESS was in big, fat bold letters near the top. Didn't need to see the fuckin' fine print.

I almost ripped the saloon doors off on my way in. Only took a second to scan the small crowd, and found my brother in our usual spot, at one of the corner tables next to grandpa.

"Why didn't you tell me this place was closing up shop?" I asked, sitting down as Piece looked up, and pushed an extra beer over to me.

Took a long sip. Thick, bitter, and dark. Just the way I liked it, second only to good southern whiskey. Could've used the harder shit today, when we were taking a kick to the nuts like this.

"Figured you'd both be here to see her off yourself,

boys," Grandpa said, twisting his old Marine cap, full of crests and honors from Vietnam. "They're having their last big bash today before the whole thing goes belly up. Latest victim of the rot chewing up the poor damned town."

Yeah, fucking right. Seventy-five years old, and our hard as nails grandpa had never talked more truth.

"What's Dusty doing?" he asked, folding a fist around his scotch and looking at us. All those fancy changes better pay off quick if the club ever wants stakes in Georgia again."

"Shit, Grandpa, that's what we're here for," Piece said, slamming down his glass. "We haven't given up. Long as this patch keeps coming across the border, fuckers will talk about us. All the other assholes will know we're here, and they'll keep the fuck out of our territory."

"Ain't always that easy, boy," the old man snorted, pausing to swallow more scotch. "The men moving in from Tallahassee, they ain't like the old clubs. No code. No limits. They'll slash your balls off just for the pleasure of it. Been hearing about them sending more scouts up here lately from Atlanta. They'd own the whole damned city by now if it weren't for the gangs and the Torches."

"Yeah, yeah, we've heard it all, too. The Deads are dirty motherfuckers, but they don't know the lay of the land like we do. These roots go deep," I said, bristling at the thought of another club taking our hometown. "Home field advantage. That don't go down easy."

"Our roots are dying on the damned vine," Grandpa snapped, giving me a hard look. The old man had the same bright hazel eyes I saw in the mirror every day, a Taylor trademark that bound us all by blood.

"No, they ain't," Piece growled, shaking his head fiercely.

"Cut the crap, boys. If you can't see we're in trouble, you're both gonna get yourselves wiped when you step into the wrong shit. Deadhands MC isn't just mean as a snake. It's bigger than a grizzly, so big it'll be chewing up half of Dixie in a few more years and shittin' it out. We'll be lucky to hang onto East Tennessee"

"Nah, Grandpa, you don't understand," I said, stiffening in my seat. "Dust has got all kinds of plans to rebuild our coffers, get us into the gun trade. We're off the nasty shit. No more drugs. Early fucked up keeping us in a dirty, dying business for too damned long. Now, we got ourselves a second chance. Something cleaner, without as much blood."

"Jackson, son…" He paused, gripping my shoulder, shaking his head sadly. "Freddy."

His other hand pulled at my brother. When he used our real names, shit got real. *Really* fuckin' real.

Grandpa lived and died by the club before he got too old to ride, and he respected the road names we'd carried for four long years.

His pause lasted a little longer because Johnny Cash started screaming on the jukebox, his favorite, kicking off the last songs our favorite bar would ever have.

"I'm too fuckin' old to watch either of you boys get yourselves axed. You're young, arrogant, full of piss to sling around. I remember that feeling like it was yesterday. In case you boys forgot, I made your old man a promise before he died in that wreck." Piece and me both turned to stone, knowing what was coming, and hating it.

"If shit comes down to building the club or saving your lives, you know what I'll choose. Have your fun here boys, and go the fuck home. Don't come back here wearing that patch. You get seen by the Deads, or surrounded by a train of 'em when you're working your way south, trying to talk to mobsters out in Savannah, you're as good as gone. That ain't happening while I'm still breathing."

I locked eyes with my brother. Our eyes slid to Grandpa and we both nodded, too resigned to his touchy-feely shit to argue. We'd humor him.

The old man loved us like our father couldn't because he'd been six feet under for twenty fuckin' years. We loved him back, and respected him to hell, even when he said shit that made us want to spit bullets.

Most of what he said had been dark as hell lately.

There wasn't time for tears, or pig roasts with the brothers. Barely enough time to knock back brown honey or to get my dick sucked, though I always made time for that.

There definitely wasn't time for a drag out fight with Grandpa, the man who'd raised us, or holding hands and singing songs like one big happy family.

Freddy and I had a feeling this shit was coming before we rode down. We shared a quick look. Our signal to throw one arm each around the old man's neck, hugging the shit outta him, showing him we'd read him loud and clear.

And we weren't gonna fuckin' listen because the stakes were too damned high.

"You've got nothing to worry about, Grandpa. We hear you."

Fuck, I hated lying to him. Both of us did.

But he didn't even know half of how desperate, how fucked up the ass we really were.

Piece and me didn't have a prayer of going all the way to Savannah. We were setting up shop here in Seddon for the next few weeks, waiting while Prez phoned every fuckin' mobster on the southern half of the eastern seaboard.

If any of 'em wanted to meet us here to hash out an agreement, we'd do it. We'd bring it all home.

And we'd get the fuck out before the Deads caught up to us.

We'd be keeping one part of our promises to the old man for real. Leaving this town for the last time was gonna hurt like a bitch.

Grandpa finished his drink and hung with us for awhile, getting into better spirits as the music rolled on, believing our bullshit.

We talked about his old dogs, the shit he made in his shop for the local VA. We listened to the stories he'd told us a hundred times before about the good old days, before the Pistols were swamped, desperate, and nearly broke, when he used to tear down the roads with Dust's old man and Skin's old man.

"You boys have entertained me enough for one evening. Just be careful," he said with a wink, yelling through the commotion of people dancing and country music blasting all around us. "If I turn you loose on the girlies around here, one of you might make me a great grandpa yet before I'm done."

Piece laughed loudly through the racket. "Hell, Grandpa, don't hold your breath."

Seemed like the whole damned town had turned out to see end of Robby's bar, the last light going out in this wasteland.

I just shook my head. *No, no, and fuck no.*

Having a kid was the last thing on my mind. My dick got hard for fuckin', not warming up bottles and changing dirty diapers.

Sometimes, the old man's jokes went too far. They still had a way of making me squirm even though I was blowing toward thirty way too fast.

Shit, thinking about any fucking at all right now – especially the baby making kind – was a distraction we didn't need.

Grandpa stood up and we helped him work his way out through the drunken, rowdy crowd. Tina stopped to chat with him for a minute as we helped him to his truck. He'd been one of the regulars here over the years.

I stood by, watching him start it up and back out. He took off his cap and waved to me before I headed back inside.

Piece already had another drink in his hand. In thirty seconds flat, he was grinding up against some nameless bumpkin, a blonde bitch who was easy pickings with beer in her veins.

What we'd come here to do weighed on my mind too heavy. I'd had my romps with a couple sluts before leaving Knoxville, everything I could do to knock that shit outta my system, so we could focus on business.

I sat down with a tall shot of Jack and let the music wash over me, wishing I'd spent more time here. I'd been coming to this place since I was old enough to booze. Shit, Piece and me had even snuck a few drinks before we were legal.

This was our first real watering hole, the only one that really mattered, outside the clubhouse's bar. All the fights, the ass kickings, the night I'd saved that honey from those drunken fuckin' college kids...all about to be fuckin' history.

Shit. I told myself I wouldn't think about Summer when I came to Seddon.

It was easy to keep her outta sight, outta mind, except when I rolled by her house, or hit the bar. She always went in the back as soon as she saw me, handing off our table to somebody else.

Sometimes, I saw her first. Saw her looking, when she thought I wasn't. Knew she had her greedy little eyes all over me.

Last time, it was at her house. Piece and me blew by on the road without slowing for a single second, but she was out near the road with a realtor, the new FOR SALE sign at her ma's place swinging in the breeze.

Didn't need to ask about her to know shit hadn't gone right. Fuck, nothing had gone right for anybody in Seddon since the bastards on Wallstreet crashed the whole economy, foreclosures devouring the countryside like locusts.

Summer didn't have a fair shot at staying a good girl...right?

Fuck if I knew. Fuck if I cared.

I had too much club biz on my mind, and too many bitches back home lining up to feel my dick for another night to worry about a chick I'd kissed three fuckin' years ago.

But hell, *what* a kiss.

I still tasted those lips when I fucked sometimes. Tasted them even more when I laid in bed alone on the long summer nights, bringing myself off when there wasn't a bitch around.

Her eyes begged for my dick, and now they were burned into my brain.

So was her smell, the silky feel of that black hair I wanted to pull harder, and yeah, that taste. That *goddamned fuckin' taste.*

Something about little Summer's fire pushed my cock into overdrive. Any time I jerked off, she was the one I did it to.

Over and over. Pinched my teeth tight like boulders crashing together when I spent myself in the shower, thinking about those palm sized tits she'd had against my chest that night, begging to be teased, licked, and sucked to perfection.

I thought about her whole sexy body here at the bar, wondering if it was close.

No, fuck that. I'd kept my promise to stay the hell away for almost three years. Even told her to look me up if a man never stepped up for her, and she hadn't.

We kept our distance. Exactly how it was meant to be. She sure as shit didn't need any drama, however good it would feel to get between her legs, and neither did I.

"Fuck me," I swore underneath my breath, standing up for another drink, noticing how hard I was.

Common sense wasn't helping tonight. The memories were killing me. So were the roads I hadn't taken, every damned time I'd thought about going by her place, banging on her door, and taking her out for another ride on my bike.

All the woulda-coulda-shoulda bullshit stung more now that our old hometown was completely fucked. Seeing this place go to the jackals made me wish I'd taken a few more mementos, like Summertime's cherry.

This place is only fucked for now, I told myself. *Ain't forever. We'll be back someday, when the club's grown bigger, stronger, and its hauling shovels to bury the Deads.*

We'll be back for grandpa, for Tina, for soon-to-be bankrupt Robby.

For Summer.

I went straight behind the bar this time and grabbed a whole bottle of booze. The lean, wiry man playing bartender tonight didn't stop me when he saw my patch.

The ship was going down, and I doubt he'd have cared even if I weren't wearing the colors that taught everybody instant respect. I took a swig of pure fire and plowed through the double doors, heading through the kitchen for the back of the building, where I could take in some fresh air and sauce myself alone.

Burgers and sausages cooking up punched me in the nose. The sizzle on the grill reminded me of the last time I was back here, the night I'd kicked that grabby little asshole's dick off with Piece.

Wasn't just me back here. My eyes scanned the scene in front of me, taking a quick nip from the bottle, looking at something fine.

When the fuck had this place added the chick with the ivory skin and the pert, plump ass rolling out her jeans? Old Robby took on too much help, one more fuck up driving him into the ground.

The new girl working the grill had her back turned toward me. She worked alone. Long, smooth, dark hair rolled down her shoulders in waves.

Spitting image of little Summer, if she'd plumped up and filled out the way a woman oughta, pushing into her twenties.

Then she turned around and I nearly dropped the fuckin' bottle. Familiar green eyes hit me harder than the whiskey soaking my system.

Shit, fuck, and damn.

Her eyes lit up, went wide, and a soft smile tugged at her lips. Same lips I'd kissed like no tomorrow, imagining how good they'd feel wrapped around my cock.

Fuck.

Fucking hell and a half.

If the urge to pick up where we'd left off that starry night didn't blow my brains out, the need to get her sweet ass naked might do it first.

"Hey," she said, her voice as soft and pure as ever.

Clenching my bottle hard, I kept my cool. All I could do not to drop it when I started to think about slapping, grinding, and bouncing that ass off my balls.

"Didn't know you were working tonight," I said, shaking off my stupor and slamming more whiskey down my throat.

She raised an eyebrow. "Didn't know you were coming into my kitchen to stand around and drink."

Fuck, that mouth. My eyes went straight to her lips, and then trailed lower.

She quickly turned over a few burgers before throwing her spatula down, walking over, sizing me up.

Yeah, no mistake. The girl had filled out *real* fuckin' nice the last few years. I hadn't realized how nice 'til I saw her up close, marveling how her baby fat turned into curves.

Curves I wanted to grab, slap, and shake underneath me. My cock pulsed like a charge about to blow.

"Thought you might show up to see us off. Your granddad's been here every day all week, ever since he heard about it from my uncle."

"Yeah, well, shit changes," I said, feeling the sweet burn of whiskey roiling my guts, radiating to my greedy fuckin' middle. My dick strained in my pants. "Sorry to hear this place is closing. Helluva blow for this town. Shit, a man'll have to go twenty, thirty miles outside town if he wants a drink."

"I know. Uncle Robby can't hack it anymore. The hours are too long, and expenses just keep rising. He'll be lucky to shore himself up in retirement at this rate. I was going to take over the bar, do the drinks, originally, but...you know." She shrugged, her shoulders rolling soft and sad as her voice.

Yeah, I knew.

Pitch black depressing shit had become the norm in Seddon. This place was a goddamned black hole, and it wasn't getting any brighter as the years rolled on.

Twisted my guts up in knots, but there wasn't shit I could do about it.

Not yet, anyway. Someday, that was gonna change. Saving this place wasn't in my reach, but the club's? Maybe.

"How many more sandwiches you got to finish up?" I asked her, nodding at the grill.

"Just a couple, the works for all the regulars who asked. Everybody else is too busy out there drinking and dancing to throw in an order. Tina's closing up the kitchen early tonight so we can party."

"Make one more," I said, my stomach growling.

I needed a snack to distract myself from the greater hunger nipping at my balls. Last thing I'd wanted tonight was getting myself into trouble with this woman, and the urge was growing every fuckin' second I looked at her, all her young beauty raising my cock like a flagpole.

Hard to believe nobody had taken that cherry yet, if she hadn't fucked around on the side.

Surely, she had. No fuckin' way she was a virgin – but the slim possibility she might be kicked me in the dick so hard I wanted to slam her against the wall, shove my lips on hers, and find out.

"Excuse me?" she said, folding her arms. "You know, wearing that patch doesn't excuse good manners."

"Another burger," I growled. "Please. I'd like a bite. Nobody makes that shit like you and Tina. Having a taste of something good will give me one more memory to chew on before this place goes belly up."

"Oh, all right. On the house. Lord knows you and your family have helped us over the years." Satisfied, her lips quirked and she turned around, walking back to the grill.

I watched her ass bobbing the entire time.

* * * *

I ate my burger at the usual spot, watching Piece make a fool of himself. He was practically fucking the blonde bitch out on the dance floor now, hugging her ass with his hands, dragging her into him so he could grind.

They'd be taking off any second for somewhere more private. Wrinkling my nose, I tossed my crumpled up napkin on the last few crumbs of my food, pissed that it hadn't done anything to fix my real hunger.

I hadn't seen Summer since I'd left the kitchen. My eyes scanned the crowd, piercing through the drunks. Found her by the back register, talking to Tina.

Didn't look like the girl was having much fun, and that was a damned shame. Even bigger shame I wasn't making it happen for her.

I stood up, ignoring the last couple shots in my bottle, ready to sober up.

Tina and her both saw me coming. The older woman backed out of the way, giving me a suspicious look.

"Joker! Why aren't you out on the dance floor like your brother?"

"Ain't found a woman worth dancing with tonight," I told her, eye-fucking Summer the whole time.

She held my gaze a lot better than the last time we'd met. The shy little girl was gone, the one who'd drop her eyes to the floor the second she felt mine crawling all over her.

Tina wasn't an idiot. She realized what was happening real quick. Caught her smiling outta the corner of my eye. Pinching my shoulder, she gave me a quick shake, and then mumbled a few words before taking off.

"Be nice to her, jackass. She's had a rough couple years. I know all about that night you dropped her at her mama's place, too," Tina said, leaning up and whispering into my ear. "Don't leave her hanging again. I'm coming after you myself if I find out you've hurt her. She ain't another floozie to dine and dash, you hear me?"

"Yeah, yeah, loud and clear," I said, pushing past the barkeep as she walked off.

Just me and Summertime now. Alone.

Just the way I wanted it.

"It's a beautiful night," I said, reaching for her hand. "Been a few years since you've rode on a bike, I bet. Let's go for a ride."

"Oh, you really think so, huh?" she asked, flicking back

her hair. "Actually, I've kinda gone on a few more rides with the guys around town. Hoping to get my own bike soon."

No fucking way. My fingers tensed around hers, trying to form a fist.

I wanted to slam it deep into the faces of any other fuck who'd taken her on his bike, anybody who'd had those little hands around his waist while he pulled her into the night.

Fuck, what if she'd gone bad, and I hadn't been around to see it?

What if some worthless pissant had popped her fuckin' cherry, the one that should've had my name on it, while I'd been jacking myself off in Knoxville, thinking about all the shit I'd do to her as soon as I rammed my cock inside her?

Then a more serious thought hit me, and I saw red. "Better not be riding with the Deads, babe. They're bad fuckin' news."

"Do I look like an idiot?" her sweet little tongue razzed me between her teeth. "I know all about them, Joker. They come through town sometimes. Everybody keeps their distance."

"Yeah, you fuckin' keep it that way, too. Those boys won't think twice about dragging you out in some field, having their way, and leaving you for the crows to pick."

The sass on her face withered. Fuck, I'd gone too hard, too soon, but I didn't regret it.

I'd drill it into her head over and over and over again if that's what it took to keep her safe.

Jealous? Shit, no.

This was about the Deads, I swore to myself, club biz

she'd unwittingly gotten caught in.

Didn't have anything to do with those suckable lips, or the urge to flip up her skirt and rip her panties to her ankles, spank her fuckin' raw for mouthing off before I fucked her brains out.

No, sir. Fuck no.

"Forget it," I growled. "You ain't stupid. Come on."

She moved reluctantly, but the point was she *moved* when I pulled her along by the hand. I shook off the last of my buzz from the booze and we got on my bike.

"You remember to hold on tight, baby. Don't want you falling off when you're gawking at the stars. Look up there too long, you'll get dizzy."

Summer laughed. "Jesus, Joker, I remember how to ride. Already told you, I've been doing a little bit of it since the last time we hung out."

I refused to let her shit about riding with other men get underneath my skin. It really was a beautiful fuckin' night, a big summer sky hanging overhead as big and bright as the excitement in her eyes.

Fuck, those green gems in her face sparkled when I watched her strap her helmet on in my mirror.

Soon as her hands went around my waist, we roared outta the unpaved parking lot, tearing down the road leading to the main highway. We left Seddon behind, heading into the countryside, between the hills at the butt end of the Appalachians snaking down from the north.

My cock hammered in my pants the whole damned trip.

I snuck glances at her in the mirror every few miles,

catching her doing the same to me. Her fingers moved along my abs, pressed tighter with every turn when the mountains bent the roads.

I'd sworn I wasn't gonna fuck her. I'd blown town and left her behind, ignored her for three fuckin' years because I wouldn't be the bastard to bring her more grief.

Tonight, I was very close to smashing that promise into a thousand pieces.

A man had needs the faceless sluts back at the club couldn't satisfy. They could suck me off a thousand times.

None of them would be half as exciting as having her pretty little lips wrapped around every inch of me.

I could fuck the whores 'til my limbs gave out and I collapsed, drenched in sweat, gasping for air. But spending myself in their well fucked cunts wouldn't be like lightning crashing through my skull – exactly how it'd be with Summertime's smooth, milky legs wrapped around me, watching her eyes roll back in her head when she came on my cock.

Fuck, fuck, fuck.

My eyes darted around the countryside, looking into the fields between the valleys. It'd been about a year since I'd come down this route. Last time, it was just a night drive, when we were staying at grandpa's place, Piece's fuckin' snoring keeping me up.

There had to be an abandoned farm around here somewhere. My memory was hazy, but I pressed on, going by faith I wasn't wrong.

A couple miles later, I found it, taking the overgrown

path up toward the ruined buildings.

Summer put her face against my shoulder and whimpered a little from the bumpy ride. Sounded a lot like the sound I imagined her making when she blew. My blood became lava.

Christ, I *had* to fuck this girl tonight, and deal with the consequences later. At this rate, I'd crawl over broken fuckin' glass for a piece of her.

Just one intense, unforgettable night out here in the country, between me, her, and the stars.

Pulling to a stop, I killed my bike's engine and helped Summer off, throwing her helmet in storage.

"Perfect spot for a beautiful night," she said.

"No." I held up my hand. "Perfect spot for a beautiful lady."

I tested her, trying to see how well she could hide her attraction. No surprises, she flunked. Summer's cheeks went beet red, reminding me of that poor, sweet kid I'd passed up years ago. Her eyes dropped to the ground 'til I took her hand again, leading her toward a hill behind the collapsed barn.

A quick climb later, we dropped down onto the grass, laying there like some shit out of a movie. The pinprick stars in the sky glowed like snow that wasn't ever coming down.

"What kinda boys you been riding with while I've been away?" I asked, turning toward her.

She smiled. "Just the older guys down at the VA. Saw your granddad a couple times, too. He's doing well for a man his age."

"Fuck yeah, he is," I growled, a little too enthusiastically for my own good. "The man's pressing eighty and he'd still be riding himself if we let him. Just works in his shop and rents out his kennel now. He's paid his dues and earned it."

Summer nodded, the same mysterious smile hanging on her lips. Damn it, she knew too much what was going on in my head.

It was nothing short of a relief to find out her motorcycle riding was limited to the old farts going for joy rides in the country.

But, fuck, *why* was it a relief? This shit wasn't good for me.

I could deal with the animal need to fuck. This other feeling, this jealousy, the green anger I kept trying to ram down into my guts – this bullshit was new.

"What's happened to you? How's your ma?" I already knew the answer wouldn't be a good one, but I had to know what the fuck had happened for sure.

Her face went dark. "She passed away about six months ago, about the time Uncle Robby decided to call it quits with the bar. Screwed up colon. She hid how bad it was from me up until the last year, when she went into hospice."

I preempted that teary look on her face, pulling her into my arms. Grabbing her chin, I twisted Summer's face to look at me, taking in every little feature here in the moonlight.

Fuck me, the girl was beautiful. No, not just a girl anymore – a woman.

One who'd taken a couple real punches from life.

Something about that sadistic hurt caused me to love how she looked even more.

"Babe, there was nothing you could've done. Don't you dare beat yourself up." She nodded, slowly opening her eyes to meet my gaze, sucking gently on her bottom lip.

"I know. I don't blame anybody. I just wish things were different, Joker. I wish she didn't have to die so young, or at least that she didn't go down fighting it so hard for so many years." No hiding the stinging wet gleam in her big green eyes now. "It isn't fair. Just like the bar closing down, right before I was about to take it over."

She let out a heavy sigh. I held her face, tightening my grip, watching the dew forming on her eyelashes.

"Life ain't fair, Summertime. Nothing else to it. You don't get shit unless you reach up, grab it by the fuckin' nuts, and yank it *hard*."

"Thanks for the pep talk," she snapped. "Not what I needed right now – especially when some things can never be yours, no matter how hard you push."

"Whatever. Just wanted to give it to you straight before I lay down exactly what you need, woman." My hand grazed her cheek again, brushing back a stray lock of hair. Remembered it wasn't no different than the one I'd tucked behind her ear years ago.

We were strangers. This shit shouldn't feel so familiar, but hell, it did.

Her eyes softened. I stared into them, fighting the wild instinct to take her in the next five seconds.

I'd wanted to kiss her before. It overpowered me now,

and I wondered how many more seconds I'd need before I crushed my mouth on hers, reigniting the explosion we'd had that night when she was too young, and I was too stupid to come back sooner.

"Everything keeps changing, Jackson." I gave her a sharp look when she used my real name. Her hands moved across my chest, soothing the frustration. "You're Joker now, I know. You have been for years. But I remember back before you weren't, when it was just you and Freddy, two young guys kicking ass around town."

I let myself smile. "Yeah, babe. I remember those times, too. Funny how fuckin' far away it all seems."

She didn't have a clue. Hell, I barely understood it myself.

I'd killed for the club since I'd put on my prospect patch years ago. I'd hauled drugs for Early a couple times, Dust's old man, and now we were trying to get gun deals with the mob. Fucked an endless train of bitches I couldn't remember to save my life.

I'd done some good, too. I'd stood up for my brothers. I'd lived free, and helped everybody else with these colors do it too.

Whether it was those nights when Skin started talking about his old man with tears in his eyes, or keeping Sixty off his bike when he'd gotten his second fuckin' DUI, I'd been there. I'd bumped beers with Piece a couple hundred times, cheering the club's small victories, and stood in a straight line when Dust became the new Prez, burying his father.

Ashes to ashes. Dust to fuckin' Dust.

The world kept turning with its blood and fire, its fuckin' and killing. Lived my life in the thick of it, taking one road at a time, and a dozen women a month.

Tonight, I just wanted one thrashing around on my cock, giving me her body like I was the last man she'd ever fuck.

"How many boyfriends you had?" I growled, narrowing my eyes.

There went those fires on her cheeks again. Pure crimson.

Her eyes looked around nervously and she licked her sweet lips. "Joker, come on. You can't just ask a girl that, especially when you haven't seen her for years."

"Bullshit. Treat it like that ride home was only yesterday, 'cause that's the way it feels."

"Whatever. Not a whole lot, Mister Nosey. There's been too many other things in my life to worry about besides chasing boys."

No way. No goddamned fuckin' way.

She was talking like she hadn't been kissed since that night, much less fucked.

She couldn't be a virgin. She couldn't…or else my dick was gonna blow in my pants like a fuckin' kid.

I'd pulled myself off too many times, thinking about taking that cherry. If I had a chance to do it, to do her for the first time, tonight…

Fuck my promises. Fuck that shit about me being too bad for her, giving her a chance with the men she deserved.

She needed to be fucked good and proper. And nobody could put it to her like me.

No more bullshit. *None.*

My hand roamed up her back, fisted her long dark hair, and pulled 'til I heard her suck in a sharp breath.

"Admit it, Summertime. Whatever else has happened, the good and the bad, you missed me."

"Maybe a little," she said shyly. "But you turned me loose. You wanted me to stay away. So, I did."

"Yeah, we did. That was a big, fat, fucked up mistake." I stared at her, and she blinked, shocked beyond words at what I'd just said.

Hell, maybe I was shocked, too. Whatever, this wasn't the time for any regrets.

"Something else you missed, too," I growled. "Same thing I've been missing, if you wanna know the bitter truth. Something we never got a chance to taste in full."

"Yeah?"

Yeah. I jerked her face into mine without a second thought.

Our lips collided like thunderheads coming together.

Lightning in my mouth. Steam in my blood. Molten steel just twisting and turning through every channel in my body, churning fire in my balls.

I'd be in her soon, laying a claim I should've put down three goddamned years ago. Fuck, she tasted sweet. Couldn't stop for anything now. Wouldn't fuckin' stop.

Her little tongue melted against mine, and I took it. Could've twirled that succulent flesh around in mine damned near forever.

Only, this time, forever was about ten more seconds before I started tearing her clothes off and taking what was mine underneath the moon and the stars.

The countdown started the second our lips locked.

Five. Four.

Three. Two.

One.

III: Flash in the Pan (Summer)

As soon as the bastard kissed me, the last three years were gone.

Obliterated in his magnificent lips, his tongue, his power, his passion. The energy he'd only given me a teasing taste of on a summer night so long ago returned.

Except this was more than a tease. This kiss said he wasn't letting up, wouldn't turn me away for stupid reasons like innocence anymore.

Not this time. His kiss was too serious, too hot, too hellbent on mastering mine.

If I let him take what he wanted, there wouldn't be any going back. *Oh, God.*

"Damn it, Joker!" I whispered, jerking my face away. "I can't...I can't do this."

"Babe?"

Before he could grab me, I was up, climbing over the hill as fast as I could go. I didn't care how serious his kiss seemed, or how good it tasted.

I couldn't let him do this to me again. Not after all the heartache and disappointment.

This kiss could work wonders, like a spell that could charm me, make me believe he'd changed. But it couldn't make me stupid, reckless, ready to be destroyed by him a second time.

"Fuck, Summer, come back!" he yelled after me, plodding down the hill.

After all the things going upside down in my life, I hadn't changed enough.

I'd stepped up and taken more responsibility, sure.

Mama, Uncle Robby's bar, and the family house were all history soon. My meager wage couldn't begin to pay the bills that would've let me hang onto the place – not with her collectors hounding me for every last penny.

I had a head start on Joker, and he couldn't move as fast with his bigger body, taking the steep hill in slower strides. I used my advantage to put more distance between us, heading for the broken down storage shed I saw in the distance.

For the first time since we'd gotten here, I wished for fewer stars. The ones hanging overhead showed too much, made it all too easy for him to trail me like a wolf, across the curvy countryside and the winding fields.

My legs gave out just before the shed. Rather, something on the ground caught me, spun me around, and slammed me down so hard every bone in my body shook.

The pain ripping up my ankle didn't hit my brain until a second later. Wincing, I grabbed the muscle, right about the time he ripped me up in his arms, pulling me close.

"Put me down already – it hurts!" I whined, flailing against him.

"Bullshit, babe. You're gonna settle the hell down and tell me why the fuck you just took off screaming."

I stopped fighting him. There was no use hiding the hurt anymore.

He'd already seen how easy it was to get close to me. He had to know about the fantasies I'd nursed for three years, the memories I'd held onto from that lonely night when he'd brought me home from one tragedy, only to get my hopes up before he brought disaster down again.

"I told you! I can't do this again. I can't have you come in like a tornado for just one night and leave me hanging. Too many things have gone wrong. I've lived too many nightmares, Joker."

My body went limp. I bit my lip, fighting the pain spiking through my ankle.

Damn him, he tightened his hold, wordlessly wrapped me up in his biker embrace. My chest rattled as I tried to breathe, inhaling his scent for the first time in three years, that strong, heavenly smell of raw masculinity I thought I'd lost forever.

"I ain't a toy," I snarled in his ear, when he rested my chin on his shoulder. "It's not fair, treating me like one, coming back in my pants without a hello – and no, don't you dare give me another lecture about life. I'm telling you, I need something *nice* to happen for once. Not another train wreck."

"Quiet, babe. Quit moving. Only time I wanna see your lips moving is when they're on mine." He pushed my cheek into his, making me feel the sandy stubble there. "Didn't realize I did so much damage last time we hung out. I left for your own good, just like I told you that night. You were too young. Too fuckin' pure for me, Summertime. Too damned innocent."

That word! Anger flashed through me, and I shook, trying to pull myself away while he continued to talk to me like a kid.

"I don't do girlfriends and I don't fall in love. I still don't." His voice softened. "I *fuck,* baby girl, and if you want something to happen, that's gotta be the end of it. You oughta ask for more, but your body's telling me something different. Only thing worse than getting fucked is not getting fucked at all. I can give you that, Summertime."

He was giving me an ultimatum. A wicked, ridiculous one – but at least it was honest.

Could a man be a complete bastard and still talk like he cared?

"I haven't ever been with a man," I said, slowly pulling away from him. This time, he let me.

His handsome face lit up like I'd just offered him three wishes. "You're an asshole, but I like you, Jackson. You scare me because I can't stay away. I'm sorry I freaked out."

No, really, I thought. He didn't deserve an apology. But I didn't deserve to lie to myself any longer, living on nothing except fantasies and fears.

Choosing my next words very carefully, I looked at him softly, and let honesty roll.

"Whatever else this is…maybe I do want you tonight. Just to get it over with. Get rid of this stupid crush, and get on with my life."

"We can make it happen, babe. Make all your dreams come true tonight, and so much more." He smiled, stepping toward me, running his big, powerful hands up my shoulders again. His fingers curled up my neck, cupped my chin, and held me. "You're too damned beautiful to waste another night a virgin, Summertime. You give that pussy up, I'll make it purr. I'll make you scream. I'll make you come on my cock so fuckin' hard you see more stars up there than dim lit sky. You'll forget all about the shit that's eating at you, and you'll walk away a woman, no worse for wear."

Why I believed him, who the hell knows. I let him kiss me, softer and slower than before, and soon he led me outside into the night.

By the next kiss, I surrendered. How could I do anything else with my heart smashed up in a thousand pieces and the immaculate night sky glowing above?

Any woman would do the same. Anybody young, who hadn't had a good thing happen since that night he took me out three long years ago, and buried my woes in his lips.

"Baby, baby, fuck. I'm gonna make you feel so good. Better than any man ever will," he growled, taking his hungry lips off mine just long enough to gaze into my eyes.

His were so dark. So hungry. So wild.

"Big promises," I said, moistening my lips with my tongue. "Why don't you shut up and show me?"

I offered him what I'd wanted to give up for three damned years.

His hand pushed against my back, bringing me home.

Our lips connected, hotter than before, melting what little resistance I had left.

He could pretend to kiss me like a lover, a man who cared, the other piece of me I'd been missing for so fucking long.

Well, so could I.

I'd give him the hot, wild time he wanted tonight, before he left me behind for a second time. He'd love my body like he wanted more. I'd fool myself into thinking he did, knowing this might be the last time I'd have something I truly wanted, or at least an illusion so real I could hold it.

My lips moved against his, opening for his tongue.

Faster, harder, sweeter. His kisses came in waves, all consuming and all conquering.

Joker's hand swept up my thigh, rounded its way to my butt. He cupped one side of my ass and squeezed, feeding the wet craving between my thighs.

Whatever else he'd do to me tonight, he'd worship my body the way it deserved. I'd give myself to a man who knew exactly what he was doing, who'd probably done it a thousand times to a thousand different women.

That thought made me hate him. But as twisted as it was, I wanted him even more just then.

"You fuckin' been lying to me, or what? I have to know," he snarled, suddenly pulling his lips off mine. "You kiss so damned hot it's hard to believe you ain't never been fucked before, beautiful."

I blinked in surprise, noticing how badly I was panting in his arms. His fingers clenched my leg so hard I thought it would bruise, and I shuddered.

Lying? No, hell no. I shook my head.

"I like you, idiot. Enough to tell the truth," I said, staring into his eyes, fire roaring through every part of me. "I want you. *Badly.* Joker, dammit, no more games. I've been waiting for this for three long years. Haven't had time for anybody else. I've been waiting for you to come to your senses. Waiting for you to come back and take what's been yours since that night when we kissed, when I was just a high school kid…"

If he walked away now…*holy shit.* My hands crawled up his back, stopping along his shoulders, where I grabbed him and dug my nails in.

I wouldn't let him leave. We'd gone too far to give this up a second time.

He moved like a panther. Snarling, ripping at my clothes, jerking me onto his lap.

"Three goddamned fuckin' wasted years," he rumbled, sliding my jeans down around my ankles, then reaching for my panties. In one furious push, they were down my legs, leaving nothing between my wetness and his hand. "Been waiting for this a long ass time, little Summer. I've been jerking off thinking about you, and thinking about you again when I'm balls deep in those sluts who can't even hold a fuckin' candle to what you've got…fuck me alive! You've got it all."

His breath became a harsh whisper. Shoving my skirt up, his face stopped near one knee, and slowly began kissing up it.

I didn't know whether to love him or hate him just then.

Thinking about the glorious bastard moving between my legs with other girls made me see red. But he'd said it was *me* on his mind, the whole damned time, and he'd said it with such a storm in his voice I knew it was true.

My fight died the second he sucked at my inner thigh.

His hands moved above his head, aggressively plumping my breast through my shirt. The other grazed my pussy several times, sliding through the sopping wet center, brushing my clit for a split second every time.

Joker's stubble needled my skin like nails. Everything collided here.

The good and the bad. The rational and the senseless. All my better instincts, wiped out in one flash by his heat, his kiss, his promises in every deeply sexual movement.

No, make that *flashes,* plural.

I saw lightning when his mouth moved up again. He growled, stopping with his lips next to my core, pouring molten breath all over it in the worst tease I'd ever had.

My fingernails fought, scratching through his leather and his t-shirt. Slowly opening, my eyes went down, and caught the raging desire in his bright hazel eyes.

"Lay the fuck back, woman," he growled, reaching for my thighs with both hands, pulling them apart. "I ain't saying another word 'til your hot little cunt's blown itself up on my face several times. There's no going back once you feel this tongue. I ain't going back – I'm swallowing every drop. I *own* you tonight. This night and maybe every last fuckin' night you've got here on Earth…"

Shit, shit. He made me believe.

My heart banged in my chest. Almost caused me to pass out when he finally made good on what he promised.

His lips moved, planting one more kiss on my right thigh, moving to the center. Then his tongue was in me, sliding through my folds – so much more direct than it had been before.

My legs began shaking, and never stopped as his rough licks quickened. His tongue lashed me there again and again, going a little deeper every time.

"Damn!" I sputtered, already seeing the stars in the sky multiply. Except the new ones were hot red, just like the hellfire I imagined pumping in my blood.

Joker's elbows pinned my thighs. His hands moved to my center, pulling me open, all the better for those licks to land deeper, deeper, so fucking deep my insides clenched like a vise before the hot release hit me.

I screamed into the night when I came.

His lips wrapped around me and his tongue found my clit. All about a split second before I started coming my brains out, bucking and riding his face, wondering how the hell he could keep going with me thrashing underneath him.

Oh, but this man was strong. A beast wrapped in his tattoos, his leather, his cocky attitude that turned panties into ashes.

Mine were just a distant memory as I gave it up to his mouth. He licked, sucked, and pulled at my clit with his tongue, holding it between his teeth, holding down my center with nothing more than his rough, gorgeous face.

Was he seriously growling the whole way through it, making me feel his feral energy echoing in my body? Yes, God yes, he was.

I came even harder. I'd never expected my first time to be with someone who was more animal than man, wilder than the fierce country wind beginning to kick up around us.

The tall grasses on the hillside blew, tickling my face. One more sensation I couldn't handle with the dynamite going off inside me.

I never realized how numb my fingers were until he finally eased off. He lifted himself off me, slowly devouring me with his eyes, giving me *the look*. That one made me believe his utter crap about how he owned me tonight.

Made me believe that maybe, *maybe,* he wouldn't walk away when this was all through. But I knew better.

It started to get the best of me before he pushed his lips on mine, still slick with my juices.

He kissed me, pulling me onto his lap, his hands roaming my body again. This time, they were more deliberate, dragging away the rest of my clothes one piece at a time. He undid my blouse, kiss by kiss, growling when it fell off my shoulders.

My bra popped like nothing underneath his fingers. Free breasts felt his fingers for the first time, and he stopped to suck one nipple, lightly rolling it against his tongue, teasing me.

"Please!" I whimpered, scratching at his neck.

No more. I couldn't take this, the anticipation, the

piecemeal way he played my body like a damned fiddle.

If this was a warm up, then it worked. I was hotter than the summer sun, taught and limber, ready to do anything and everything to feel him deep inside me.

Growling, he tightened his teeth around my nipple, quickening his tongue strokes. He used the way I melted, surrendering totally, to push me flat underneath him again.

He sucked and lashed each breast until I couldn't think. My brain shut down, lost in this delight, my body rising and falling and always asking for more, more, *more.*

I squirmed underneath him, wide eyed, caressing my hands up his back like scaling small mountains.

His legs pushed between mine. He rubbed the hard, needy bulge in his jeans against the wet, tender skin he'd just tormented so deliciously.

"This is really it, isn't it?" I whispered, more to myself than him.

"Summertime, you've got no fuckin' clue. I'm gonna teach you everything a woman your age oughta know about her own sweet body by now. First things first – shut up and taste yourself on these lips."

He kissed me, forcing another growl into my mouth. His tongue swept over mine, more possessive than before, and that was saying something. His lips moved like a firestorm, scorching every millimeter, taking what they wanted.

So hard, so swift, so sweet.

Joker pressed me into the earth, dry humping me with rougher strokes, making my wetness soak into his pants. I'd never been so thankful for the cool bed of grass below us, or the soft breeze caressing my skin.

If it wasn't for that, I was sure we would've burned alive.

"You on the damned pill?" he growled, his fingers tangled through my hair when he jerked my face away from his.

Desperately, I nodded, my hips still bucking, rising to meet his, begging.

"Good. 'Cause I'd have taken you raw even if you weren't, beautiful. Nothing's too good for this pussy but skin-on-skin."

He lifted himself up and I watched him roll his shoulders. His cut came off. He lifted his t-shirt, taking away everything with the violent skulls and smoking pistols.

There were plenty more waiting on his skin. Dark, jagged inks rolled down his rock hard chest and tight packed abs, the one I'd caressed all evening on the back of his bike. The Pistols' skull leered at me, a strange dance between beauty and death, everything that was quintessentially Joker painted on his magnificent body.

I never thought my first time would be with someone like him, looking like a pirate.

But there he was, on top of me, larger than life. I watched as his belt buckle came loose, slapping gently on his jeans.

He shuffled out of his denim and hooked his thumbs below his boxer's waistband, wearing the most arrogant smile I'd ever seen on his face. Then they were down too, and I saw what he'd been hiding.

I gasped when I saw the little silver bullet gleaming on top of his huge, throbbing manhood.

"Is that –"

"Fuck yeah it is, baby, and you're gonna moan yourself hoarse when you feel what it does to you," he said, fisting his cock in one tight hand. "Just got it last year. Precision made to stroke your little pussy 'til it creams, screams, and creams some more. It hits all the right buttons and then some. Don't start drooling before you feel it…"

Asshole. Who did he think he was? Really?

Apparently, the man who was about to fuck me out of this universe.

Leaning up, I slapped his chest, and he caught both my hands. We tumbled down into the grasses again together, him wrestling his way between my legs, pushing the angry, pierced head of his cock against my opening.

He held his length there, wedged between my folds, teasing me as he shoved my hands over my head.

No going back now.

Hell, I couldn't even think about it, feeling the burn, the ache, the agony rising in my core. Muscles I didn't know I had tensed, whining to be fucked like never before.

"This fuckin' cherry…mine," he growled, angling himself up, cocking his hips backward like a trigger on a gun. "Your lips, your tits, your whole fuckin' body…you guessed it, babe. *Mine.*"

As soon as he said it, his hips punched forward, pulling him into me. I jerked underneath him, overwhelmed by the sudden sensation of him invading, stretching, pulling me apart.

Pleasure mingled with the slight discomfort. Something tore the deeper he went, snaking to my womb, claiming everything he'd promised. My pussy tingled, hotter than ever, struggling to adjust to his huge size.

When he'd gotten as far as he could, he stopped, holding himself in. Both of us stared at each other, our chests rising and falling, taking as much of the coolness into our lungs as we could so we wouldn't combust from our inner heat.

"Fuck, you're tight. Roll with it, baby girl. Feel me fuck you every time I dig in and out, and you fuck back. This is the best fuckin' night of your life, and I'm gonna make damned well sure you remember every smokin' second."

Lofty promises that could've put the devil himself to shame. The evil skull on his chest with the smoking guns next to it seemed to agree, grinning wide.

This cocky biker bastard and his promises.

I should've known by now he'd make good on every single one of them. His hips rolled, and I watched his big slab of a chest swell as he inhaled new breath.

Joker's cock dipped back before pushing into me again. Then it happened again.

Again.

Again!

Each thrust a little harder, a little more strewn with his hot, thick breath warming my face.

He dipped his head and kissed me. We twined tongues while the fire in my body rose with every stroke.

He rocked me like the machine he was, completely built for this, made for fucking a woman's body into full submission.

And God, did I surrender to it all.

I gave it up, gave him everything, moaning while my greedy pussy tightened around his cock. My body wanted to pull him deeper, feel him explode inside me.

We rocked, sweated, and gasped in between fresh kisses on the grassy hill. Even the coolness underneath my back couldn't quell the heat now.

It came ripping through my veins like liquid fire, calling for release, turning my muscles to stones one thrust at a time. I bucked desperately into at his hips, fighting through the initial hurt in my body.

His thrusts turned pain to pure pleasure like coal turning to diamond. I was the anvil, and he was the hammer, his huge, beautiful body slamming into mine until every part of me glowed and ached.

A minute later, I had my hands around his neck, tightening my legs around his back. He was fucking me so hard and fast it should've hurt. His thick balls punched my ass each time he drove into me, quickening the staccato rhythm between us.

My mouth opened a little bit at a time, too full of shock and awe to brace for his kisses. He must've sensed what was happening. He stopped mid-stroke to reposition us, raising himself up, throwing my trembling legs over his shoulders.

When he drove into me again, that fiery itch I'd had rising erupted into lava.

Sweet. Merciful. Fuck.

Pleasure couldn't describe the ecstasy tearing through me anymore. His body swept mine up and crashed into me again, smothering me with pleasure, igniting every nerve I had with a delicate, needy sweetness that hit my brain in a fireball.

The flame building in my belly exploded.

Yes, yes, shit yes!

My mouth formed a perfect circle while I clenched him with everything I had.

My hands, my feet, my poor little pussy, totally overwhelmed with every thrust...every part of me, I wanted tangled up with him, so lost in his body that I couldn't find where mine ended and his began.

His stamina was relentless. I expected him to slow, to crash, to climax with me, like two great waves crashing together.

Instead, he fucked me straight through my climax, smashing his mouth down on mine and pushing his body faster.

Yes, faster. I lost my mind, feeling him spiking in and out of me, pounding my hips into the soft, sweet earth.

Halfway through it, I bit into his bottom lip, desperate to keep breathing as his earthquake shook me apart.

His fist pulled angrily at my hair. "You're fuckin' lucky I love those little teeth, Summertime. Next time you do that shit, you better draw blood. I'll fuck you even harder when you do."

Harder? *Harder?!*

Was he out of his mind? When his hips sped up again, I knew he wasn't.

My legs could barely stay tangled around him as he

pistoned his hips full throttle.

Joker fucked me into the ground. My hips slid against the earth, tearing up the grass, consumed with the pleasure swallowing me whole.

Bastard. Even during sex, I wanted to keep fighting him. I couldn't let go of the love-hate insta-connection we had.

Nothing – not even this mind blowing sex – could wipe away three years of mixed emotions in one go.

And so, I held on tight, fucking him back as hard as I could. When he kissed me, I returned it like a whore, throwing off the shy, virgin shackles that ruled me for so long.

He wanted teeth? I let him have them.

I bit his lip so hard I tasted a metal. He growled like an animal into my mouth, fisted my hair, and pushed both our heads to the ground. The leverage only got his cock inside me deeper, like a railroad spike slamming through steel.

God, that piercing on the tip of his cock, I could *really* feel it now. The soft, silvery little bullet attached to him caressed me from the inside out; hot, tingling, and magnificent.

My nails racked his back. He grunted each time he thrust, all the way to my womb, shaking me with all the force his hips had.

"The fuck's gotten into you?" he whispered, tearing his face away from me so I could see that tiny cut I'd left on his bottom lip. "You wanna play rough, Summertime? You *sure* you wanna fuckin' do that?"

"You know I do," I said, speaking through the lightning

coming quicker in my body. "If that's what it takes to make you come with me this time…"

"Fuck," he growled. "Fuck!"

Next thing I knew, he'd pulled out, flipping me over like a tornado.

He pushed his palm on my back and grabbed my hair, causing me to arch onto all fours. His palm cracked across my ass before he pushed inside me again, snarling as he did, my hair more tangled than ever in his hand.

"Fuck me like the greedy little bitch you are," he said, his voice as rough as his hips crashing into mine. "Fuck me. Make me come. Show me what you've got, Summertime, or I'm gonna tan this little ass 'til you can't sit for a fuckin' week."

God! The savage threat ruined me.

Orgasm rose up and lodged in my belly, stretching to my throat. I dug my fingers into the ground for precious support and rocked my knees as fast as I could, slamming my ass into his pubic bone, fucking and grinding him like I'd lost it for good.

Hell, maybe I had.

Good girls didn't fuck like this.

Virgins never did.

They didn't give into all the filthy, nasty things they'd read in dirty books and fantasized about when the man they desired stepped into their dreams.

They didn't surrender this easy, this crazy to a man who'd use them as nothing more than another notch in his bedpost.

But out here on the grassy hill, with his pierced cock wrecking my better senses, *nothing* was off the table.

I became someone else underneath him. And after all the bad news I've lived through these past three years, I loved it.

I let it happen.

Panting like a mad woman, I started growling too, thrashing with my hair in his fist every time he filled me with his cock.

"Fill me," I said, barely recognizing my own voice through the chokehold pleasure had on my neck. "I want to feel you come. Do it, goddamn you!"

"What the fuck did you just say?" he whispered, slowing his strokes just enough to leave me on the edge, burning up.

"You. Heard. Me."

"Yeah," he said, making his throats slower, shallower, his free hand reaching between my legs. "Maybe I did, babe. Maybe I fuckin' did. Maybe you're about to get shot so full I knock your pussy up."

Damn! Why did he say that?

His thumb found my clit and my entire body seized. His fist jerked *hard,* pulling my face up to the open sky, where I saw the stars above us becoming bright and thick as a blizzard.

"Joker! Jackson! Holy hell!"

Never knew how I managed to sputter through the blinding pleasure picking up and slamming me back down again. I barely felt Joker's thumb brushing my clit anymore, but I knew it was there from the shocks exploding in my body.

His insane talk about knocking me up, that had to be fantasy. But in the heat of the moment, my body didn't know that. I gave in, and let him ravish me, anyway he wanted.

He fucked me fierce.

He fucked me rough.

He fucked me until I came crashing down, wrapped around his cock, panting his name through clenched teeth.

I didn't think it could get any hotter. But then he came. *Oh, God. Shit.*

The bastard buried himself to the hilt and roared, lifting my face to his with my hair locked in his stern fist. His lips touched mine the second he swelled inside me. He sucked every last desperate sound from my body when he erupted.

"Fuck, little Summer, I'm coming! Spilling the whole fuckin' load inside you!"

Fire. Hot and brilliant and intense as the stars spinning above us poured into me.

My pussy clenched and convulsed all over again.

Locked together, we thrashed and bucked and came.

Kissing and biting. Gasping for air. Calling each other's names in guttural, scratchy voices so wracked with pleasure they were barely coherent.

But my body understood with every shallow stroke he made inside me while he emptied his balls.

I finally understood what this was really all about as his seed leaked into me, flooded me, filled me so full I could feel him pouring out the crevices in our flesh.

He fucked me so hard I tilted my hips, giving up one

last round of bliss, before we both collapsed, exhausted and overflowing.

Sometime later, he rolled off me. We both sucked the sweetest tasting air ever into our lungs, staring up at the star scape rolling by above.

"It's beautiful, isn't it?" I asked, tilting my face toward him.

"Not half as pretty as the shit happening down here on the ground," he growled, so convincing I thought he was serious.

I slapped him on the chest with my hand and laughed. "Oh, come on. Stop. We've already done the deed, Joker. You don't have to keep saying that stuff."

"Don't fuckin' have to, but I will, babe. It's true. All of it." He wrapped his arms around me, pulled me onto his chest, cupping my ass with one hand. He squeezed.

"You know, you're kind of a dick, but so far...I don't regret this," I said, mulling over my words. "I was afraid I would, as soon as it was all over."

"Over?" He quirked an eyebrow. "We ain't half done fuckin' tonight, babe. I'm thinking I won't be done even then, neither."

"No?" I said, surprised.

"Nah. Piece and me are gonna be held up here in town for the next few weeks, staying at Grandpa's place. Club business," he growled darkly. "Sure I'll find some time to slip away for more enjoyable shit. Now that my favorite watering hole's gone bust, I'm gonna need more than just knocking back shots at home."

I laughed, squealing playfully as he tightened his hold on me.

His words were enough to make me want to put the brakes on, to keep my hopes checked before they soared like rockets. Except that glint in his hazel eyes...I couldn't ignore it.

It was a bright, honest shine. One that meant everything he'd said, his need for more than one night at a deep, primal level beyond any speech.

"Why don't you help me move while you're here? Assuming you can spare an evening, of course," I said, giving him a sharp look. "I need to be out of mama's place before the bank comes next Friday."

"Sure. Where you going next?"

"Little apartment on the edge of Seddon. I scrounged up just enough for a deposit and some new furniture. It'll do, until I can find another gig. Maybe I'll just take something easy like ringing folks up or stocking shelves, then wait for another opening at a bar."

"You really wanna do retail your whole damned life?" he asked, narrowing his eyes.

My smile melted. No, of course I didn't, but it was just about the only good option I had in this tumbleweed town, pummeled by a crap economy.

"We can't all just ride off into the sunset and make our money other ways," I told him, shaking my head. "Christ, Joker. If you're about to offer me some kind of strip job or worse, don't even go there. I don't want it."

He stiffened underneath me, tightening his hold on my

back. I laid a finger on his chest, giving him one firm tap, right across the winged skull darkening his skin.

"I want *you,* Jackson. Not the club. Whatever else is happening between us, that's as far as it goes."

"Babe, don't be fuckin' stupid," he said, following the kiss I'd laid on his chest with one on my forehead. "You think I want any of my brothers seeing you naked, then I'm gonna think I truly fucked your brains out. I want you happy, square with your money. If you ain't finding shit here for work, you oughta look elsewhere."

"Where? Like Knoxville?"

He smiled, cocky and sly as ever. "Something like that. Helluva a lot more opportunities out there than Seddon. Even more in the Tri-Cities, not too far over."

I didn't answer him then. There wasn't anything to say when my brain was still processing, overwhelmed by everything that had happened tonight.

So, I just buried my face in his chest, freely breathing that scent I'd remembered for three terrible years.

Maybe I'd have to move, if it kept him a little closer, and paid me, too. I'd wanted to put down roots in this town because it was all I knew, but it wasn't working out that way.

Here, the ground was barren.

Not that I'd be making any fly decisions tonight.

All the misery of mama, poverty, and the bar hadn't turned me into a fool. We'd just see how well the next few weeks went.

By the end of them, if he wasn't just playing me – a very

huge if – then maybe it'd be time to think about finding somewhere new.

His fingers pinched my ass, causing me to look up. That mischievous smirk on his lips turned into a hungry one.

His hand slipped down, pushed between my legs, and pulled them apart like he owned them.

Tonight, I suppose he did.

He jerked me up, moved me over him, until I was straddling his cock, already rock hard.

"Enough fuckin' around with the future, Summertime. We've got the whole damned night ahead, and I'd rather hear you screaming than giving me shit any time. You've got nothing to worry about, long as you're in these arms."

One push of his hands on my ass cheeks lowered me on his cock. Then I couldn't think about anything at all except how good, how right, how incredible he felt deep inside me.

* * * *

The next few weeks should've been a total nightmare. Instead, they'd become a dream.

All thanks to him. Joker.

The bastard who'd taken over my head for three long years roared in, wooed me, and conquered my life.

He came to me every other night since our first beneath the stars. I'd climb on his bike with a grin, feeling my heart skipping a dozen beats per minute. He'd introduce me to half a dozen new secret spots around Seddon I hadn't known before.

Now, I knew them like his body, intimately acquainted with every single one of them when we were naked and horizontal in the tall grasses, the broken down barns, the little nook next to the stream.

That last place, he'd held me up in the air the entire time we fucked, banging me into the boulders behind us each time he thrust deep.

It should've hurt, being flung around like a ragdoll, but of course it didn't.

Basically, the story of this whole insane romance that sprang up between us. Assuming you could call motorcycle rides, doe eyes, and hard sex any kind of love story.

What should've been agony became delight.

Pain turned into pleasure.

Risk blossomed from barren fear into a beautiful certainty.

Forbidden? Impossible?

All of the above, plus so much more.

Nothing about us should've worked, especially at this awful crossroads in my life. But it did, damn it.

We were working, hooking up for more than just a fuck. I truly believed we had more to ourselves than sheet soaking sex.

He was exactly what I needed when I left mama's place forever, watching as the sheriff and the moving crew from the bank moved in and roped off the place where I'd grown up.

Joker helped me christen my new apartment the very first night, throwing me down on the mattress between the boxes.

I sucked his cock on the worn floor, practicing everything he'd taught me. Then he slipped between my legs, fisted my hair, and covered my mouth with his free hand.

I bit him to keep from screaming, just shy of making my new neighbors hate me on day one.

Three weeks blurred by in a blissful storm.

He went back to Knoxville, satisfied he'd finished whatever he'd come here to do with his brother.

I didn't ask. He didn't tell.

"Club business," he'd growl, whenever I got too close to wondering what he did on that bike without me. "We'll talk about anything in the fuckin' world, babe, except for that."

I wasn't stupid. I knew he did bad, illegal things because he wore that patch. Busted up bigger bastards than him when they asked for it, and earned his money by the sweat of his mystery.

Hell, I'd known it from day one, that first kiss we'd shared when I was just a stupid kid.

Both the Taylor boys were bad news. But to me, he was the best I'd ever gotten, and I wasn't going to let it slip away without giving it a chance.

Joker kept coming, making the long drive down from eastern Tennessee, usually just for me.

One weekend, Piece came with him. Both of them were here to handle more of that growl-worthy *club business* that always put me on edge, however much I tried to pretend it didn't exist.

I'd just started working at drugstore in town when he

picked me up. Even through the noise and at least forty feet to the lot, I heard his motorcycle.

Who knew that harsh sound could make a girl smile every damned time?

Then he was there, in front of me.

When this man walked into a room, everything came to a screeching stop. Customers and other employees froze and stared, watching him swagger in between the registers, decked out in dark leather covered in his fearsome patches like a modern day knight.

"Babe, hurry the fuck up and finish your shift," he growled. "I'm taking you out tonight."

I looked at the old woman I'd been ringing up apologetically. Surprisingly, she smiled and shot me a wink, readjusting her glasses. I ran her credit card and scooped her stuff into a plastic bag.

"My, he's a big one," she said, looking at my man like a piece of meat.

Seriously? I blinked, gingerly lifting the bag and passing it into her hands.

"Get out of here and have some fun, girl," the granny said with a smile. "Men like this don't come around except once in a blood moon."

She was gone. Thankfully, there hadn't been anyone else behind her, so I turned to Joker.

He'd been giving me that arrogant, hungry look the whole time, the one that pulled at my nipples like an invisible set of clamps. *Mercy.*

"Did you hear that?" I asked. "Blood moon? What's she

talking about?"

"Sounded like blue moon to me." He shrugged. "Fuck if I know, beautiful. Old spinster's too damned smart for her own good. You heard the woman. Punch the fuck out and let's go."

Smiling, I sighed and looked over his head, staring at the huge clock mounted on the wall. I had about three more minutes left, but it probably wouldn't hurt to close up a little early.

We passed a rack of cheap tabloids on the way out, filled with the brain candy everyone reads in waiting rooms. Yes, stories about the royal family renting a spare room to Elvis, or how Martians are behind rigging the next election.

One of the magazines had a huge red moon on it. That made me stop and stare, scanning it for a second.

PROPHECY! The headline screamed. *Will you survive the next blood moon, or crash and burn?*

So, that was where she'd gotten it. I kept walking, following him out to his bike, inwardly laughing off the creepy coincidence. The old lady had to have seen them on her way out, too, and maybe she'd slipped up when she meant to say "blue moon." Just like Joker said.

Out here, the moon hung big and brilliant red in the sky. Even Joker stopped for a second to stare up at it, whistling into the darkness.

"Fuck me with a bottle. Ain't ever seen a big, red bastard like that hanging in the sky for years. Maybe never." He turned to me with a wicked smile on his face. "Might be the end of the world tonight, babe. We'd better fuck like rabbits."

"Oh, please." I rolled my eyes, locking my hands tight around his powerful waist, resting my chin on his shoulder so I had a perfect angle to whisper into his ear. "Is that how you celebrate the end? We were going to do that anyway, right?"

"Damned straight," he growled, reaching behind us for a second to squeeze my thigh.

My pulse quickened. Blood moon or not, we were getting into some seriously sexy mischief tonight.

Yeah. If only things had gone down that way.

When we took off down the road, I didn't know I was living the last happy moments of my life. It took me a few more weeks to realize how deadly, ominous, and hungry that evil moon in the sky really was.

* * * *

"Joker, no! Their lights are on – this place isn't abandoned at all!" Giggling, I flattened my hands on his chest, pushing desperately. "We can't do it here with people around."

He'd already buried me underneath him, staring down at me with that feral gleam in his hazel eyes. "Fuck if I care. You can bury your face in my palm again if you want so Farmer Jones don't hear you screaming."

I kicked my legs. "I *do* care – especially if they come out here with a shotgun to kick us out!"

I didn't have a clue who owned this place. Normally, his judgment was spot on finding secret places for us out in the country.

Fucking outdoors certainly hadn't lost its charm since I'd gotten my own place. We did it often, whenever the urge took hold while riding through the countryside.

"Babe, trust me, there ain't gonna be any trouble tonight," he growled, silencing me with a long, sticky kiss. "Calm your sweet ass down, or I'll pull down those pants and spank the shit outta you 'til you do."

I stuck my tongue out. He talked like an animal – and I must've gone insane because it turned me on.

"Don't fuckin' tempt me, Summertime. You think I'm bluffing?"

Heavens, no.

I nodded anyway, pulling back when he tried to bury his lips on mine again.

Teasing a man like this was playing with fire, yeah, but it was the most exquisite kind of fire a woman could get.

That did it. I tried not to squeal as he lifted me up, throwing me over his shoulder, just enough to undo my belt and yank down my jeans. I kicked hard, thrashing so he couldn't get them all the way off.

He loved the bad girl act. So did I.

Hell, he'd already introduced me to a lot of things I hadn't expected to ever love. The biggest one was staring at me, the bastard himself, giving me a look that said this was way more serious than foreplay.

"Stop moving or I'll hoist you up right here in the field while we fuck," he rumbled in my ear, hot and low as summer thunder.

"No!" I whimpered, shaking my head.

"Yeah, fuck yeah, baby girl. I don't bullshit, and you know it. Keep wrestling, your pants are gone. I'll spank the shit out of you, fuck you where the bastards in the house can see, and leave your clothes here in the dirt. You can take the bitch seat my bike completely naked."

Oh. My. God.

I stiffened in his arms. The insane threat lit every nerve I had on fire.

He couldn't possibly be serious – could he?

Between the panic, my pussy gushed, lost in the heatwave of anger and filthy desire smashing together.

His threats scared me, aroused me, and tempted me all at once.

I was still trying to decide whether to slap his face and see if he'd make good on it when his hand caught the back of my jeans and pulled.

Cool wind kissed my bare cheeks. His eyebrows shot up. I drank in the surprise on his face and grinned.

"No fuckin' panties? Shit!"

"Told you, I'm full of surprises. You haven't gotten me figured out yet, Joker."

A low growl began building in his throat. I'd heard it a couple dozen times by now, and I loved it every single time. I braced myself, ready to be thrown down on the ground while he tore at my clothes, hurled into a desperate heat to fuck me senseless.

But a loud ringing went off next to us.

I gasped. My heart leaped into my throat, and for a bitter second, I thought we'd really been caught by the people who lived here.

No, it was something else – his phone. He carefully set me back on the ground. I reached for my pants, pulling them up while he turned his back, staring at the phone he'd jerked from his pocket.

"What the fuck? Grandpa's number?" Joker muttered. He tapped a key and held it up to his ear. "Grandpa? What's up?"

I leaned in. There was nothing but static on the other end, a faint crackling that didn't resemble voices.

White noise. Vague and chilling.

After another few seconds, he killed the call and redialed. My brow furrowed as I wrapped both my hands around his, listening in, hoping it was nothing so we could get back to the filthy, crazy things we were about to do.

Somehow, my heart knew it wouldn't be so simple. I had that sinking feeling deep in my stomach. The kind I'd got when mama brushed off her sickness like no big deal, even when she couldn't keep down toast and water.

"Fuck. We have to go," Joker said finally, pushing his fingers through mine. "Ain't like him to call when he knows I'm out. Never heard his line acting up like this. Something's up."

"Let me come with, Joker," I said. I'd been itching for a chance to get closer to his family, to test where we were going. "I'll stay outside if anything's up. Promise."

Smiling, I crossed my heart. He hesitated for a few seconds, but finally nodded.

"All right. Let's fuckin' go."

We flew down the highway leading back into Seddon.

His grandpa had a cozy little house on the outskirts of town.

Soon, we were parked outside it. A faint light was on in the window. Joker's body hardened underneath my hands when we pulled up, and I saw him looking at his brother's bike, parked next to the old man's truck.

He killed the engine and we listened quietly to insects droning in the night. Tucking my helmet into the storage compartment, I stood there next to him, eyeballing the mad tension souring his face. He inhaled deeply several times, turning his head.

"Jackson, what is it?"

"Smoke. Somebody's been roasting the shit outta something in the fire pit." He took off toward the small ring of stones at the side of the house.

I ran after him, putting my arm over my mouth so I wouldn't cough. The stink of something strange and sickly hung in the air. I'd barely noticed it at first, but now that I was closer, it was withering.

I found him at the firepit's edge, crouched on a ground. He held a long stick in his hand, and the burned tatters of something leathery hung at the end.

"What is that?" I asked nervously, hesitating to put my hand on his shoulder.

"Nothing good," he whispered, squinting at the thing on the stick. "Looks like somebody's fuckin' cut's been burned out here. Can't make out the damned colors…"

No kidding. The leather vest barely resembled anything now, looking a lot like a skinned animal singed to a crisp. He shook it off and kicked off the grill sitting over the fire, pushing his stick through the ash and debris.

It looked like there were rocks mixed in with the coals and cloudy ash. Bone white rocks, covered in scorch marks.

Bone. I trembled.

No. It couldn't be human…

"Jackson?" I looked at him intently, clutching his sleeve.

He pressed a finger against his lips, flashing me a sharp look. My eyes went wide when I saw his free hand pulling his gun from its holster.

"Quiet, babe. Some serious shit's been going down. You wait here, back behind the tree." He stopped and pointed to the large trunk several steps away. "Grandpa doesn't go to sleep so fuckin' early, and neither does Piece. Sure as fuck don't come out here to grill after dark, except when Piece is looking for a midnight snack…and the shit in here ain't anybody's dinner. It's too quiet. Too fucked up. Hang tight. I'm goin' in alone. You hear anybody else moving out here, you scream, and I'll come runnin'."

I wanted to cry out, but I didn't dare. My heart pulsed frantically in my chest. For the first time since we'd shown up here, I knew we were in real danger, something I wasn't ready to handle.

I hung back behind the big tree out front, obeying him word for word, my hand on my pocket. First sign of trouble, I'd call the police.

Depending on the biker code to handle whatever was happening out here wasn't going to do. I couldn't let anybody else get hurt.

God. Swallowing a lump in my throat, I let the evil possibilities wash over me.

There'd been so many rumors about the Deadhands moving into town, the rival motorcycle gang that had eaten up most of Georgia.

What if they'd found out about Joker and his brother? What if they were here?

Just relax. Breathe, I told myself.

Up in the sky, the big moon glowed, still holding a little of its blood red tinge from the eclipse earlier this evening.

The first gunshot exploded inside the house a second later.

I jumped at the sound, hugging the tree for support. Two more loud bangs echoed through the night, one after another.

My fingers shook as I pulled out my phone, desperately trying to get it up to my face, so I could dial.

The last few drops of blood in my body that weren't already glacial became ice when I saw the dark, lifeless screen.

"Shit!" I cursed myself, remembering that it'd been low on charge at work. I'd fucking forgotten to plug it in.

Stuffing it back into my pocket, I peaked around the tree, staring at the house. If there was any sane way out of this, I'd find it inside, however hellish it might be.

I had to move. I had to find him.

Walking into the house made me feel disembodied. I hadn't had that sensation since mama's funeral, the one where it seems like a woman's soul is going to leave her body forever, and there's nothing she can do about it.

The screen door creaked loudly in my hands, making me

silently curse the whole evil situation one more time. As soon as I was in, I heard...a slapping sound?

Someone banged on something soft. Like the way I remembered mama slapping bread dough.

"Joker?" I whispered, creeping around the corner.

There wasn't much to the place. Just two tiny rooms, a kitchen, and a main living area.

Someone had left a blanket and several empty beer bottles on the floor, next to the couch. I carefully avoided tripping on them and pressed forward, perking my ears up again, listening for anything.

I heard him when I was near the first little room. Joker's voice sputtering in a harsh whisper.

Desperate. Horrified. Enraged.

"Grandpa, come on. Come on. Come the fuck on!"

Fingers trembling, I gripped the edge of the door, and pushed it open.

First thing I noticed was the broken glass all over the place. Someone had shot out the window – probably the gunshots I'd heard.

Joker leaned on the floor, bent over the old man, frantically pumping his granddad's chest.

I was about to drop down and help when I noticed the strange, round object perched on the bed. At first, it looked like a pumpkin in the shadowy darkness, but it was only July. Jack-o-lanterns weren't close to being in season yet.

Pushing the door just a little more so I could get light into the room, the shadows moved. Then I saw the detached face staring at me from the bed.

Joker's face, missing his brilliant hazel eyes. They'd been plucked from his head, leaving two neat spiderwebs of blood curling down his sunken cheeks.

Both my hands went straight to my mouth. I tried not to hyperventilate as I realized I was looking at Freddy's severed head, ripped from his body, mutilated in their own house.

Beneath me, the old man sputtered, gasping for breath, finally alive again.

"Fuck, fuck, fuck, fuck, thank Christ," Joker groaned.

The next few seconds happened in slow motion like some kind of horror movie. He stood, shaking as he got up on his knees, his phone in one hand. He looked at his twin brother's severed head on the bed, and then turned to me slowly, wiping away the hot, brutal tear rolling down his cheek.

"Joker...Jackson..." I tried to say more than just his name, the only two I knew them by, but the words wouldn't come.

What the *hell* do you say to a man who's just lost everything? What the fuck could I possibly say that would mean anything?

"Get. Out," He growled, stepping toward me until I backed away, filling the empty doorway with his huge body. "Old friend's coming to take you home."

No, let me stay! I want to help! I thought, but my tongue was completely stiff when I tried to speak, my mouth hanging open like a total fool.

"Joker..."

"Do *not* fuckin' argue. You heard me," he said, his warm, cocky voice turned into a killer's ice. "This ain't for you, babe. You don't belong here. You never did."

Those cracks in my heart deepened. Split. Shattered.

Dashing out the door, I held in a scream, feeling the sharp pieces of my own heart clattering against my ribs, tearing me in two.

The rest of the night passed in a stupor. Somehow, I forced myself onto the porch, where I sat there and waited. Eventually, an old truck pulled up, and an older man wearing a military hat waved.

He asked me where I lived. I told him. Those were the only words we exchanged until he was at my door.

"Out," he said, reaching past me to pop the door.

I turned, giving the asshole the dirtiest look I had. "Really? After all that, you fucking tell me to –"

"You've got ten seconds, doll, before I shove you out that door and take off. I don't ask the questions, just do favors when the club asks me. If you've got any sense in your pretty little head, you'll do the same." He looked at me, his eyes dark and angry, like I was the biggest chore he'd ever had. "Go home. And don't you *ever* tell anybody what the fuck happened out there tonight."

He had me. He won.

I couldn't deal with this shit. Not after what I'd seen, death and destruction, the love draining from the face of the man I'd started to believe in.

I didn't walk. I ran, all the way to my doorstep, jamming the keys in so hard I nearly snapped them in the locks.

Bed was my only sanctuary.

My face hit the pillows as soon as I was home. I buried it there, drowning in my tears, hoping they'd pull me completely under so I'd never have to wake up. When I did, it was going to be one long nightmare.

Oh, if only that hell was the end of it. I had no idea how terrible things were about to get.

* * * *

Present Day

Three years this week. Three blinding, painful, monstrous years.

It seemed like it passed in the blink of an eye.

The days I cried for him, too scared to anywhere near his grandfather's house. All the rumors I heard at work about the murder, the decapitation, the worst crime this town suffered for generations.

People talked about how they'd been scared shitless. But I also heard the relief in their voices after a few weeks, when they knew the crime was too big to bring any outlaws back to Seddon anytime soon.

And they were still talking, gossiping, holding their children a little tighter each night when I started to get sick.

Really sick. Every damned morning.

It took me a full week before I could manage to sit down with the pregnancy test, and prove what my body already knew. It only took a day after I saw that neon pink line staring me in the face to decide what I'd do.

I had to keep it. This baby was a miracle grown in darkness, and he deserved a chance to fight, no different from me or Joker.

Joker. Jackson. The devil and the Adonis stuffed into one mortal man, now somewhere very far away, shattered in his grief.

I didn't know if he was alive or dead. As much as my heart cared, my head didn't. Not anymore.

It took all my energy to keep myself from getting in my car and driving up to Knoxville. I knew it wouldn't be hard to find him if I did, somewhere at the Pistols' clubhouse.

I thought about it a thousand times. How I'd break the news, and plead with him to come home, or at least give me a space here so we could start a life together with our child.

But he wasn't Joker anymore. He wasn't the man who'd swept me off my feet and carried this town on the Taylors' strongman reputation.

The man who'd looked at me, spoken to me, and forced me out of that cursed house was someone else. Someone I'd never let myself truly recognize.

His eyes were so vacant. His voice, so cruel. Dead to the world, and to me.

It was like he'd lost his soul in the hot tear I'd seen rolling down his cheek. Our love had gone with it.

A man this broken couldn't be my lover. And he damned sure wasn't going to be a father to my son or daughter.

It wasn't just Piece who'd been killed and buried that night.

Joker, the man I'd begun to love, was dead. So were the pieces of my ruined heart, driven into the ground for good, one shard at a time.

All we had left was our suffering. Both of us alone, condemned to our private hell.

I didn't have to think hard to imagine what he'd become. No man who wore the patch let something like this go lightly. He'd be hellbent on revenge.

He'd be reckless. He'd live for nothing besides blood, until he got back at the men who killed Freddy, or they killed him, too.

All the reasons I didn't dare put myself and the baby between him and the monsters who'd consume him every waking minute.

I had to live my own life. Had to raise my son. Just had to forget the man who'd helped me create him.

That's exactly what I did for three numb, lonely years.

* * * *

I was standing over Alex, still staring into the building's parking lot, when I heard the knock at the door.

My hand went to my chest, soothing my ferocious heartbeat.

Jesus. Who the hell could it be pounding away at this hour?

I checked to make sure the sound hadn't disturbed my baby too much. No, he laid there quietly, sleepy and peaceful as ever. Thankful for small favors, I moved out into the hall, my feet growing heavier with each step toward the door.

The bolt had fallen off the shoddy lock about six months ago. Now I *really* wished I'd bothered to replace it, especially when I cracked it open just enough to see the huge, dark silhouette standing there.

"Yeah? Can I help you, sir?"

He didn't answer with words. I was too stunned to scream when he shoved the door hard, slamming me into the wall. The door crashed against my shoulder and I fell over, bracing myself against the TV stand.

I was quick, but he was faster. The bastard wrestled me to the ground like nothing, his hand flying across my mouth as he kicked the door shut behind him.

It slammed like a bullet. I heard Alex, startled awake, crying over the insane thud of my heart pounding my ears deaf.

"Listen to me, and listen fuckin' good, dolly. This is the way it's all going down, and you don't got a choice. You scream, I gut you here on the floor. You start crying, maybe I knock you the fuck out, and head straight for your kid's room. You're gonna lay there like a good girl, look at me, and keep your damned mouth shut. It's easy, long as you don't do nothing stupid. You follow?"

I did. He'd just threatened the only thing I cared about.

My fear turned into a supernatural calm, the kind a person probably has in the wild when they're being stalked by a lion.

"Good. Fuckin' knew it wouldn't be real hard to drill it

through your skull." He let me go and stood up straight. I got a good look at him for the first time.

Even though it was dark, I could see the patches. DEADHANDS MC, GEORGIA. PRESIDENT.

A huge severed gray hand was stitched on his side, identical to the one he had on his back. Red was all over his cut, like thick spatters of blood sewn into his leather, and so was a half-skinned cartoon skull with one eye hanging out.

He didn't look like much. Hair slicked back on his pony tail, a couple scars on his face, nothing I hadn't seen before in Uncle Robby's old bar.

Except for his eyes. One blue. One green. Both more sinister than anything I'd ever seen.

He was big. Mean. Brutal in every breath and every movement, a smug smile hiding behind his salt and pepper beard as he thumbed his switchblade.

"Let's talk business, doll. What I'm looking for is easier than a pig rolling in shit, and we can be best friends if you do me a solid."

I put my hands on my knees, bracing myself, listening very closely without saying a word to this demon. I would've killed him if I thought I had a chance.

He had to know that.

It only made him smile wider as he slowly crouched, until his face was dead center with mine. "Name's Hatch. You don't know me, Summer Olivers, but I know you very fuckin' well. I know everything about anybody I want in this state, right down to the times they piss and fuck. My club's got eyes and ears fuckin' everywhere. You fuck up, you get a laser crawling across your tits. Only warning you get before a bullet blows through your heart. Or maybe you come home to find your brother's head hacked off and laying gutted on your bed, smiling from the holes where his eyes used to be..."

The asshole trailed off. My heartbeat quickened, taken back to that night when Freddy, Joker, and my last chance at a normal life died.

Murdered. Killed by this animal staring at me like a tiger. Hungry, taunting, and merciless.

"What?" I whispered. "How could you –"

"Don't play dumb. I know you were there, bitch, and so was that old man rotting away in a nursing home. So was your old boyfriend, Joker, now the Deadly Pistols' Veep. He's moved up in this old world, and left you in the fuckin' dust by the looks of it."

God damn, he was good. Ripping open old wounds and rubbing salt in deep.

I kept my eyes glued to his, trying not to shake, not to cry, not to open up any weaknesses that would risk my Alex.

"Aw, come on, keep the waterworks off. I ain't here to patch up shit between fuck buddies. I'm here because you're bait."

The only thing I'd ever hated more than this man was the single ruthless tear that finally escaped, rolling down my cheek. He reached out, catching it on his fingertip, staring at it like a bug he'd just caught.

My stomach turned when he raised a finger to his mouth, making a show out of licking it off. "Fuck, that's good. Makes me wanna do all the shit I came in here squawking about, especially with Betty G being so goddamned fuckin' hungry tonight..."

He held up his switchblade, shifting his fingers to the side, so I could see the name scrawled on it in a cursive script. *Betty G.*

Jesus, he was talking about his fucking knife like a person. Psychopath confirmed.

My eyes were bigger than the saucers stacked in my cabinet, just several feet away.

If he took a step toward Alex's room, I'd have to make a run for it.

I'd run, fling the cabinet open, or pull one of the knives from the block, whichever seemed easiest...

"Shit, little mama, don't worry your pretty head. I ain't here to fuck with you and the kiddo unless you say no to anything I tell you. That, doll, is a very, very, very fuckin' serious offense." Smiling, he stood up, running the finger that had been in his mouth across the edge of the blade.

He winced, exaggerating his pain. "Ouch! Betty's been sharpened up. Bitch almost cut me, and I can't have her making me bleed all over your carpet."

"Why?" I whispered, hearing my own voice from a hundred feet away. "Why are you here? I haven't seen or spoken to Joker for years. You have to know that's true."

I couldn't take him toying with me a minute longer.

"Yeah, and thank fuck for that, Summer. He won't see you coming 'til you're right on his doorstep, shoving his kid in his face. He'll trust you. He'll open up. And that's when you'll find out every fuckin' thing I want to know about his club and feed it back to me, straight down the pipe."

It all made sense now. And I wished to holy God it didn't.

"Don't, please," I said, shaking my head, feeling more brutal tears rolling down my cheeks. "I'm not a spy. I just want to be left alone."

He looked at me for a long second, his face turning white. Then he tipped his rough head back and laughed, so loud he made Alex cry harder in the other room.

"Okay, okay, okay." Hatch shrugged. "Have it your way. I'll kill the kid first and throw your worthless fuckin' carcass on top of his."

I lunged, wrapping my arms around his boot, before he could even take one step toward my baby's room. Alex screamed, bawling louder in the other room, as if he could sense the evil coming.

"No, no, no, please! I didn't mean it that way. I'll do anything you say. Anything. Just please…don't go in there."

Hatch stopped, his boot halfway raised above my fingers. He looked down at me.

"Give me your fuckin' phone. Right now."

I looked around, moving my shaking hand down to my pajama pocket. I pulled it out and handed it to him. His nasty face got nastier, twisting into a sadistic smirk as he hurled it against the wall so hard I heard it splinter. It left a dent in the wall, going out with a flash, before the pieces bounced on the carpet.

"Here's your new one," he said, stuffing a newer, crappier flip phone into my hand. "You use that shit to check in with the only number on it. You see it ring, you drop whatever the fuck you're doing, and fuckin' answer. Even little Alex. Understood?"

"Yes," I said, nodding painfully.

Yes. Somehow, someway, I'm going to fucking kill you, I thought to myself.

"Awesome. You're pretty smart for a bitch without a man," he growled, turning around. "You leave tomorrow for Knoxville. We'll tell you the place you're staying when we hear you're on the road, and then you'll get the orders I know you're waiting for with baited fuckin' breath."

"Okay. I understand," I said, each word drying my throat like a desert.

"No, that's the shitty part, Summer, I don't think you do." He looked at me as I blinked in confusion, his mismatched eyes shining. "I'm gonna walk out that door, get on my bike, and fuckin' leave you with your brat. You just stay on the floor for the next hour before you start cleaning up the mess."

I stared at him dumbly as he licked he gazed straight through me. "This is the part where I get to have some fun, and show you how fuckin' serious this is so you don't do anything stupid."

There wasn't any time to wonder what the hell he was talking about. His hand struck the side of my face like a head-on collision.

I blacked out before I even hit the floor.

IV: Down and Dirty (Joker)

Sometimes I thought about what a fuckin' idiot I used to be.

Thought about that night I lost Piece, my grandpa lost his freedom, and I left behind the shithole town that had the only woman I ever gave a shit about fucking more than once.

Those thoughts drove me to the range, or else the closest bottle of good Tennessee brown honey.

Today was one of those fuckin' days. I'd just got outta church, listening to the Prez yammering about the latest big plans.

Bingo was on his leash. Had to hold him tight to keep him from galloping around like a tornado when he felt the wind brush his face.

The big hairy Irish Wolfound licked my face when I leaned down to put him on his chain. Damned dog loved to run all the fuck over, and we normally let him, but not anywhere the brothers were shooting their guns.

"Good boy," I growled, reaching into my pack for a fresh bone. He barked excitedly as I tossed it on the ground in front of him, watching as he dug into it, happier than any creature had any right to be from something so fuckin' simple.

If I could still smile, that shit would've done it.

Didn't take much to please a dog, long as he was fed, stroked, and walked. Took a lot more to please a man.

Took even more to undo the bad shit. And good fuckin' luck ever wiping out the truly awful, tragic stain on a man's soul.

I hadn't figured out how. All I had was a release valve for the blinding rage out here.

Soon as my nine was in my hands, that demon energy flowed out of me, bit by bit. Flamed out in each and every bullet I fired at the torn wooden targets and weather mannequins we used for practice.

Taking aim at a half-cracked face peeking out behind some old boards, I fired. Missed. Gritted my teeth 'til they almost fuckin' broke and tried again.

Had to kill these venom thoughts, one shot at a time.

One bullet for the good times in Seddon, at Robby's old bar, places and people as done as this plastic motherfucker was about to be.

One more for the sick, sorry fucks who still owed a blood debt to me. They'd ripped apart the only fuckin' family I'd ever had, killed my twin brother, and burned him in a barbecue pit. Put the old man in a place where he couldn't take a fuckin' piss without some nosy cocksucker leaning over his shoulder.

Pulled the trigger again for Summertime. Whatever the

fuck I'd said to her that night when I was blind to everything except raw bloodlust, revenge, and hate, it worked.

The dummy's head exploded into a thousand pieces on the third try. I grunted to myself, satisfied, knowing it'd be at least ten minutes before the urge to kill swept over me like a fresh tidal wave.

Those evil words stayed with me, even after I stuffed my gun in its holster and watched the dog, chewing his boney treat to a mess.

Evil or not, they'd done their job. They'd kept her the fuck away. They'd saved me from the demons for a few more hours.

Only goddamned thing I ever asked for.

I'd been outta my fuckin' mind to think I could ever bring a girl like her into this sick, toxic life. Sure as shit wouldn't pull her deeper, drowning her, painting a goddamned target on her back like Freddy and Grandpa, or all the other boys in this club and their old ladies.

Fuck the past. Fuck it all.

"Bingo, you big damned badass," a voice growled. I looked up to see Firefly standing there, our big Enforcer, a new rifle hanging over his shoulder, leaning down to pat my dog on the head while he snarled into his bone.

"Leave him be. He's chewing his heart out."

Firefly smiled. "Don't take much, does it? I'll bring him a new one next week. Whole fuckin' club might as well get its jollies in before the Prez takes us to the grinder."

Drawing my switchblade, I stiffened up, standing over a

stump with a spare sharpener we used to keep our shit stabby. "He ain't taking us anywhere, brother. It's the goddamned Deads screaming for blood."

"Can't argue. Won't be easy, though. Some of our boys got a good chance of getting shot to shit on this run. Deads got the numbers. We've got the brains, the balls, and bigger fuckin' bullets. Only question is if it'll be enough."

I snorted, ripping the sharpener up and sliding my knife through it. "You're going soft like Skinny boy, Firefly. Ever since you married that chick and knocked her up. You're talkin' like you're afraid."

"Afraid? No." I could practically hear the steam hissing out his mouth. "Fuck yeah, family changes a man. I'm gonna have a kid hanging on my arm in five or six months. I ain't going back on anything the Prez orders, and neither is Skin, because both of us have got a fuck of a lot more to fight for here than you do."

My eyes tried to dig a hole through his skull. He didn't have a fuckin' clue.

Firefly and Skin, they'd go off like bombs for their women, their kids, putting the patch last. For me, these colors came first, second, and third, equal partner to the bloodlust boiling me alive for over three fuckin' years.

None of the brothers knew what really happened to Piece.

They didn't know about the blood oath Prez promised me the night I reported in. Didn't know he'd told me to keep it quiet because we didn't have the strength to fight like we needed to in those days.

Dust slapped his big arms around me, pulled me close that night, promising we'd rip the throats out of the sorry fuckers who'd done my brother one day, when the time was finally right.

Prez got me drunk. Held me back. Stopped me from going deep into Georgia on a suicide run, with nothing but my gun, a pack of grenades, and enough rage to blast myself to kingdom come.

Would've done it, too. Would've driven into the Deads' clubhouse and blown myself up like something outta the shit overseas.

Firefly's rifle cracked. I blinked.

We'd stopped talking. I slid my knife against the stone hard and fast, thinking about skinning the fuck outta every sick motherfucker I could find who wore the bloody hand on their cut.

His shot went straight through the boards hiding the dummy whose head I'd taken off, and kept going. The mannequin's body joined its head in a million pieces, shattered beyond redemption.

"Goddamn, this baby's got a kick. Helluva a scope on her too," he said, more to himself than me. "Haven't had this kinda firepower in my hands since the army days."

"That's one big fuckin' check mark in our column," I said. "Quit worrying so much about the op. We're gonna kick their asses so hard into the ocean, the Grizzlies will be on their damned knees, begging for our routes. Haven't ever let death stop us before, and we're not gonna start."

"Brother, I'm telling you, you've got it all wrong. Ain't

death I'm worried about." He looked up, anger in his big blue eyes. "It's my wife and kid coming up without me that's making me stand here and practice the shit outta this gun 'til I've got it right. It's a motivator – not a damned detriment."

"Whatever. We'll see about that." My fingers began burning.

I had to test my knife. Firefly's mad eyes stayed on me the whole time as I laid my hand against my tree bark, taking the freshly sharpened blade in the other. I started stabbing that fucker right between my fingers like a jackhammer.

All the brothers winced when I did it. Turned their stomachs, expecting me to lose a finger or two every time.

Fuckin' pussies, all of 'em.

They thought I was outta my damned mind.

Maybe I was, ever since that night when the lights went out forever.

My blade stabbed faster, faster, dangerously close to carving off one of my digits, closer on the next thrust. Fucked up as this shit was, it *always* took the edge off.

Reminded me how close death and dismemberment lurked every day, wearing this patch. Reminded me to be fearless, hard as a stone, ready to do whatever it took to keep my Veep patch and mean it.

Reminded me that giving yourself something to lose was fuckin' stupid. With two brothers going soft thanks to their girls or babies on the way, it'd be up to me to pick up the slack, to charge in and cut every throat we needed to, without any second guessing.

Some of those sick bastards probably had old ladies and kids, too. That family shit would make them hesitate, and it'd be fatal when my knife went through their throats, before they put theirs through mine.

Firefly sat on a log, cleaning his gun, when my fingers finally cramped up and gave out. I dropped the knife, letting it clatter against my boot. Picked up some mud when I reached down to grab it, and I wiped it on my thigh, feeling a little hate streaming out my body.

Wish there were a whole lot more going with it, but fuck if I hadn't stopped wishing long ago.

Bingo started barking just then. He'd dropped his bone, causing it to roll down the small incline, just outta reach from the spot where he was straining on his chain.

"Shit. Hold up, boy." I looked down, noticing how the fuckin' thing had gotten lodged in that little pit we used at the to hide our spare guns.

Not an easy climb. I got down on one knee and slid, turning to see Firefly standing by my dog at the last second.

Lost my grip somewhere along the way and fell three feet, smack in the mud, right on my ass. Overhead, Firefly and Sixty looked down at me, laughing their asses off.

"You need a rope down there, bro?"

Fucking shit. Sixty's crap didn't deserve a response, so I reached into the muck, digging around the cold metal box to see where that damned bone had gone.

Took about a solid minute for my hand to come up with that chewed up, dirty, mottled white stick. That was when the wrecking ball crashed through my brain.

I toppled back against the wall, twitching like a current went through me. My eyes weren't seeing the club's spiderholes anymore.

Instead, I saw the *hell* in grandpa's fire pit three goddamned years ago.

My brother's bones. What was left of his scorched cut. They'd burned him, bones and all, incinerating his leather, his clothes, his flesh. His whole fuckin' body.

Everything except the head I'd found, next to grandpa, who was barely breathing after his heart attack.

They'd ripped out his fuckin' eyes. My eyes, the same hazel set we shared as twins.

That sick, soulless grin from my own flesh and blood haunted me. Stalked me like a demon through time and space, always sideswiping me like this during the most mundane bullshit.

Damn. *Damn!*

I quietly cursed the shit out of everything now, swinging the bone, holding my muddy face up to the sky and screaming.

"Joker! Fuck's sake!" Firefly's booming voice cut through the nightmare. "Get a damned rope. We're coming down for him."

"No!" I snarled, shaking my head.

Holding the bone between my teeth, no different than my dog, I pushed my fingers deep into the muddy walls of the pit where I could find the wooden boards. They were rotten and dirty but they held a man up. I climbed through the slippery shit with brute force, one push at a time, hauling myself over the ledge about two minutes later.

I ignored the hands my brothers held out. The bone plopped outta my mouth and the big dog started growling, staring at me all covered in mud.

"Shit, Veep, you okay?" Firefly asked, shaking his head.

"We've gotta get a fuckin' gate around that thing," I said, standing, shaking off the muck clinging to my jeans.

Picking up the bone, I carried it over to my dog and took him off his chain. He plucked it up in his mouth as we made our way through the clubhouse, heading for my room.

Time to go. I'd drop Bingo off and then hit the showers, blast all this crap away, before I hit the bottle or my bike.

Didn't know about the order just yet. Shit, maybe I'd ride into town, check out the new skin shop, the Ruby Heel. The girls there were easy, desperate to suck the cock of any man wearing this patch.

Probably thought it'd bring 'em more money than what they got in tips at our joint. Or maybe they just got wet for any man with a bike, a cut, and a dick between his legs that could fuck them to high heaven.

I stopped by the sink near the back, jerking the bone outta the wolfhound's mouth one more time. Rinsed that shit off before I gave it back to him, stroking his head. "Savor the fuckin' flavor, wolfie. Took a little detour through hell to bring it home. You're welcome."

He looked up, wagging his tail. Bingo whined through his clenched teeth, snug around the bone. We walked into my room and I left him by his bed, gently closing the door behind me.

Skin stood at the end of the hall, looking at me like he'd just seen a ghost. "Christ, Veep, what the fuck happened to you?"

"Just a spill," I said, wondering why the fuck the universe was conspiring to keep me dirty. "What's your deal?"

"You've got a visitor." His smile jerked up, following the scar going across his cheek, and I sure as hell didn't like it.

"Visitor?"

"Yeah, some chick, showed up at our gate and called your name. Lion and Tin were gonna chase her away 'til she insisted she knows you."

"Better be Honey-Bee," I growled, thinking about the skinny little stripper with the sweet ass I'd fucked three times the other night.

"*Definitely* isn't Honey-Bee, brother. Meg's been busy telling her you're bad news."

Stopped myself just short of telling his old lady to fuck off. Woman had no business telling her girls who they could and couldn't fuck in this club. Would've said we'd fucked up making her lead manager at the strip joint, but she had the business end down, better than any of us.

Besides, I really didn't need a fuckin' fight when I was still dripping mud on the floor.

"Fuck me, Veep. You've got your hands full," Skin said, his eyes following a clump of mud sliding off my jeans to the floor. "You want me to tell the boys to send her away?"

"Nah. I'll do it myself, jettison whoever the fuck she is so I can clean up." I walked past him and Skinny boy shrugged, careful to sidestep so I didn't brush my muck on him.

Rage nipped at the back of my brain. Fuck, why today? Why now with these damned disruptions?

Wanted nothing better than to hunker down in a nice, hot shower, before I decided to figure out how I'd un-fuck my head tonight with the usual distractions.

Lion and Tin nodded at me in the garages. They still manned the gates most of the time, even though we'd made 'em full patch a couple months ago, both the wounds they'd taken in our dustup with the Torches MC healing nicely.

"She's out there, Veep," Tin said, pointing to the shitty, rusted blue hatchback sitting by the gate.

I marched right past them, already muttering under my breath.

What the fuck was this? Who was it? Why hadn't the bitch been smart enough to walk the fuck away after we'd finished?

Every girl in the county oughta know by now I didn't touch the same pussy twice unless it was fuckin' amazing. And it damned sure never went beyond that.

When I saw the little honey step out behind the car with her long, black hair rolling across her shoulders, my dick twitched. She held her face to the side, and I forgot all about Honey-Bee and the other bitches at the Heel, wondering if I'd found my fuck for the night without having to leave the clubhouse.

Shit, whoever the fuck she was, maybe I'd be giving her another ride on my bullet after all.

Then she looked at me, full frontal, and my blood turned to ice.

Summer. Fuckin'. Olivers.

Like a ghost who'd reached through the past, caught me by the throat, and slammed me against the pavement with the force of a thousand suns.

"Hi," she said softly. Just husky enough to ring my ears. Like I needed another shot through the heart. "Uh, holy shit. What happened to you?"

I stepped up to her, my jaw clenched, trying to stop my heart from tearing out my ribs and slapping her in the face.

"What the fuck you doing here, Summer?"

Her face soured, causing her bottom lip to stick out.

I remembered biting it. Fuck yeah, I did.

Feeling its softness. The little curl it'd make beneath my tongue when she moaned. Tensing for the hot air rushing out her mouth, all the pleasure I swallowed, all the times I fucked her 'til she collapsed.

"I came to see you, Joker. It's been awhile. But maybe this isn't a good time...looks like you have your hands full. I can come back, whenever it's better for you."

"Babe," I started, and stopped. Balled my hands into fists for using that word. *Fuck!*

Old habits never died easy. They died harder than most men.

Her big green eyes widened. I shook my head, coming closer, making her back up so she wouldn't touch my muddy fuckin' chest.

"Summer, ain't never a good time to see me. You oughta

know. Get in your rusted out box and go the fuck home. Whatever you've got to say, I'm not hearing it."

I kept moving. Backed her straight into her car. She stood up straight, making herself a little taller, but she still fell at least a foot short of me. Those defiant little eyes I'd rolled into the back of her head those summer nights so long ago went off like firecrackers.

"I don't care," she said, defiant as ever. "I've been thinking about the past. About us. You told me to back off after the horrible things that happened that night. I don't blame you. But I can't stay away forever, Jackson. I haven't forgotten. I tried. I can't. I *can't* forget you."

That shit struck deep, found its target somewhere deep inside me, and exploded. If it wasn't for the nervous tremor in her voice, I would've believed every word.

Maybe I would've grabbed her, thrown her against my chest, and held her the way I'd started to when I took those trips to Seddon for more than club biz. Maybe I would've pushed my lips on hers, searching for the spark I'd smothered for three fuckin' years, trying to find out if I was still human.

I didn't. Something about her voice was strange, off by half an octave, strained. *Off.*

Something that stank like desperate bullshit.

"Jackson, please," she whined again, when I went too long without giving her an answer. "I can't forget, I'm telling you –"

"I can, Summertime." Pain criss-crossed her face like spiderwebs when I called her that name. "You wanna use names you really shouldn't around here, then so will I."

Her lips popped open, shocked and kissable as ever. I pushed my palm against her mouth, held her face, silencing her.

"Go the fuck home, Summer. There's nothing here for you. The shit we had three summers ago – it's as dead as my poor fuckin' brother. So's the man you knew. Last warning you're gonna get."

"Joker...Jackson..." She looked at me intently, her bright green eyes going dark. "Goddamn, why do you have to be so stubborn? Is it asking too much to just sit down and have a drink with me? We shared something once...something beautiful. You're hurting, and so am I, ever since you left me alone that night. We can talk this out. We can catch up. Maybe we can find each other again."

No. Fuck no.

I reached for her shoulders and pulled her in. Pressed her against the muck caked all over me, ruining the shit outta that pretty little blouse covering up her body.

First, she gasped. Then she squirmed while I held her, fighting me, whimpering in disbelief.

"No. We. Can't," I whispered. If she didn't understand what I said with words, then the dirt would make her.

This woman had already taken a roll in the dirt with a bastard. She'd been lucky to walk away with nothing but bitter dirt, rather than blood.

Wasn't changing. Wasn't fuckin' letting her open me up, get back in my blood, and heat everything to a thousand degrees 'til I did stupid, dangerous shit that could get her killed. Hell, maybe me and my brothers, too.

She fought with her hands, slapping my chest, trying to stop the muck from getting all over her.

Too damned late. Her fight was easy. Mine, it was all on the inside, and it burned like a nuclear fire.

Took everything I had to keep from cracking, to hold my fuckin' dick down, as soon as I felt those perfect tits I'd had a dozen times pressed up against me.

Fuck, a dozen times too many. I let go.

Summer flew backward and banged against the car door when I pushed her away.

"Fucking asshole! I drove all this way for *this*? What the hell is wrong with you?"

"You know damned well what," I snarled, giving her one last jagged look before I turned my back.

Had to leave her. Let sleeping fuckin' dogs fuckin' lie.

Had to let her fade away one more time.

"Lion, Tin, let the woman out. Make sure she never gets back inside these gates."

The two new brothers looked at me. Had to be watching the whole ugly scene, even if they didn't know shit about it.

"You got it, Veep," Tin said, getting up from his bench. Both brothers disappeared behind me, heading out there to make sure the little girl I'd left behind never showed her face here again.

Wouldn't let myself look back. No goddamned regrets.

She had to stay buried. Deep in old, evil, blood soaked ground.

Same as everything else , 'til it was time for the brothers

to kill the bastards who'd murdered Freddy. Even then, nobody had the full picture.

God willing, they never would. Nobody needed the fine details that ripped my fuckin' heart out, nobody except the Prez. Dust did a noble lie for the club, for me.

He'd told the boys my brother died in an accident. He'd dropped pure bullshit so we wouldn't go in hot and crazy, waging a blood war we couldn't hope to win just then.

Someday, he'd promised. *Someday* was coming sooner, too, soon as we ironed out how to hit the Deads hard, and when.

"Fuck you! Take your hands off me. I'll go out the gate," Summer screeched. I was almost to the club's door.

I stopped with my hand on the handle. *Don't turn around, asshole. Let her fuckin' go.*

For a second, I pinched my eyes shut, listening to her tires burn rubber as she tore through the open gate. After the mind-fuck I'd given her, she'd never be back. She'd leave me to my hell, just the way it was meant to be.

Before I could pop the door, Skin opened it, staring at me from the other side. "Already done out here? That was fast. Who the fuck was she?"

Didn't say a damned word as I pushed past, shoving my muddy arm against his cut. "Aw, fuck!"

His curse echoed after me, barking through the open bar, as I continued down the hallway to the showers.

I'd need a fuck of a lot more than hot water and good whiskey to wash away all the filth today.

V: Crash (Summer)

"Asshole, asshole, fucking asshole!" I slammed my fist on the steering wheel again, adding one more muddy streak to the worn pink cover.

I couldn't believe he'd turned me away like I was nothing.

I couldn't believe I'd stood there and taken it, expecting a miracle, when I'd learned to stop believing in them years ago.

I *definitely* couldn't believe he'd rubbed his filthy body against mine, caking me in dirt, forcing me to feel those hard edges all over him one more time. The ones I'd tried so hard to forget.

For years, I'd wondered how much I'd hurt confronting him like this.

Now, I knew.

It killed me. Tore out my soul a second time, dashed it to tatters before my eyes.

God damn him. My love had turned to *hate*.

If it weren't for the monster holding the gun to my head, I wouldn't have come back. Ever. But that demon, Hatch, reminded me why I was here every few hours, pinging the phone he'd left me with a text or another nasty voicemail.

He'd made himself deadly clear. It took a lot of makeup and even more aspirin to cover up the blow to the head.

Then I'd gotten in my car and driven, non-stop with Alex, stopping only for gas. We checked into the hotel this morning, where I fed him and let him nap, before finding the closest babysitter.

If Hatch were a reasonable man, I would've moaned about how much this was taking out of my pocket. Naturally, I didn't say a word, fearing what would happen if I so much as asked for a penny.

Everything was going down, down, down.

My life. My bank account. My poor, sweet baby's future, handed off to strangers while I pleaded with a man who thought nothing about shredding my heart for the second time.

I picked up Alex at the little daycare in town, ignoring the dumbfounded looks from all the women, wondering how I'd gotten smeared with mud. Then we headed back to our room, where I took a long, hot shower, ignoring the hunger pangs ripping at my stomach.

Joker wouldn't leave my head. I couldn't get over the contrast, the change in the man I once knew. Where had he gone?

He'd been replaced with a killer robot wearing his skin.

His gorgeous hazel eyes didn't shine anymore. They just glowed like dull stones, dead and cold to everything they saw.

That tragic night three years past killed both the Taylor boys – just one less literally. Joker walked the earth and rode his bike like a shell, lost to his humanity, his love, and me.

Before, he'd been a deadly angel with a beautiful soul underneath.

Today, he'd looked just as handsome as before – maybe more so with the extra edges and tiny scars the last three years had given him – but now there was nothing underneath except ugliness.

Watching the last few bits of grime and soap disappear down the drain, I turned the nozzle, only to hear the damned phone I'd left in my jeans vibrating.

Sighing, I stepped out of the shower and started toweling myself off while I reached for it. "Yeah?"

"How'd it go, bitch? You were supposed to check in."

An evil chill swept up my spine. Hatch's voice had that effect, just pure, vicious poison. My battered temple throbbed, remembering how he'd knocked me out cold.

"Not well," I said. There wasn't any point in lying. "It's going to be tough to find out anything. He doesn't want to talk to me."

There was a pause on the other end of the line. I could practically see his nasty, leathery face pausing to take a long drag on a cigarette. His mismatched eyes must've trembled with rage.

"You're gonna do better, Summer-Bummer, or you're gonna get your fuckin' guts hanging on a clothesline, mixed with the kiddo's. Quit fucking around. We're paying for your room. Wasting the club's good money."

Fuck you, fuck your money, and fuck your club, I wanted to say, but I bit my tongue. Tasted blood.

"I'll try again. Give me another day or two. I'll find out where he goes, follow him, try to pin him down somewhere outside the clubhouse."

"Yeah," he said calmly. "You will. Because if you don't —"

"Hatch, please!" I flattened my hand against the wall, propping myself up so I wouldn't pass out. "I know what you'll do. I don't need another reminder."

"Good. 'Cause if you fuck us over, you little fuckin' skank, what's coming ain't just talk. It's blood. You've got three days to drain him dry before we drain your skin in the nearest ditch."

The line went dead. I closed the phone and angrily threw it down on my clothes, promising myself I wouldn't let him set off another chain reaction of ugly crying.

I couldn't fight this hellish noose he'd slipped over me. But I could control my own reactions. Getting upset about his sickening threats wouldn't do anything to keep Alex safe.

And that was the only reason I was here. After today, I didn't have another.

* * * *

"Mama!" Little Alex sat on my lap with some stupid kid's show on the background, tugging at the bottle.

"Sorry, little man. Here you go." I helped put the tiny

juice bottle up to his lips, watching while he took it.

He sucked his sweet drink without a care in the world. For a second, I wished I'd brought along something a whole lot stronger for me to drink,, but that wouldn't do me any favors either.

You can't give up, I told myself quietly. *Look at him. You're his mom, for Christ's sake. His everything. The only defense against these sick bastards he's got.*

My baby slurped the apple drink, staring up at me the whole time, his eyes as big and bright as his father's used to be. They were the same color.

I wouldn't let that fire in his little eyes go out. I'd keep him safe, keep him alive, and I'd damned sure keep him happy. He was too young to see me killed over nothing, this biker nonsense.

Leaning down, I kissed his head, and thought about how I'd make good on the lofty promises in my heart. It didn't come to me until after midnight, when I sat awake in bed, watching him turn around in the tiny play pen I'd set up.

Everybody was restless tonight. I wondered where Joker was, and if he was just as upset in his own bed.

Then I instantly covered my face, hating myself for thinking it.

Today, he'd ripped away any reason left to ever sympathize with him. Hell, I hoped he was suffering somewhere tonight, torturing himself for the way he'd treated me.

Talk about wishful thinking. I shook my head, knowing I'd have another brutally early morning tomorrow. I had to

121

be up and out near the clubhouse if I wanted a real chance to catch him.

God help me, I would. There wasn't another option.

I'd sell out the bastard who'd wiped his filth on me in a heartbeat. I'd do whatever it took to keep my son safe, even if it meant watching the monstrous killers threatening us put a bullet through his father instead.

* * * *

The next day, I had Alex at the daycare as soon as it opened, before I took off in my rusted out car for the clubhouse. I parked just around the corner, careful to keep myself out of sight.

Hopefully, he'd take the opposite road heading for the highway when he came out of there.

If he came out, I meant. Nothing was guaranteed, but there wasn't a better option.

I'd decided to risk the entire day scoping out the only place I knew for sure where he'd come and go.

After three long hours in the car, I finally heard the motorcycle roar that got my hopes up.

"Shit," I swore to myself, watching the scruffy brother who'd let me through the gate yesterday roar out instead.

Ten more minutes, I sulked, contemplating all the roads I could use to flee the south for my life if I couldn't get close to Joker again. Then there was another growl.

I stiffened in my seat, inhaling a sharp breath as I saw the unmistakable outline of the big, bold man I'd once loved drive through the gate. He was in his truck this time, and I swore I saw a massive dog at his side, heading for the highway.

My hand turned the key in my ignition before I could think. I counted to about ten and then took off.

I hoped I'd hang behind him close, but not so close he'd spot me, and throw me off, or worse.

It worked. My heart pounded a little harder with every mile, heading down the short stretch of highway to a new exit, where he took a sharp turn. I almost lost it when he disappeared.

Soon, I saw his truck turn into a nearby parking lot, next to a squat building that looked like an old post office with flowers out front.

I pulled into the gas station across the street, keeping my eyes on him. No, I hadn't been mistaken before.

Joker went over to the passenger side and pulled out the biggest dog I'd ever seen on a leash.

What the hell? Seeing the animal didn't compute.

The cold, dead-eyed man who'd pushed me away didn't look like the type who had any room in his heart for a pet. I wondered if it could be a guard dog – but then, what was waiting inside the building if he felt like he needed to bring one along?

Whatever, I had to find out. When I was sure he'd entered the building, I darted across the street, parking behind the building.

STERNER PLUS RETIREMENT HOME, I read on the sign.

There wasn't time to stop and think about what that might mean. I grabbed my purse and headed inside, only to be stopped by a burly looking old woman at the front desk.

"Visitor sign in, ma'am," she said. "Who are you here for?"

Crap. I hesitated, wracking my brain for a name, the only reason I could think of why he'd be here.

"Donald Taylor?" I said, grabbing the pen, scrawling my name and number before she could tell me there was nobody here by that name.

"Oh, of course! Mister Taylor. It's about time he had somebody coming to see him besides his grandson…"

Of course! I echoed in my head. I could've dropped to the floor with relief.

"Have you been here before?"

I shook my head, watching as she beamed and stepped away from the desk. "Cheryl! Take over while I show the girl around. Right this way, ma'am, he's probably hanging out in the commons like he usually does this time of day."

My knees grew heavier with every step I took, following her down the long, egg white corridor. I saw them sitting together as I rounded the corner.

The lady smiled and pulled away, giving me a friendly squeeze on the shoulder.

Honest to God, I needed it, knowing this was going to be the last peaceful minute of my life today.

A shitstorm brewed ahead. And I was walking straight into it as soon as I came into their sight.

No time like the present, I thought. *Go.*

Forcing my way forward, I plastered the biggest, fakest smile I'd ever worn on my face. The old man saw me first, turning his head, muttering something about his hearing aids.

"You heard me, boy. This damned place creeps and crawls with everything. I ain't gonna be able to hear shit if you don't move your ass, and fix it for me."

"Grandpa, that's the fourth fuckin' time this year. I – "Joker stopped.

He froze as soon as he saw me coming. I didn't stop.

The huge, hairy grey dog laying on the floor must've sensed his master tensing up. He stood up and let out a loud bark, forcing Joker to look down. Rather than stand up and beam that hatred at me, he crouched on the floor to sooth the do, before it turned the nursing home into a total circus.

"What the fuck you doing here?" he growled, running his hand over the beast's furry head.

"Oh, Joker, I knew I'd find you here. Visiting your grandpa, huh?" I looked at the old man and winked.

His weathered face pulled up in a smile, amused by my interruption.

"Summer, you don't know shit. If you've got any sense in your head, you'll pack it in, turn the fuck around, and – "

"What's gotten into you, boy? That's no way to greet a woman," his grandfather snapped, turning his wheelchair toward me. "Sorry, we haven't met."

"Hi, I'm Summer," I said sweetly, taking his hand. "It's a privilege, Mister Taylor, I don't think I ever met you straight up while you lived in Seddon. Just served your table a few times, back at Robby's bar. He was my uncle."

"Shit on a shingle! You're a hometown girl?" He slowly turned to Joker, glaring the entire time. "Jesus, boy. What else you been hiding from me? I might be cooped up in this damned place, but I ain't pushing goddamned daisies yet."

I laughed. Genuinely.

The old man had a lot of the Taylor twins in him. He had fire. Plenty of Alex, too, judging by the sharp hazel eyes that hadn't worn down a bit with age.

Joker and I shared a look.

Don't upset your grandpa. Follow my lead. Listen to me, I told him with my eyes.

"Haven't been hiding nothing, Grandpa," he growled reluctantly. "She's just an old friend. Didn't know she was in town 'til now."

"No? I tried to come by the clubhouse the other day. Didn't your brothers deliver the message?" I came closer, reaching down gently to stroke the big dog's muzzle while Joker dodged the question. "My, he's so big. What's his name?"

"Bingo!" Grandpa Taylor yelled. "Named him myself. Seeing this boy's the most excitement I got to look forward to all week, outside the weekly games."

"Yeah, Grandpa. You picked a good one," Joker said. His icy voice matched his eyes each time he looked at me. "So, why'd you come by? Could've waited for me at the clubhouse."

"And keep an old friend waiting? I don't think so, Joker.

I'm only in town for a little while. Gotta make the most out of every moment."

The dog softened with both our hands on him. He tilted his massive head, opening his mouth to lick my hand. Through all the anger and anxiety eating me, I smiled.

Grandpa looked up, pointing at me with his thumb. "I like her. You still live in Seddon? What's the old place like these days?"

"Oh, same old, same old," I said, making light of how hard we'd been hit by the bad economy.

For the next minute or two, I truly enjoyed making small talk with the old man, forgetting about the dagger I'd have to drive into Joker's back before long. My ex-lover sat there in silence, stroking his dog, his eyes boiling like angry seas whenever our eyes locked.

I held his gaze. Showing any weakness was going to be fatal.

"You two were hanging around for all these years, and you never said anything?" Grandpa growled, turning to his grandson. "I can't believe you!"

"She was before Piece," he said darkly.

The old man's anger melted. The air around us seemed to curdle, turning thick and toxic. I looked around desperately for a distraction.

"Hey, there's some soda and coffee. Can I bring you boys something?"

"Black coffee," Grandpa Taylor said quietly.

"Joker?" Gingerly, I reached out, trying not to feel horrible that I'd caused him to lay down his dead brother's name.

I couldn't think about that night. Jesus, I couldn't forget why I was really here, what was on the line, all out of some sick, misplaced sympathy for a man who had *none* for me.

"Water," he growled, subtly shrugging me off by leaning down to fix his dog's collar.

I nodded and stepped over to the long table, keeping my ears perked up for their voices.

"You don't gotta be so damned surly all the time, Jackson. She's come a long way to see you. Let's not dig into the past again. Ain't bringing him back," I heard the old man say.

"You think I don't know that?" Joker's voice was low, like thunder.

Bingo let out a tiny whine as I turned around with a tray full of drinks. Just in time to see Joker grab his grandfather's hand, pure death shining in his eyes.

"Jackson..."

"Don't fuckin' call me that here, old man. I'm Joker 'til the job's done. Promised Freddy I'd kill the sick fucks who did him in, and I'm going to, real goddamned soon. I'm keeping my promises, just like you wanted."

Grandpa Taylor tore his hand away from him, shaking a little when I put the tray on the table. "It's all here, boys. Enjoy."

I sipped my orange soda quietly, trying to make small talk about the dog, and failing the whole time. Grandpa guzzling his coffee down, without waiting for it to cool, told me the visit was nearing its end.

"Okay," he said, putting down his empty cup. "Think

it's time I got some rest before the real bingo starts up tonight. Pleasure meeting you, Summer. Joker, wheel me back, and take the lady out for a real drink. Life's too damned short to spend it not having any fun."

So much truth from the tough old man. Too bad I was in no position to take it to heart.

"Meet me out by the bench," I said to Joker. "I'll be waiting."

He nodded, wrapping the dog's leash around his hand while he pushed the old man. I watched the three of them head down the hall, finishing my soda before I collected the cups.

Then I sat down at the bench and waited. I thought about what I'd say, bounced around a dozen openers. None of them left me feeling better.

I had to let it happen. I couldn't let him walk away this time, or I'd be letting down Alex, and myself.

Time to make it or break it.

* * * *

"Tell me why the fuck you're really here," Joker growled, standing over my shoulder. "Couldn't have made it fuckin' clearer after yesterday, mucking up your shit."

Bingo stood at his side, his mouth open, breathing loudly. Blissfully unaware.

I stood up, looked him dead in the eye, clenching my purse. "I came all the way from Georgia to talk, Joker. I'm not leaving until we do. Go ahead and push me down on the sidewalk if you have to. I'll get back up and I'll be at your doorstep again tomorrow."

He snorted. "Fucking-A, you've really lost it, Summertime..."

That name again. Goddamn, *that name.*

It took everything I had not to break eye contact, my heart doing a full, painful loop in my chest, blurring past and present.

"I lost my best friend," I said, stepping toward him. "Look, I know my odds. They're crap. But I'll die if I don't try to get him back."

"You really want him back, babe? That's what you came all the fuckin' way from Seddon for? Why didn't you say so sooner?" He stepped closer, his voice softening.

My heart leaped into my throat. We hadn't shared this closeness, this intensity, for three lonely summers. The way he looked at me took me back to those hot nights when we'd made Alex, the son he didn't know he had.

The bitter lump in my throat tightened. There couldn't be something there, shining in his eyes...right? And if there was, then why the fuck was I letting the Deadhands use me to get to him and his club?

"I just...I mean...I want..." I stuttered, completely lost for words, not knowing what I wanted anymore.

"You don't know what the hell you want." Joker put one hand against my cheek, tipped it up, thumbing the corner of my lips. "Don't fuckin' talk, baby girl. Pucker up. Let's see if there's anything left in this fuckin' chasm I used to call a heart."

His finger brushed aside. His mouth came down on mine, hot and rampant.

Moaning, I melted into his tongue, twining mine with his for the first time in an eternity.

This kiss devoured worlds. I forgot all about the brutal threats, the pain, the loss.

For the next minute, there was nothing except Jackson and me.

Two lips.

Two tongues.

Two hearts.

One pulse, the one and only synchronized rhythm pounding in his flesh. It didn't stop until Bingo brushed up against our legs, and then I looked down, smiling.

This kiss was beautiful. And it was also very dangerous bullshit.

"There. How was that?" he whispered softly, running his hand down my cheek, stopping at the end to clutch my chin.

"Just like old times," I said weakly, staring at him, one hand on his neck to hold me up. The other hung at my side, being gingerly licked by the giant wolfhound. "What about you?"

"Nothing," he said. The spark in his eyes snuffed out, obliterating the magic.

"What?"

"There's nothing here, Summertime. Absolutely fuckin' nothing. I tried." He tugged on Bingo's leash and stepped away, pulling his cut flush against his chest. "For the last goddamned time, get your ass home. You're wasting your time here chasing a crush that's never coming back. You show your face around my grandpa's place or the clubhouse again, I'll make sure a couple prospects give you a ride back to Georgia."

I stood there like a dumb statue about to fall, watching the whole time as he walked to his truck without looking back. He put the dog in the passenger seat, got in, and took off, driving right past me without even turning his head.

"Bastard!" I whispered, balling up my fists, fighting the hot tears.

A chubby middle aged couple came close, staring intently, one more humiliation I didn't need. I'd been a complete fool for the second time since I'd shown up here.

And yet again, I'd failed to make any progress getting closer to whatever Hatch wanted. I'd put my life and my son's one step closer to a horrific end.

"Jackson Taylor...go to hell," I whispered, taking long, angry strides toward my car.

I promised myself I wouldn't feel guilty about putting him there anymore, if it kept us safe. Now, if only I could figure out how the hell to do it.

* * * *

"Brrrrrrrr!" Alex sat in the corner at our hotel room later that evening, playing with a couple toy planes I'd brought along on the trip.

I smiled feebly at him, trying to enjoy the little things.

At least he was happy.

If only that meant something. With the sword hanging over our heads, even my son's little laugh and *vroom-vroom* noises couldn't cheer me up.

My phone buzzed a second later. I picked it up and sighed, wondering how badly he'd torment me tonight, stepping into the bathroom so Alex wouldn't have to see the horror on my face.

"How'd it go today, bitch? You suck him off yet, or what?"

"No. I'll try again tomorrow."

"Try? Try?! Try, try, fuckin' try?" Each word hit my eardrum, more explosive than the last. I held the phone away from my ear.

"Jesus fuckin' Christ, woman. You're even dumber than I thought. Sure wish that sonofabitch picked a smarter cunt to fuck all those years ago. Some bitch with a bigger fire under her ass over the fact that, fuck, her own fuckin' son is gonna die in front of her!"

"Please, Hatch. You don't understand. It isn't as easy as you —"

"Shut up. From where I'm sitting, you're the stupid fuckin' slut who ain't hearing me. Let's try this again…"

No, no, no, I mouthed, shaking my head. *You've tortured me enough. This isn't making it any easier, you bastard.*

"You fuck me over, you waste my club's money, then you and your kid are dead. Dead! Fuckin' offal. Carcasses we'll drag out into the woods and feed to the bugs."

No more. I flung the phone away from my face and cut

him off, ending the call, slamming it down on the counter next to the sink.

He must've called back at least five times while I sat at the edge of the tub, hands over my face, trying to think of some way out of this maze from hell.

This was hopeless. There wasn't truly a chance at ever satisfying this demon out for blood.

Come tomorrow – hell, maybe later tonight – I'd take my chances on the open road. I'd flee until we were several states over, turn ourselves into the police there, and hope that taking down the Deadhands was a big enough deal to get us into the best witness protection a confession could buy.

On the sixth angry, vibrating ring, I picked up. I had to stall him, see how he'd react to the realization that he'd already lost me as a pawn.

"Listen to me, you fuckin' bitch –"

"No, you listen!" I snarled into the phone, pressing it against my ear so hard it burned. "I want to know something from you. Why are you such a fucking monster? These stupid gang fights are really so important that you're using an innocent woman and her baby? Is that what you always wanted?"

There was a pause on the other end of the line. Then he began to laugh.

Jesus.

His long, drawling chuckle was just as evil as the rest of him. But it gave me a tiny sliver of hope that maybe, just maybe, he wasn't so pissed I'd have a nice head start before his men came.

"Really, Summer-Bummer? You think you can lecture me? Me? The man who's fuckin' mowed down bitches and brats several times over?"

"Why?" I whispered, begging for an answer, truly wondering through all the terror smothering my heart.

"Because I'm God, bitch. G-O-fuckin'-D. I decide who lives, who dies, and who sucks my damned cock. It's just me and Betty G, together, and we are both hungry motherfuckers. Right now, the ones who die are the motherfuckers who ain't paying their dues to the only club that belongs in Dixie. The Pistols are fucked because they're bad for business. That's it. So are you."

I couldn't tell if he was genuinely insane or just eaten up with greed like a bad cancer. Honestly, that made him even more terrifying.

"Whatever. I can see what god you really worship," I said.

"Fucking shit, didn't call you up for a talk about theology. Here, why don't you do me a favor and get off the pot. Go by the TV and take a good, long look at little Alex."

What the hell was he talking about? How did he know I was in the bathroom?

Jesus, he wasn't here, was he?

In less than a dozen words, he destroyed what little desperate courage I'd pulled from my depths. I stood numbly, leaving the bathroom, the phone blazing against my blood filled ear like a glowing coal.

"Little closer. Easy, now. Ain't gonna pop any heads unless you give me a fuckin' reason to," he growled, urging me forward.

Alex was still holding his toy planes, taking a break from his vigorous play. He looked up at me and smiled. Such a beautiful, innocent grin.

One I would've normally beamed back – if only there weren't a killer whispering in my ear.

"You see it yet?"

I didn't until it moved. Then the red dot, like something from a laser pointer, except dime sized, crawled across the toy jumbo jet on the ground next to Alex's little thigh. It crept across the floor slowly, about as slow as my eyes bugged out of my head, stopping just short of landing on my son.

"What you're looking at, bitch, because I know you're too fuckin' dumb to know, is the laser attached to the gun that puts your kid in pieces right in front of you."

"No…" I barely made a sound, shaking my head, not sure whether I should throw myself over it or try to grab Alex and run.

"I know you're getting restless. I know you're thinking about taking off on me, running before you've done the job we sent you up there to do. I know your panties are filling up with shit right now, wondering what the fuck I'm gonna do." He paused. "Believe it or not, I don't wanna fuckin' kill you, or the brat. I want you to shut up, get with Joker, and do whatever the fuck it takes to stop me from telling my man to pull the trigger. Sooner you figure out you don't have a choice, we're all better off."

The bastard was right. I really didn't.

He was one, two, maybe five steps ahead of me.

Always, god damn it. Always.

There wasn't any running while he had this man following us, ready to shoot whenever Hatch told him to.

"Okay," I said, feeling myself floating above my body the instant I said it. I'd come uncoupled, the only thing I could do to survive the horror. "I'll try again."

"Yeah, you will. You'll try harder. Because if you don't…" He stopped, inhaling a deep breath. "Bam!"

I winced. The red dot on the floor flashed one more time, and then disappeared.

"You've got two more days, Summer-Bummer. Corner him, fuck him, show up at his doorstep asking to borrow a cup of sugar. Whatever the fuck you have to do to get good with him, you fuckin' do it. Nothing less. You get close enough to count how many fuckin' hairs he's got on his balls. Close enough to ask him anything, and jump when we say go."

The line went dead. So did my soul.

"Mama?" Alex looked at me, a tiny frown on his face. He couldn't understand any of this, and thank god for that.

I walked over, scooped him up, and held him tighter than I had since before all this began. We sat on the bed while he lazily played with my hair.

Tomorrow, another level of hell waited. Tomorrow, I had to do anything and everything I could think of to save his life.

Mine didn't matter anymore.

The biggest mistake of my life wasn't the demon who kept calling and threatening me. I'd already made it six years ago, when I'd let myself fall for the rough, dirty boy who'd given me a ride home.

It wasn't Hatch's fault. It wasn't mine.

Goddamn it, this was Joker's fault. If he hadn't gotten so close, given me this kid I loved, driving me to my wit's end...

Closing my eyes, I sat there holding my baby boy, just reflecting. No, maybe I'd been too harsh. Too crazed.

Whatever mistakes I'd made, Alex hadn't been one of them. He was the only good thing that ever happened to me.

I had to keep him alive and smiling. Fucking *had* to.

He gripped my hand, his eyelids drooping in that sleepy, lovable way they always did when he got tired. I rocked him gently, hoping he'd go to sleep.

Hoped even more I'd force a miracle. There had to be some combination of words and actions on this earth I could use to get close to Joker.

Didn't stop my poor, savaged brain from drawing a complete blank. I was still struggling to fight through it, kicking myself, drowning in my frustration when I heard the motorcycle growl in the parking lot outside.

Alex woke up, jerked in my arms, and a man screamed outside. I held my baby tighter, standing up, trying to see what was happening out there.

Then all hell broke off its chain and came flying through the window.

VI: Restless (Joker)

I fuckin' lied to her face, lied to myself, and even lied in front of my dog.

When I put my lips on Summer's, I'd been more at peace than when I cracked a hundred skulls. She brought me back to the time before Freddy died, before things went to shit.

The past was supposed to be dead. Gone. Standing next to her, it sure as hell wasn't.

That freaked me the fuck out.

I had to keep her away. Had to tell her I was as dead as I pretended, before she got her hooks into me. Had to avenge my brother, the only fuckin' thing that mattered, and I couldn't handle any goddamned distractions right now.

Soon as I pulled outta the parking lot, I headed for the Ruby Heel. Twenty minutes later, I had a mug of beer in my hand and I sat under Honey-Bee, watching her snow queen act.

She swung across the stage on a high swing, wearing those heels I wanted stabbing my ass, blowing handfuls of fake snow across the tiny crowd. From the corner of my eye, I saw two old ladies staring at me with sour puss frowns on their faces.

Meg, Skin's old lady.

Cora, Firefly's wife, her belly swelling by the day with the kid they were having.

Fuck them both. They didn't own me. If I wanted to bang Honey-Bee backstage tonight, they weren't fuckin' stopping me.

Only trouble was, I couldn't get hard. Not even when Honey-Bee came down to the floor, floating on her strings, giving every man here a perfect view of an ass so round I wanted to sink my teeth in.

That's what I would've wanted any other night, anyway. Tonight?

Fuck, it was different, and I didn't know why. Even flashing her long lashes at me and blowing a kiss didn't do shit for my cock.

What the fuck was wrong with me? Bingo sat by my side, his tongue hanging out. Damned dog looked more interested in the stripper than I did.

I took a long pull from my beer, grabbed a bone in my pocket, and put it into his mouth.

"Helluva mutt you got there," an old man in a leather jacket with a Harley emblem said.

I looked at him and snorted. If these fucking casual riders weren't filling up the Pistols' coffers with the money they spent here, I'd have stood up and walked the other way.

"He's no mutt, asshole," I growled, hating how he looked at my next fuck with more intensity than I did. "Pure bred Irish Wolfhound."

"Shit, man, what's eating you?"

I stood up. Soon as he saw the patches on my cut, his face lit up, and he quickly moved several chairs over.

Nobody was stupid enough to start shit with a full patch brother. These wannabe badasses always ran just as soon as they came face to face with real outlaws.

Didn't take any pleasure in scaring away the chickenshit. Like most nights, I just wanted to be left the fuck alone.

Honey-Bee still had her hungry little eyes on me as her act wound down. I wasn't looking at her anymore, dead to feeling it, thinking about Summer the whole damned time.

Fuck.

"Come on, boy. Let's get the fuck outta here." I took the bone away from Bingo and hauled him up on his feet, walking him outta the bar.

Meg was standing by the door on my way out, a tall brunette who always dressed too fuckin' fancy for any brother. Fancy, yeah, except for the PROPERTY OF SKIN jacket she wore like a second skin.

"What's going on? Leaving already?" she asked, like she couldn't believe it.

"Yeah. Put the beer on my tab."

"Smart choice, Joker. Honey-Bee doesn't need any trouble. She's been jerked around enough by you and Lion lately."

Lion? The beat up, scruffy motherfucker we'd only patched in about a month ago?

Shouldn't have been surprised she was taking whatever cock she could get. The woman was voracious.

Shit. Whatever urge I had left to fuck the stripper totally evaporated. If only she'd known he'd had his cock buried in more of the bitches here than I did.

"She's a big girl," I said, pushing past her on my way out. "Don't think she needs her boss playing big sis, telling what she should and shouldn't do."

Meg called after me, but I wasn't stopping.

I'd lost sight of the real mission for too long. Kissing Summer and sending her packing only reminded me of that, and I'd be damned before I let it fuck me over any longer.

* * * *

"Joker, for fuck's sake!" Dust grabbed his pipe, blowing smoke in my face. "Knock it off. You're gonna fuck up the new silestone if you keep that shit up."

Looking up at the Prez, I finally stopped slamming the blade between my fingers, faster and harder than I usually did. I sat the bar with the brothers in our clubhouse, a little while after I'd gotten back and put Bingo down for a nap.

"Cut him some slack, Prez," Firefly said, knocking back a whiskey shot. "It's too fuckin' dark for him to hit the range. He's gotta blow off steam somehow."

We locked eyes. I had a weird understanding lately with

the big vet who served as our Enforcer.

Wasn't so long ago I'd tried to tell him he was making a big fat mistake getting in so deep with that Cora girl. Fuckin' ship had sailed on that months ago, with him marrying her and knocking her up, the whole club taking out the Torches MC in the process.

Too damned bad the Torches were just one more distraction.

Our old friends fucked us over, coming after his girl for some shit debt her dead daddy ran up. They'd been the only thing keeping Atlanta outta the Deads' grip, and now the fuckers owned it about as hard as they had Seddon locked down.

"No honor in staying sober night, Veep," Skin said, sitting on my other side. He passed me the bottle of Jack he'd been swigging. "Go ahead. This shit'll wash away the stick up your ass."

I held the bottle, staring at the amber liquid, already feeling the sweet numbing fire before I raised it to my lips.

"No." I pushed it back into the brother's hands, shaking my head. "Ain't the right time for Jack."

"Aw, shit, Veep. What's the matter? Don't tell me you gotta be fuckin' sober to walk the dog!" Sixty's goatee twitched as he looked at me with a shit-eating grin, one man over from Skin. He slapped Crawl on the back like he'd just cut the best joke in the world.

I gave him that look. *Shut the fuck up, Mister Comedian.*

Took my sweet time folding up my knife. It never took more than a crazy look to shut these boys up when they threw their shit, and Sixty was back to nervously talking to the brothers, soon as I stood up.

I headed for my room, too fucked in the head to stir the pot tonight, much as I wanted answers from Dust about facing down the Deads. Fuck, I needed those answers soon, before I decided to suck face again with an old flame I needed to smother.

I only got to the hall before I smelled the Prez's tobacco trailing after me. "Hold it, boy. Where the fuck you think you're going? We barely get the whole crew together anymore with half of 'em running their asses off, and the other half fuckin' around with their girls."

He grabbed me by the shoulder and swung me around. I looked into his cold gray eyes, trying to hold in my rage. Trying, and fucking failing.

"I know that look," Dust growled. "You've got some serious shit on your mind. More than just the usual venom gnawing at your bones. Let's talk."

Reluctantly, I let the Prez push me a little further, guiding me toward his office.

A minute later, we sat down and shut the door. My back pressed tight into the beat up chair across from his desk.

"Better start talking, Veep. This club don't need any more shit running under the surface with the big op coming together."

"That's what's pissing me off, Prez. All this talk about taking down the Deads, doing deals with the Grizzlies and the Devils, and you haven't said shit about your promise."

"The fuck?" Dust straightened up, blew out his pipe,

and slammed it down on his worn desk. "What do you think I'm pulling, brother? Taking the fuckers down in their home state does everyone a solid. Club gets its money and flexes its nuts. Wrecks its biggest threat. I get Hatch's fuckin' head on a pike, and you get the bastards who murdered Piece and put Don in a fuckin' nursing home. What's missing here? Nothing!"

His fist came down. I stood up, rage flashing in my eyes.

Crazy as I was, I wasn't about to accuse the Prez of dragging his feet, fucking me over because his eyes were purely on the cash 'til now.

Prez's rage caught me by the throat and squeezed. He wasn't wrong – wiping out the Georgia Deads technically fulfilled his promise. The op missed the spirit of what he'd sworn to me that night, when I came in, ready to ride off alone, straight to certain death.

"You promised me peace, Prez. That's the word you used that fucked up night. Peace."

It still smelled like bullshit coming outta my mouth. Had I been a fuckin' chump? How the hell was I ever supposed to have peace, really?

Even tearing the throats outta those sick bastards wouldn't put Piece back together again.

He was gone. Lost to Heaven or Hell. Forever.

"Yeah, I promised, all right," he said quietly, standing up. "You know I keep 'em, too."

Prez stepped out from behind his desk, walked straight past me, and flopped down on the torn leather couch in the corner. Our gaze never wavered.

He was about ten years older than me and still a fuckin' mystery. He'd survived more death than any other brother, had his damned throat slashed just a couple months ago, and walked away from it alive.

And that was probably nothing when he'd been born in this club's blood.

The prince who was always meant to lead it when his old man's gavel fell. Nothing on the pirates he'd said he fought overseas, an ex-captain in the U.S. merchant fleet.

"Boy, you're looking at me like I fucked you over, but you know it ain't right. Every brother here respects you, Joker. Every brother loves you. You're walking around town every damned day with a chip on your shoulder the size of fuckin' Jupiter. You do that shit with the knife every damned day. And every fuckin' day I'm watching, waiting for you to slip, carve off a perfectly good finger."

My jaw clenched. Dust's voice came steady, cool, and calm. He leaned forward, folding his hands.

"You need to pull your head outta your ass, VP. You wouldn't be wearing the patch if I didn't trust you to have some reason mixed with the psycho killer bullshit. You were smart enough to listen to me that night you showed up, asking for blood, telling me you'd go for it yourself. That would've been suicide – we both know it. You were patient. You were fuckin' smart. And now, it's almost time to get what I told you. Everything I promised."

"I ain't getting shit, Prez. Let's face it. Even if we kill some fuckin' animals, yeah, I'll feel better for a few hours, maybe a week. But once the party's over and I finally sober up, cleaning their blood off my knife…Freddy's gone. Grandpa's fucked. My hometown's a goddamned shithole that won't ever welcome anybody with a patch again – not after the dirty shit the Deads have been pushing there. Putting the motherfuckers down won't un-fuck anything."

"That's why you gotta reach inside and feel your own guts. Don't fuckin' wait for the final battle, Joker. Do it sooner. Now. 'Cause if you wait, we'll win like we always do, and you'll still walk away empty fucking handed." He leaned forward a little more, his steely eyes boring into me. "Bullets and knives only kill the demons outside you, Joker. The shit underneath your skin – that's where you gotta use your brain, your heart. You're the only one who can."

"Prez –"

"Shut up and listen for a second, brother. You think you're the only one who misses Piece?" He paused, just long enough for the anger to burn hot in my eyes, trying to ignite the gray ice in his. "Fuck, Joker, you miss him most. Fuck yeah, you do. But goddamn if the rest of us don't. You were both hell on wheels. Both of you made this club stronger. Shit, both of you were there when my old man bit it. Your votes gave me the gavel, helped keep this club in one piece when it'd been rocked to its fuckin' core."

What the fuck was he saying? Trying to pretend he understood? Trying to tell me he could even fuckin' fathom one tenth of the deep, hellish loss ripping me to shreds every goddamned day I opened my eyes?

No, no, *hell no.*

"He was my brother!" I roared, standing up, halfway to

hallucinating Freddy sitting next to him, smiling on that damned beat up sofa. "By blood, by patch...maybe by fuckin' soul. They took him, Dust. Tore his fuckin' head off, ripped his eyes out. I walked in and saw my grandpa on the floor. His poor heart snapped like a twig when he saw those holes where Piece's eyes used to be. I gotta watch him flinch a little every fuckin' time I see him, and he looks me in the eye, knowing he's still seeing Freddy when he looks at me."

Big goddamned mistake, spewing the poison like this.

It flashed before my eyes, a hundred times more intense than most days.

Even now, it was all a sadistic blur.

My hands on grandpa's chest, pumping furiously, fighting the molten tears in my eyes.

Freddy's fuckin' severed head sitting on the bed, taunting both of us, worse than seeing my own dead face looking back at me.

Summer walking in, freezing up on the spot, horror in her eyes. Didn't take me two fuckin' seconds to tell her to leave.

And Summer...fuck.

Fucking goddamn it to hell! That's what this was all about, wasn't it?

I couldn't lose anyone else. I couldn't lose her again.

Fucking couldn't! I'd pushed her away because I had to, get her the fuck away forever.

"Joker," Dust said, sitting up straight in his seat, his pipe in one hand. "Look at me."

Took forever to finally do it. I fucking hated how well he knew me, knew every man in this club, like the father most of us never had.

"Time to be straight. It ain't just Freddy or the war with the Deads eating you like a case of fuckin' termites."

"No!" I growled, still denying it, even when it caused my damned heart to beat a million miles an hour.

"Yeah, fuck yeah. I know about the girl," he said. My head jerked up, and I looked at him like hot death given a human face. "Skin told me the other day. So did Lion. Said she worked you over good, got you madder than a fuckin' hornet, so pissed off you covered the bitch in mud."

Goddamned Skin. Fucking Lion.

I'd put our Treasurer into a coma for ratting me out, and that scruffy motherfucker, Lion, back in one.

"Honestly, makes me wanna crack your jaw for fuckin' with a lady like that," Dust snarled, holding the flame on his skull-tipped lighter to his pipe. "Especially when she's the only one who's been able to get shit outta you for three years, only one besides that damned dog."

"She's nobody," I said coldly.

Yeah, another lie.

"Bullshit," Dust said, taking a long pull on his pipe. "She's somebody you fucked and didn't wanna walk away from, or somebody who fucked you over. Maybe both. Point is, she's pulled your pin like a damned grenade, and that's dangerous as a knife to the throat when this club's about to swing its nuts harder than we did in a generation."

"So, what, Prez?" I growled, shaking my head. "What

the fuck are you telling me to do?"

"Ain't telling you shit, brother. You're a grown man. That's for you to figure out. You can put two and two together. You know what you've gotta do already. That's not coming from me. It can't, and it won't." He held the pipe, tipped his face up, and blew a strong string of thick smoke toward the ceiling, where it hung like a thunderhead.

"Straighten your shit out," he growled. "Clear your head as much as you can before we ride into Georgia, guns blazing. Do whatever the fuck it takes so that when we return to Knoxville with bags of bloody Deads colors in our saddlebags, you can live with the brothers. Life with yourself. Live with us again, Joker, without acting like you're three goddamned seconds away from ramming your blade into some poor bastard's throat."

Sage advice. Wise, ruthless, and completely fuckin' infuriating.

"We done here yet?" I said, standing up.

"Yeah. Don't let the door hit you in the ass," Dust growled, clearly disappointed.

I headed out, and went straight for my room. Last thing I wanted was rejoining the brothers drinking and laughing at the bar.

A couple girlie voices cut through their chatter. Somebody's old lady must've shown up. Or maybe a couple bubbly sluts for the single guys, bitches who'd just as soon as ride a brother's cock for a jolt to their pussy and a hopeless stab at being a club wife.

One big, happy ass biker family.

Turned my stomach.

I couldn't relate. I couldn't fuckin' have it.

The last three years, I'd drank and fucked and joined in the big roasts with all my boys. But I didn't fuckin' smile. Didn't feel it when the men I'd sworn my life to sat around me, didn't even feel it when I was buried in some bitch to my balls, hate fucking her in between swigs of booze.

Riding helped. So did the dog at my feet, who came over when I dropped on my ass, rocking the shitty bed. Bingo whined, forcing me to scratch his head.

Aw, fuck it. Today, I sat up, leaned down, and hugged the greedy bastard.

He licked my face once before I pulled away.

I loved him because he didn't ask stupid fucking questions, or bust my balls over the past. He loved my sorry ass because he didn't know any better. Didn't understand how permanently fucked up I'd gotten three summers ago.

Damned dog knew too much about me. Only one person walking this planet really did.

I'd pushed her away. Fuckin' *flung* her outta my life like she'd burn me down.

Just like I swore I always would if I ever saw her face again. Summer had the only face in my memory as cruel and unforgettable as Freddy's.

I couldn't get her killed, letting her back, and I'd make her hate my evil ass more than she already did.

But fuck, *why* had she come back? Nothing made sense about it.

Why the hell had she tracked me down after three

damned years of nothing?

Bingo whined again, licking my hand, just like he could sense the hell roiling my mind. I looked down into his sad, dark eyes, smoothing his fur 'til I saw that tail wag.

"Don't worry about it, boy. I'm just flushing some shit."

Some shit. Yeah, fuck me.

If only it were as easy as pulling a damned lever.

No, ever since she'd come to me, not once but fuckin' twice, pushing deeper into my world at Grandpa's home...I'd been the one who walked away covered in shit.

Five more minutes, I sat with my dog, the same nightmares stewing in my brain. Decided I only had two choices.

I could throw the dog a bone, walk out to the bar, and steal a bitch from Lion, Tin, or Sixty for the night. I could try for the millionth time to bury my ruined life and wake up with another hangover and an awkward little girl hanging around my neck.

Fuck that. It hadn't worked before, and it damned sure wasn't gonna start.

Option B was even more fucked up, but at least it'd be a stab at something different, instead of the same old shit that never worked.

Right about now, Option B sounded pretty fuckin' good, because it meant answers.

Standing, I patted the big dog's head, then walked him over to the cushion in the corner, laying him down for the night. "I'll be back in a few hours," I said, reaching into the cabinet and pulling out a treat.

A couple minutes later, I had my helmet locked on my head. My bike droned steadily on the open road.

Normally, the purr comforted me, no different than every other brother wearing this patch.

Didn't do a damned thing for me today except ratchet up the tension, add to all the bitter questions sticking like gum in my throat.

I had to find Summer. Had to ask her why the fuck she'd come back. Had to know why she still wanted these lips on hers when it was totally obvious she'd kissed a dead man who wanted nothing to do with her.

Something about all this didn't add up. And if I couldn't figure out my own shit, like the Prez wanted, then at least I'd take a crack at hers.

* * * *

Seddon never paid anybody shit. Knowing how harsh our old hometown could be, plus seeing the rusted out shitbox she drove, I knew she had about two places she could be staying with her money, if she hadn't blown town already.

I came up empty handed at the first place, a run down dump just a few blocks from the Heel. The ratty looking bastard at the front desk told me nobody named Summer Olivers ever checked in.

Second motel, a strong runner up for cheapest shit stack in town, turned up the same damned thing. An old, middle aged woman with a thick European accent told me there wasn't anybody with Summer's name staying there, even when I asked her twice.

What the fuck? She'd either changed her legal name – not too fuckin' likely – or somebody else had brought her here on their dime, under their name.

The hairs on the back of my neck pricked up.

If she was here, then I definitely wasn't leaving empty handed.

I'd walk the whole damned lot, crawl up on that cracked balcony, and look through every fuckin' window if I had to, just to find her.

Figuring out what the fuck was going on here wasn't just about me anymore. It might easily be club biz, too, and I never defaulted on the patch.

I'd parked my bike next to the front door. Decided to take it down the next street, put it out of sight, in case there was anybody here waiting for the Pistols with a bullet. I was rounding the corner, pulling out toward the road, when I saw the shit in the bushes.

A greasy looking sonofabitch crouched down. Hiding. A rifle in his hands, perched on his shoulder, one eye on the sights.

The laser cut straight through somebody's window. How bad did I want to bet that was Summer's?

Revving my engine told me. I didn't stop, didn't think, didn't second guess as I plowed my bike straight into the shitty crop of trees.

Fucker never saw me coming. He screamed when my front tire rolled over him. I punched the brakes, stopping me from skidding into the wall.

I jumped off, holding my arm over my mouth, fighting smoke and dirt kicked up in the air while I went for my nine. Had to kick a couple branches aside before I felt the gun on the ground.

My boot knocked it further away from fuckface, who was on his side, his leg torn to shit, looking at me.

He was holding a pair of shitty looking night vision goggles. One look at his cut told me everything I needed to know – the severed hand sewn into his side.

Our mortal enemies were here. In our own goddamned territory. Maybe aiming through my fuckin' girl's window!

"Fuck, shit, please," he sputtered, holding a hand over his face. "Hatch is gonna –"

There wasn't time to contemplate all the fuckin' whys, and not a spare second for mercy.

My gun barked, slamming a bullet through his brain. Easy.

Finding Summer and getting her the fuck outta there before anybody else saw this shit show wasn't gonna be as simple. I stood up, dusted myself off, took one look at the window he'd been aiming for and ran.

Never bothered knocking. My boot slammed into the door and flattened it, leaving me a clear path.

I stepped in and saw – what the fuck? Summer in the corner. With a kid. Clutching him close to her chest, his little face tucked into her bosom, her hands across his ears.

"Joker?" she whimpered, her eyes going wide, as if she couldn't believe it was me.

Well, fuck. That made two of us.

Couldn't *believe* the fuckin' shock and awe I was seeing right in front of me. Shit that stirred up a hundred more questions than there were answers.

"Who else?" I growled, stepping into the room, coming up to her, trying to do my damnedest not to startle the kid.

"I thought we were done for," she said, tipping her head for a second to kiss the little boy through his dark hair. "I mean, when I heard the bike, and saw him go down, I expected it to be one more of them. I need to –"

"Babe, you're gonna shut your fuckin' mouth right now, is what you're gonna do."

Boom. Lips sealed. Still just as sweet and biteable as ever before, but fuck if they didn't make my blood boil, because I had proof right in front of me that she'd been lying about an awful lot.

Shit, what else was she hiding?

"Where are your keys? You're coming to my place. I just killed a fuckin' man out there. We've got about ten minutes, maybe less, before some jackass here phones it in and every cop in Knoxville hits us like vultures."

She didn't dare fight. Just looked at me, stopped breathing for a second, and then closed her eyes and nodded.

"Over there." Her little hand pointed to a big green purse over in the corner.

I walked over, ripped it up, and carried it over to her, pushing it into her free hand. "Listen, when I say go, you're gonna get in your car. Follow me every fuckin' mile like your life depends on it. Because babe, I ain't shittin', it absolutely does."

The toe of my boot pushed against something on the floor. I looked down, saw it was a busted out screen. A shitty looking cellphone, like the kind the club used for burners, now smashed into a couple pieces.

"Um, there's an explanation, Jackson. I promise you, it isn't what you —"

"Quiet," I growled, pushing my hand over her mouth. "Didn't tell you to start squawking to me about a buncha fuckin' questions I haven't even asked. That comes later. Right now, you walk the fuck out behind me, strap in the kid, and don't move 'til you see me pulling out on my bike."

The kid looked up just then. I looked away just as fuckin' fast, hoping she'd think it was because I didn't want to startle him.

Had to follow my own advice. Had to get them out of here. Had to take them to my apartment, put the kid down for a nap, before I laid into her.

But Jesus Christ. One second was all I needed to see it, to see the eyes that blew my world apart.

Fucking fuck.

I stopped every nerve in my body from having a conniption fit 'til I was on my bike. I walked her out like a robot, covered her while she put the kid in his seat, then climbed into the driver's side herself.

Then I hauled ass to my bike, got on, and roared out, checking the mirror carefully to make sure her rusted little car hung close.

Small miracle I didn't lose my shit on the way back. The sharp, numb focus that always came over me when I'd dealt with life and death before triumphed again. But it got the biggest fuckin' test in my life since the day after Piece died, when Prez had to hold me back, before I went lone wolf against his killers and got myself wrecked.

That kid. That beautiful, mysterious, spear-through-my-fuckin'-chest toddler...I'd grill her about it later, no bullshit.

But I didn't have to. Deep down, I already knew the answer.

The second I saw that bright hazel glow in his eyes, I knew he was mine.

He was my brother.

He was my grandpa.

He was me.

He was a Taylor by blood.

The only man in this world who could've made him was looking back at me in my bike's mirrors, his fucked up eyes flashing with a thousand kinds of rage and a haze of tears.

I had a son. And the bitch I'd once loved had fuckin' lied to me about it for God only knew how long.

VII: Wag the Dog (Summer)

Oh, God.

Holy hell.

Oh, crap.

I tried not to hyperventilate on the long, painful journey down the highway, straight to the exit on the other side of town.

The last thing I needed was to freak out and wreck the car.

The second last thing was scaring the hell out of poor Alex worse than I already had. He'd started crying as soon as he realized something was wrong, about a split second before I saw Joker's bike tear through the bushes.

By the time I picked him up, the lone, deafening gunshot had rang out. Hatch was screaming on the phone, snarling and cursing like a mad dog. I picked it up off the floor and hurled it at the wall as hard as I could, silencing it forever.

I walked across the debris, feeling the satisfying crunch underfoot. The demon who'd threatened my son would be twice as hellbent on killing us tomorrow, but today, he'd lost.

There was about thirty seconds of satisfaction before Jackson's heavy boot kicked down the door. He came in, staring at us, his eyes glued to the baby in my arms.

I wasn't sure how I kept it together. Everything I'd tried to hide away was out in the open, lost in an instant, forever torn away from me by that wild, scary energy in his eyes.

They'd been so dead, so haunted, for so fucking long. But when he saw Alex, before he told me to shut up and leave with him, I saw something I never thought I'd see swirling in those intense hazel eyes ever again.

Life.

He knew the kid was ours. He knew I'd hid him. And I'd probably be dismembered for doing it by the end of the night.

* * * *

Joker didn't say a word when I followed him into a cracked parking lot. It belonged to a tall, worn looking building.

He got off his bike and motioned, leaving me to park the car in an empty space nearby, then collect Alex. I followed him to the door he unlocked, and we stepped into a tiny lobby lined with big mailboxes.

At least it was cleaner in here than it looked on the outside. Better than the place I'd been living, under the Deadhands' gun.

He shot me an angry look over his shoulder, checking to make sure I was following as he headed for a big, winding staircase.

Little Alex yawned in my arms. I walked slowly, careful not to wake him, hoping he'd finally get some sleep after all the excitement.

He wasn't scared anymore. That counted for something. But now it was like I'd taken his innocent terror, feeling my blood turn to ice with every step I took toward Joker's apartment.

Mine wasn't nearly as innocent. Maybe I deserved whatever was coming, the barrage of abuse, but I'd only tried to protect my son from a man so dangerous, so broken, a normal family life wasn't in his makeup.

Upstairs, he stopped next to a big wooden door, jammed the key into the lock, and threw it open. He held it open, waving us in, while he pulled out his phone.

"Sixty, it's me," I heard him say. "Feed Bingo for me tonight. Won't be coming back to the clubhouse to pick him up 'til tomorrow sometime."

I looked around for a place to sit. His apartment was surprisingly spartan, and I walked toward the big couch in the middle of the room, never seeing any of the beer bottles or busted pizza boxes I'd expected.

"Shit, bro, you okay?" I heard the other man say through the phone. "Must've found your own fuckin' party – we were keeping your bottle warm! Whatever, long as you're happy, fed, and deep in pussy. Out."

Joker killed the call with a grunt. A tense silence blanketed the small, cozy space between us. I watched him take a lap around the coffee table like a lion deep in thought, before he finally sat in the black leather recliner across from us.

I licked my lips, tasting fear in my own sweat. "I don't know where to begin," I said.

"At the fuckin' beginning, babe. You tell me a story. I'll sit here and listen real quiet – just like your little boy." He leaned forward, hands on his knees, the wild eyes he shared with my son stabbing through me. "Maybe by the time you get to the end, you can put him down for a nap in my room. Then we can talk about more serious shit."

I swallowed the bitter lump in my throat before I started. Had to do it several more times throughout my story. I told him about the Deads rolling into Seddon, coming into my store, roughing up whoever they didn't like, and walking out half the time without paying for anything.

Nobody challenged them. Nobody dared.

I told him about the drugs, how bad it got since mama died and he left for Tennessee, what life was like, living in a building half-full of junkies.

He heard about how long I suffered alone, doing my best to raise Alex on my shoestring budget and some food stamps when I needed them, how I wished every day, every night, and every minute in between that mama was still alive to help.

I didn't tell him the truth about the boy, where he'd come from. Stupid when he knew – *holy Christ, he knew* – but the words caught in my throat every single time.

He watched the tears come down in silence, sitting up a little straighter, a mix of compassion and raw hatred in his eyes.

God, what a contrast.

What a storm.

Joker sucked in a sharp, brutal breath, one that made his entire chest ripple, reminding me how incredible he looked underneath his leather cut and thin club t-shirt.

No, no I couldn't think about that, though. I had to carry on.

"Then there was Hatch," I said. "That's what he called himself."

"President of the fuckin' Deads in northern Georgia," he growled, nodding.

He already knew. Hell, of course he did. None of this nightmare would've happened if I weren't plunged into the middle of a blood war between motorcycle clubs.

"Yeah. Well, he knew about us, our history. Knew he could use me to get to you." Joker stiffened up, staring me down. I hugged Alex closer, glaring back just as angrily. "Obviously, I wouldn't have screwed you over. I didn't know how to break the news, Jackson. I had to play along, at least for a little while, anything to stop him. He threatened Alex, told me he'd kill him right in front of me!"

I forced my voice to a hush, feeling him stirring in my arms.

"Alex, huh?" Joker said, ignoring my bullshit. "That's a great fuckin' name. Strong name."

"Right," I said quietly, before I glared at him again. "Seriously, how was I supposed to tell you what was really going on? Every time I came by, you made it *very* clear you wanted nothing to do with me. You wouldn't even sit down and talk."

"That's before I knew you were sitting on the biggest fuckin' secret in the world," he growled, standing up. "Whatever, fuck it. Let me hold him. I'll put him down for a nap. Gotta learn sometime."

The big, awesome biker towered over us. Reluctantly, I sighed, and lifted my baby, offering him up to his father for the first time.

I was ready to jump in at a moment's notice, if he held him the wrong way, or moved too fast.

It never happened. My heart plunged into my stomach and smashed into a million bits, just watching them together.

Alex rested his head on Joker's thick, muscular arm, suspended against his leather chest with that wonderful, manly scent.

Father and son. One.

A sight I thought I'd never see, that I'd tried to keep for so fucking long...

God. What the hell was I thinking? If only I'd come to him sooner, told him about the little boy.

Maybe he wouldn't have been dead for so long. Maybe I wouldn't have suffered alone.

It was too late for that. Tears clouded my eyes as I watched him holding the boy, rocking him gently in his arms, staring down at him like he was the most precious thing in the world.

More precious than the bike that took him everywhere. Maybe even more than the big, hairy dog I'd seen at his side the other day.

I stood up cautiously and followed him into his room. I'd halfway expected guns on the wall, or a thousand sharp things sitting around, but there was nothing except an old guitar in the corner, a couple posters of bikes and classic cars, and a big, thick bed with a headboard going halfway to the ceiling.

I had a flash of us laying down together, instead of him putting our son down for a nap, making that headboard rock as I straddled him, hands on his immaculate chest, sinking down onto the only cock I'd ever had inside me.

No. Hell no. There were so many strange, twisted things running through my mind right now I had to fight, but I definitely had to go after *this,* tooth and nail.

"Make sure you check up on him often. He isn't used to sleeping in a bed like this."

"We'll only be a little while. Promise." He laid the boy down and tucked a sheet over him. We both stood there, watching as he drifted off, blissfully away from the tortured hearts and real life killers hanging over us like swords.

"Outside, Summer. Now." The growl in my ear was almost inhuman. Joker put his thick, rough hands on my shoulders and squeezed.

So much for savoring the small, miraculous heartwarming scene on the bed. I turned around and walked out, leaving his hands on me, stopping in the hall while he slowly pulled the door shut behind him.

Then, he looked at me, and I was completely alone with those feral, angry, beautiful eyes. "Why'd you lie to me, Summertime?"

"What else could I do?" Shaking my head, I swallowed, preempting another stone from forming in my throat.

"That's your defense?" he snorted. "Tell me again. Why'd you fuckin' lie to me?"

Shit.

He didn't wait for an answer. Snarling, he grabbed my hand, and jerked me deeper into the apartment, into the bathroom with him while he slammed the door shut.

"You fucked me over, you fucked yourself, and you fucked our son, keeping him from me. He's really mine, ain't he? Don't even fuckin' deny it!"

His rage paralyzed me. Before I knew it, I was up against the wall, his chest on mine, both his hands planted on each side of my head, caging me in completely.

"Yes," I said softly, wincing as what was left of my heart ripped in two. "He's yours. He's only two, just had his birthday a couple months ago. We made him that summer, Jackson. The last few happy nights I ever had in my life..."

"Last? I don't fuckin' know 'bout that. But you can be damned sure that every last night you're gonna have is mine now."

I gasped. What the hell did he mean? He talked like he was entitled to make me his property!

"I'm not your prisoner. I'm —"

"Summertime, shut your fuckin' mouth and listen. Long as my kid's under the gun, he ain't going anywhere with you. You're not taking a step outside this apartment unless I say so, neither. The Deads are coming. I'm getting the club together," he said coldly. "Murdering every last one of those filthy, sick cocksuckers. It was always personal, ever since they did Freddy, but now they're doubling down on my son?"

I flinched when he shook his head, his hands turning into fists next to mine. My ears heard the faint sound of plaster starting to crack, felt the pressure of the wall behind me caving in.

"They're fully, completely, totally fucked!" he growled, spittle flying through his teeth, landing on my neck.

"And babe," he said quietly, coming closer, touching his crazed forehead to mine. "So. Are. You."

He was right about one thing – life as I knew it was *over*. There was no coming back once I was face-to-face with a raging, handsome psychopath.

Definitely no coming back from the strange, sick tingle that ran through me, being this close to him. Even when he looked like he was about to strangle me on the spot, he was gorgeous, so rough and primal my brain couldn't stop the chemical reaction churning my blood.

My thighs pinched together, trembling, feeling my panties soften with my own wetness. His lips were only inches from mine, lips that cursed me, threatened me, told me they were taking over, and *fuck me* if I didn't like it.

Yes, fuck me.

Fuck.

"Joker...Jackson..." I said softly, finally at a loss for words. "It doesn't have to be this way. I trust you to protect us. We can talk the rest of this out. We can –"

"Bullshit!" he snapped, his eyes narrowing, boring into

mine until my eyelids fluttered, the only defense I had left. My hands went plush against his chest, ready to push him away if I had, even though I didn't have a prayer of making it happen. "What did I tell you about that fuckin' mouth, Summertime? Said I'd shut it."

It was the last thing he said before he kissed me.

That is, if a woman could call the savage pressure and teeth sinking into my bottom lip a kiss, rather than an act of total domination.

The passionate tease he'd given me the other day outside the nursing home, slamming his lips on mine? Nothing compared to this.

This was fire. This was hate. This was a man coming undone in my mouth, tearing a bitter moan out of me, and then another when his hand flew to my breast and twisted my nipple through my shirt.

My nails tangled in his shirt, raking against his chest.

Fighting him, pulling him into me all at once.

My mouth moved against his, saying things words couldn't.

But I didn't realize how much like lightning cutting across the sky this conversation was going to be until he started ripping off my clothes.

His hands roamed my body, jerking off my shirt, snapping my bra strap. My jeans and panties came down in one push, and I felt the wet trickle rolling down my thigh instantly.

"Joker..."

Big mistake, just whispering my name. He took my

thighs, slammed them against the wall, and pulled my legs apart.

Then his face was buried in my pussy.

My fingernails were on his scalp now, pushing through his thick, dark hair, feeling for precious support. And I needed it – *God, I needed it* – almost as much as I'd needed this for so long.

His tongue pushed through my wetness, taking over, hitting all the right spots. My thighs were trembling, and I leaned on him, urging him in deeper, deeper, deeper while his mouth took me through heaven and hell.

Oh, God. Deeper.

"Holy shit. Joker, I'm –"I bit my own tongue, dying from excitement.

Every time I whimpered, his mouth moved faster. My clit went between his teeth, swelled in his vice, and exploded against the first few lashes of his tongue.

He growled when I came. His rumble echoed through me, angry as a wild animal, just a steady, mad pulse of fire, hate, and sex.

Still panting through clenched teeth, I forced myself to open my eyes while he was still licking me, and saw myself in the mirror. My whole body was totally contorted. My pupils were tiny and the whites were going bloodshot, blown out by the nasty shock of the past week, and now *this*.

Whatever the hell *this* even was.

He held me while I halfway collapsed in his arms, coming up, and smashed his lips down on mine. I could taste myself on his mouth. I could taste him.

God. I tasted three fucking years worth of built up emotion, all pouring out in this torrent.

"Fuck, I missed that sweet little cunt. You on the fuckin' pill, or what?" he spat, pulling away from me, clenching my chin with his fingers.

"I've…I've missed a few days. It isn't safe. I'll start again tonight."

"Then get on your knees if you don't want another kid. You're gonna suck every last drop outta me, straight down your throat."

He pushed me down. Gently, but firmly.

My eyes went to his pants, which he pushed down a second later, along with his boxers. The pierced, magnificent dick I'd missed forever sprang out, angrier than I'd ever seen it before.

"Speak to me, Summertime. Suck me the fuck off. Blow me so goddamned hard I forget about all the lies and the bullshit and you running, hiding, lying. Suck."

"I didn't run," I said angrily, trying to keep my eyes off the rock hard cock pulsing in his hand, the little bullet of his piercing shining in the dim bathroom light.

"Suck," he repeated, reaching down, tangling his fingers through my hair. He pushed my face towards it.

Before I knew it, my mouth was full of him. Hard, hot, earthy beneath my tongue.

I bobbed my head, running my tongue along his length, searching for that spot underneath the head – the one that caused him to suck breath and growl all those years ago.

"Fuck. Shit. Goddamn, woman!" he snarled.

Bingo. I focused my tongue there, reaching up to massage his balls, amazed that these were what had given us the boy sleeping in his room.

I sucked him like my life depended on it, because maybe it did.

Ran my lips, my tongue, my teeth across his cock, erasing all the years of distance, speaking through the insane, painful barriers between us.

"Fuck, fuck, fuck," he sputtered, pulling on my hair until it burned deliciously. "Fucking shit, Summertime. Take it!"

And I did.

His head swelled, pulsed, and pumped into my mouth. I held him deep, still massaging him as he came, hopelessly trying to catch his come.

It was completely impossible. He flooded me, shot thick ropes down my throat, just pumping and pumping and pumping until his sticky, warm seed ran out around the corners of my lips.

I'd be a total mess by the end of it, and so what?

Right now, nothing mattered, except feeling him growling out his hate, his madness, shooting me full of him. *Again.*

When he finally softened, I pulled his cock out, and kissed him near the piercing. He jerked himself away, glowering at me again, his eyes as dull and dead as they'd been before.

"Clean the fuck up and let me know if you need to eat.

You can sleep in my room with the kid tonight. I'll take the sofa."

"You mean…that's it? Just like that?"

Pants pulled up, he tugged on his zipper, leaving me naked while he reclaimed his biker suit like nothing ever happened.

Jesus, I'd been an idiot.

"That's all 'til I decide what the fuck to do with you, yeah. I'll sleep on it. You rest. You're safe here, you listen to me, and that'll do dandy."

He walked out, closing the door behind him, leaving me alone for the millionth time.

I buried my face in my hands and broke down, surrounded by his scent.

* * * *

"Wake the fuck up, sunshine," a dark voice said, edging me from my dreams.

I turned, reaching one arm out for Alex, and felt – nothing.

I bolted up, heart pounding, and saw him in Joker's arms, the little boy giggling while he reached for his father's face.

It was still dark outside. "Shit. What time is it?"

"Early enough. We've got business at the clubhouse, babe, and you're coming with."

"Be careful with him," I said, feeling like a total bitch because Alex looked happier than he'd been for awhile in daddy's arms. "Let me get dressed."

He left the room, still playfully bouncing the boy in his arms. They were naturals together.

Of course they were. Why did that feel like an arrow through the chest?

Maybe because there'd never be one big, happy family. I was only fooling myself.

There was only Joker and Alex. Alex and me.

Two pairs. Never a whole.

I got dressed as quickly as I could. When I stepped out, Joker sat on the sofa with Alex on his lap, a bowl of pipping hot oatmeal at his side.

"Buckle up, little man. Here comes the Harley on its run..." His hand slowly moved the spoon toward Alex's mouth, stopping as my son laughed.

It would've been heartwarming, honestly, if I wasn't still so pissed. "You need to be careful with that! Make sure it isn't too hot."

Joker looked up, his eyes on fire. "Ain't a fuckin' fool, Summertime. It's plenty warm. Not scalding. Tested it myself. Anyway, there's more in the kitchen if you need it."

My stomach growled, forcing me to swallow my pride and take what he'd left out. I grabbed it and sat down next to them, spooning a bite into my mouth.

Anything would've tasted good. This was almost heavenly, with just the right honey sweetness, a hint of apple, and some cinnamon mixed in.

"Is this instant?" I said, eyeing him carefully as he moved another bite to Alex's small mouth.

"Come the fuck on." He snorted. "I'm man enough to wake up and do my cooking. Same recipe Grandpa used to feed us when were kids. Only fair my son has the same breakfasts I did."

My son. It sounded so heavy on his lips, so full of pride.

I softened, giving him his moment with Alex. Whatever.

There'd be plenty of time to seethe at him for using me as a doormat later, but for the next ten minutes, I was almost at peace, watching him handle our baby boy like he'd been doing it from day one.

"Okay, kid," he whispered softly, pulling a napkin off the table and blotting at the little boy's mouth. "Time to go. Keep eating like that and you'll be able to knock men out twice my size someday."

I rolled my eyes. "Oh, sure. Like I really want him becoming one of your brothers."

Joker's head twisted, aiming the second hate-fuck in twenty four hours at me with his eyes. "You're in no position to judge shit, Summer. You don't know a damned thing. Growing big and strong can turn this boy into a billionaire or a fuckin' quarterback. You're acting like everything I say has the club's stamp all over it. Ain't true."

"How do I know it doesn't?"

His jaw clenched, but he didn't say anything. I put my hands out, ready to take Alex again. Reluctantly, he passed him over to me, and I hugged him tight.

"Just need to change his diaper, and then we'll be ready to go," I said, finishing the last of my oatmeal with one hand.

"Damned straight. You leave it to me next time, I'll let you cover before we go."

"Really?" I said, standing up and wrinkling my nose in disbelief. "I can't believe you're so serious about this. I thought you'd leave the diapers and baths to me."

Joker bolted up, rooted himself to the floor, even though I knew he would've been up in my face if I wasn't holding the toddler. "He's mine, Summer. My son. My own fuckin' flesh and blood. 'Course I want to learn everything, make up for all the time I've lost thanks to you. When we get to the club, you're gonna sit down, let the kid play with my dog, and keep your fuckin' mouth shut. I'm giving you one more pass on your bullshit assumptions today – but it's the last one you get. I'm warming up the truck."

I stood there with my jaw hanging as he walked past, grabbed his keys off the counter, and then popped the door, letting it fall shut behind him with a thud.

I *hated* being put in my place by this screwed up, cocky, bloodthirsty dick.

I hated it even more that he blamed me for everything.

Mostly, I just hated him for being right, and so point-blank about it that my inner bitch was screaming.

* * * *

I kept quiet on the short ride in his truck, checking on Alex every few minutes. He sat behind us in his little seat, holding a stuffed lion, his favorite toy I'd brought along from home.

God, home. I had about another week before the rent would slip by without getting paid. The greedy old landlord wouldn't wait more than a week after that to dump my stuff and find a new tenant.

I'd left behind everything else. I was never going to see anything that wasn't in my purse or my car again.

But I had Alex, we were both safe, and for now, he was all that mattered.

At the clubhouse, we rolled through a tall metal gate guarded by two grim looking men with prospect patches. Not the same boys who'd greeted me the other day, the first time I'd tried to confront Joker, and talk some sense into him.

"Outside," he said, pointing to the door out back. "You can wait out there 'til I say it's time. Show Alex my dog."

Holding the little boy, I pushed open the screen. The big dog laying on the ground instantly perked up when he saw us. Bingo stood up, stretched, and walked over, his tongue hanging out.

I sat down in a deck chair, Alex on my lap, stroking the dog's fur. Baby boy perked up as soon as the giant dog came over, giggling while he dug his hands into his fur.

"Doggie! Doggie!"

"That's right," I said, finally allowing myself to smile, holding him closer. "You're learning so fast, honey. He's a big one, isn't he?"

"Biiig!" Alex echoed.

Giving in, I let myself smile, watching as he pushed his face into the dog's fur, stroking his sides. Bingo seemed just as happy, letting out a satisfied whine, his tail slapping the air.

These moments were precious, and so rare, especially when every hour might bring hell, ending them all forever.

I hadn't forgotten why we were here.

Hatch was out there. Seething.

He'd come for me – come for *us,* just like he'd threatened – unless the bastard who had my heart twisted in knots saved us. I hated having to depend on him, almost as much as I hated him for using me to suck his cock.

I wasn't his fucking play thing. But I definitely wasn't his woman either, and I never would be.

"Rowww! Rowww!" Alex interrupted my melancholy thoughts, trying to imitate the dog's sound. I made the same silly noise when I read him his stories, teaching him all about animals.

It shouldn't bother me so damned much. Today, my son was happy and safe. He'd made a new friend to play with, judging by the way the big gray dog wagged his tail.

So, why did I feel so lonely? Abandoned?

Why did I want to punch myself in the face every time I let my eyes wander to Joker at breakfast, still admiring his rock hard body. The fact that he could be so gentle, so patient with Alex only made it harder to stop.

I hugged Alex tighter, my embrace apologizing for how we'd never have a happy family. It was an illusion. I wouldn't keep him from Joker anymore, but after all of this was over, I definitely wouldn't be crawling back.

I'd let him protect us. I'd let him catch up with his son.

I swore I'd stand my ground. And if he ever tried to pull me into bed or put me on my knees again, I'd slap the absolute shit out of him.

VIII: Brotherhood in the Balance (Joker)

Soon as I stepped into the meeting room for church, the air was heavy as shit. I wasn't the only one dragging myself in all pissed.

Firefly sat next to Skin, Crawl, Sixty, and the rest of the boys, looking like a human hand grenade. He looked up when he saw me. I jerked outta my seat, plopping down before I pulled out my switchblade and shot him a look.

"What the fuck's eating you?" I extended my blade, ready to stab that shit through my fingers, and add a few more scratches to the beat up table with the Pistols logo painted in the middle.

"He's fuckin' my sis again," Firefly growled, slamming his fist down. "Come on, Veep. Don't start that shit. We're all on edge today."

"Easy, brother," Skin said, grabbing one of his shoulders and giving him a shake. "Already told you – Hannah's a grown woman. You can't do shit about who she drags into bed. Meg, she's dealing with the same thing all the time, watching her girls at the Heel bum around with all kinds of fuckin' scum."

"It ain't the fuckin' same, and you know it! Hannah's too fuckin' good for any man with the patch. She's a businesswoman, for Christ's sake. The kind who deals with a fuck of a lot more than some shit strip club here in town. Prez is fucking her like another whore to kick to the curb, if he isn't slipping his dick in her, trying to get her money. Greedy fuckin' sonofabitch."

Skin's face tensed, anger flashing in his eyes. "I'm gonna pretend you didn't just call my old lady a fuckin' idiot, brother. Say it again, and my fists are going in your guts."

Shit, this was bad. I looked up, my eyes quickly scanning the rest of the boys. Crawl sipped water from a canteen, or maybe something stronger, pushing his dark hair back, trying to pretend the shitshow a couple guys over wasn't happening. Sixty took a long drag on his cig, his goatee twitching, smart enough for once not to make any damned jokes.

Lion, Tin, and the three new prospects we'd invited to the table sat at the end, nervously whispering to themselves, too new to lay down the law.

Who the fuck could blame them? It was Firefly's job as Enforcer to break up fights between the brothers, but since he was in the middle of one, now that shit was up to me.

I slammed my blade into the wood so hard the whole table shook, and left it there. Good enough to throw all their eyes on me.

"Brother — brothers! — lay the fuck off Prez and each

other. Your shit's all just personal, Firefly. You wanna hash it out with Dust in his office or some shit, whatever. You keep bad mouthing him here, in front of the whole club, we've got a fuckin' problem. One we don't need when we're supposed to be here today, talking about the op, for fuck's sake. Put a goddamned lid on it – all of you!"

I ripped my knife out of the table and pointed at everybody there, one by one. Last tick of my hand stopped on Firefly, who fuckin' seethed, his blue eyes rippling like raging oceans.

Pissed as they were, everybody was also shocked. I never got this goddamned heated. Ever since Piece died, my rage came cold, went into my knife, and didn't come out 'til there was blood all over it.

I didn't go off like this. I didn't scream.

Except, now I fucking did. My blade's knife scorched my hand, and it was shaking. Shaking like a fuckin' leaf.

"Veep," Skin started, licking his lips. "What's going on, brother?"

"Yeah, bro," Sixty said, blowing a string of smoke. "Ain't just Firefly and Skinny boy ripping into each other's shit today. Never seen you like this."

Fuck. I sat there, paralyzed, knowing there was no way I could open up about Summer and the kid.

I'd decided this morning it was strictly business. I'd tell the brothers everything I knew, but I'd treat it like one more piece of business, no different than our latest hit, or the weapons we were hauling on the next run.

Getting emotional about this goddamned shit in front

of the club wasn't a choice. No fuckin' way.

I was about five seconds from feeding them a load about a bad hangover when Prez saved me. The door flew open, and he entered. Dust nodded to us, kicking it shut behind him with his boot.

All the anger in the room seemed to go to him as he sat down, giving me a quick look. "We've got a lotta shit to run through today, so we're coming to order now," he said, picking up his gavel and swinging it down hard on wood.

"First order, I've finally talked some sense into that crazy old motherfucker out west. Blackjack and the Grizzlies are giving us some guns and some guys to kick the door down."

Every man in the room collectively sucked in a breath. Crawl cocked his head, cleared his throat, more calm than anybody after the shit that just went down.

"That's good news, isn't it? More than we've been hoping for all these fucking months. But what the hell do they want in return?"

"Thirty big in mercenary fees, plus fifty percent once we've got a solid route through Georgia. They'll be sharing that shit with the Devils, too, whenever their guys head into Dixie. So, really, we're getting our asses a solid deal with both clubs, as much as they want to claw outta us." Dust reached for his pipe, tucked fresh tobacco into it, and gave it a light. "Obviously, we'll have ourselves a vote real soon. I'm telling you, boys, this is the shit we've been waiting for. Percentages can change over time. We need their firepower to kick the fuckin' door down, and once we're in, we're home."

"Count me an 'aye,' right now, Prez," I said, holding my knife.

"Yeah, yeah, I can tell you're happy. You ain't doing that bullshit with your blade going in the wood." Prez grinned, looking me up and down with his cold gray eyes. No, they were surprisingly warm today, like he'd just gotten a gold medal around his neck for fuckin' the choicest pussy ten states over.

Shit, for all I knew, he had.

Hannah didn't appeal to me — never wanted a damned thing to do with rich bitches — but he'd taken enough of a shine to her body to fuck her more than once.

Firefly glared, the shit between the Prez and his sis weighing on his mind. Dust turned to him just then, ignoring his snake eyes, taking a long pull on his pipe.

"Firely, how soon can we be ready?" Prez growled, stopping just short of rubbing his hands together in anticipation. "Blackjack said he can get some men out here by next week. They'll be ready as soon as they're in, itching for action after the cartel wars ended out west. I want everything square in five days. Earlier, if we can swing it."

"Five days," he repeated, staring at the Prez like a spider he wanted to stomp. "Doesn't leave much time to train any of the brothers on the heavier shit. We've been getting more of it in and our range ain't great for this stuff."

"Fuck the big guns," Dust growled. "We'll have manpower on our side. The Grizzlies are bringing a few of their newer toys, too. It'll balance out."

"Before we do this, there's something else," I said, sitting up in my chair. "That girl, Summer, who some of you boys saw the other day. She's got news on the Deads…"

I went through all the facts then. Told them about how they'd trashed Seddon, how Hatch wanted to use her as a mole to pry shit outta the club through me. I told them about my kid last, how I was sure he was mine, and I'd do everything I could to make up for lost time, keeping them both safe.

She'd come clean to me.

So had I, and none of this shit bothered me.

Yeah. Yeah, fucking right.

"Jesus Christ, bro. I mean, fuck, everybody knew you had secrets, but…shit." Sixty grinned, chomping on his smoke. "We've got your back. You and your new family."

His last words didn't do much to settle me down. I waited for more shit, pivoting my switchblade in my hands, feeling the sharp reflection of the sunlight coming through the old blinds peeling off it. Straight into my eyes.

"Goddamn. I'd hoped to get the fuckin' jump on those bastards," Dust said, twisting his pipe thoughtfully between his fingers. "Looks like they're gearing up to do it first. They can smell us fuckin' coming."

"Better not be a damned rat," Firefly growled, his rage shifting to something else.

My guts sank. Fuck, it didn't seem likely, but we'd only brought on the three new prospects last week, men who'd been there as hangarounds for months.

"Nah," Dust said, dismissing it with a wave of the hand. "Hatch is a brutal, sick motherfucker. He ain't stupid. He knows we're getting stronger, pulling in legit money from the strip clubs and the chop shops, buying more guns. Fucker's probably been busy moving in on the Torches' old territory for months, and he's gotta know we wiped 'em out. Nobody else would've planted Deadhands' cuts in the wreckage for the cops after we torched that place."

No, nobody else would've been so stupid and ballsy. That idea had been mine, just a couple months ago, when we saved Firefly's old lady down in Atlanta, and finished off our friends-turned-enemies. The Torches MC was dead, and we'd framed the Deads for doing it.

Too fuckin' bad the bastards hadn't taken much heat.

"Motherfuckers must be handing out bribes left and right," Skin said, like he'd read my mind. "Fuckin' FBI should've given them something to shit bricks over for months. They're not doing that."

"More reason to hit them hard, soon as we gas up our bikes and get our new troops," I said, thumbing the edge of my knife.

"Joker's right. The roadblocks we tried to put up while we got are shit together just went down. They're coming, unless we knock them on their asses first. No more fuckin' around, boys. This is all out war."

Dust looked at me when he said it, as if he finally understood me. This wasn't just about avenging Piece anymore.

This was about saving myself from losing my last shred of sanity.

Nobody was coming for Summer. They damned sure

weren't coming for Alex. I wouldn't let any of the sick, evil poison from the club's fights savage my family.

Maybe I hadn't figured out what the fuck family even meant. Right now, it didn't matter, I'd have all the time in the world as long as I decapitated the bastards who'd picked at Taylor blood like vultures.

"We can't be fuckin' fools about it, Veep. It's gonna take planning. Maybe seven or eight days instead of six. Give me the time I need to do the job right," Firefly said, still giving Prez the stink eye.

"Orders are orders," Dust said coldly. "I've given you a time line. You make it happen, Firefly."

The big Enforcer clenched his jaw, his biceps bulging as he pushed his fists together. My eyes bounced over every brother, waiting for the whole fuckin' room to go up like a rocket factory on fire.

"Listen, you've all got the big picture. We'll iron out the details later. It's time to vote." Dust brought the gavel down, moving this shit along. He looked at me first.

"Aye," I said slowly.

Aye for Summer, for Alex, for my own future, however rough or fucked up the going got. Yes to death, to avenging Freddy and Grandpa, to burying the past once and for all so I could focus on the family I hadn't known I had 'til yesterday.

Prez moved down the line. Everybody voted, except for the three prospects who hadn't earned those rights yet. We'd all be checking up on them later, making absolutely sure they weren't putting a fuckin' dagger in our backs, feeding intel to the Deads.

"Unanimous." Dust's gavel came down harder, and he blew a long chain of smoke through his lips. "Unless anybody else has anything, we're done here."

He waited a minute. The gavel slapped the wood one more time, freeing brothers to get up, mill around, and go for their coffee. More than a couple guys would be taking something stronger in their black brew after this.

"Veep, hold up," Dust said calmly, grabbing the back of my chair.

I waited 'til all the boys cleared out, Firefly going last, eyeballing both of us like a wolf waiting for its chance to strike. Well, fuck him, too.

"What's eating his ass?" Dust growled, soon as he was outta the room.

"You and his sis," I said. "That fuckin' drama ain't my business. I've got plenty to worry about, so you'd better hash it out with Firefly privately. We gotta have every man behind our backs."

"Yeah, I figured. I'm more worried about you."

My eyebrows went up. "Don't bother. You think I can't handle this fuckin' girl and my own son?"

"I think you will, long as you keep a lid on your shit and make it home alive, after we're done with these devils in Georgia. You've swept through enough blood to know how it always goes down. One mistake," he growled. "That's all it takes to put a bullet in a brother's brain, or get a blade in his spine, putting him off of anything except sucking shit through straws 'til he's gone. You can't let this shit get to you 'til the job's done."

"You're bullshitting me, Prez," I said, standing up, my blade in my hand.

"No," he said quietly. "I ain't. You're the one standing there with that nervous fuckin' tick in your trigger finger."

I looked down in horror. My knife was trembling again, incrementally, like something crawled up my wrist and gave me the shakes.

"Fuck!" It clattered to the floor, and I crouched down and picked it up, tucking it back into my belt.

"Yeah, boy. That's you coming back, after losing Piece put you in a fuckin' coma all these years." Dust blew out the last embers in his pipe, before stuffing it into his pocket. "Whatever you're going through, it ain't gonna be easy. But I need you to listen, and listen fuckin' good – the club comes first. Your little family's already a part of it, whether you claim this chick or not. If you think you're less than a hundred percent before we're supposed to ride south, come to me, Joker. We'll fix it together like brothers do."

"I'm solid, Prez. Same as always before a battle."

Goddamn, why did I deny it? Why'd I fuckin' lie? I didn't even believe it myself, soon as the words were outta my mouth.

"Fuck you, don't lie to me." He stood up, stepped forward, and slammed both his thick, calloused hands on my shoulders. Those crazy eyes in his head had seen plenty of shit, just like mine, and they always read every brothers' minds, including mine.

Didn't have a prayer of hiding shit. "Let go, Prez. I'm done lying."

"Yeah, you are. 'Cause if you're still this fucked up in another week, I'll see it, clear as the summer sun dying behind the Smokies. And if I do, you ain't going anywhere. You're staying behind with the prospects to guard the clubhouse, and the rest of us'll bring you the cuts from the shitstains who killed Piece."

Tore myself away from him, hard as I could. My guts were on fire, like I'd been chugging snake venom, full of piss and hate and betrayal.

I was gone before he dismissed me. Hell, I *had* to be, otherwise I would've spun around and clocked the Prez right in his fucking face, shattering his jaw.

Then he would've had plenty reason to fuck me up.

I couldn't let that happen. Couldn't get unhinged. Couldn't come undone when everything I'd been working for these last three fuckin' years was finally on the horizon.

The brothers were out in the bar, everybody except Firefly, Meg hanging on Skin's shoulder. They all went quiet when they saw me coming, and I didn't last long.

Just reached straight through Crawl and Sixty, grabbing a fresh bottle of Jack off the counter, and tore away the lid. I must've poured ten shots of that shit down my throat, dousing myself in sweet Tennessee fire before Skin wrestled the bottle away from me.

"What the fuck's gotten into you?!" he roared, startling Meg. "Whole fucking club's going to shit when we need every man firing on all cylinders, and you're boozing like the assholes are gonna ban it tomorrow! Goddammit, Veep. Sober the fuck up."

Snarling, I walked away, heading for the little spot where I'd left my girl, my kid, my dog.

No, not your fuckin' girl, I thought. *She's nothing but your bitch 'til you make her something else.*

Something besides a lying whore, good for sucking your cock, and not a whole lot else.

Pain stabbed through my chest. I'd been a fuckin' devil last night, hate fucking her mouth, all I could do to show her how pissed I was for hiding Alex all these years.

I hadn't had a blowjob that good for – fuck, three years? If I wanted to man up and admit it, yeah, it was the stone cold truth.

There'd been fire in her kiss. Lightning in her lips when she dropped to her knees, put my big, mean dick in her little hands, and sucked me 'til I flooded her mouth.

I'd wanted her cunt too. Shit, some sick, twisted part of me was dead serious when I'd threatened her, wanted to pump another kid in her, breed her sweet fuckin' ass so I'd know my next kid from day zero.

I hated her.

Only, I fuckin' didn't when I stepped out the back door and saw her. She looked at me with those bright green eyes, wide and restless as the first time I'd made them roll back in her head. Then she had the dark hair I fisted, softer than it had any right to be, its silky feel calling my cock to life.

"Well? Are we done here?" she asked, holding my sleeping kid. Bingo laid at her feet, offering the illusion I had a real, happy family for a split second.

Whatever the hell it looked like, I knew better.

"Yeah, we are," I told her, reaching into my pocket for my keys. "Take this shit and drive my truck home. I'll stuff myself in next to Bingo."

"Huh?" she said, looking at the mess of keys hanging in her hand. Her nose wrinkled up a second later, probably a sign she could smell the whiskey on my breathe. "Jesus Christ, Joker, are you drunk?"

"Not yet. Got about three more minutes before it really fucks me up."

"I can't believe this," she said, shaking her head. Didn't stop her from standing up, tucking Alex's head against her shoulder, and walking out.

"Come on, boy," I reattached Bingo's leash and led him out with us, walking behind her.

Thank fuck he listened like a champ, jumping up on the passenger seat when I patted it. I squeezed into the back, feeling the big dog's breath hitting me in the face.

"I've never driven a vehicle like this before," she said, strapping Alex into his kiddie seat, new frustration in her eyes.

"You'll manage. There ain't nothing to it. You know how to get back to my place, right?" I pulled out my phone, tapped a few keys, and passed it to her. "Use the GPS. It'll have us home in no time."

She started her up as I slumped down in my seat, next to the dog. Woman drove like a fuckin' grandma the whole way, leaving me plenty of time to watch the wide blue summer sky spinning through the window.

Maybe half that inertia came from inside me, the booze

and raw feeling screwing up my guts.

The other half...fuck, Prez was right. Not that I'd ever admit it to his face.

This had to be the last goddamned day I ever let myself go off the rails, processing all this shit. I had about forty-eight hours to sober up, get my head straight, and prepare for war.

* * * *

Back at the apartment, I crashed on the couch, sleeping off my imminent hangover.

There wasn't any worry about work today. The club wouldn't be taking many cars or bikes in the shops, handing over the ones we got to the hangarounds who knew about auto shit.

Most of my dollars came from the club's shared profits every brother got a piece of. I'd been saving for a down payment on a cabin or a house forever.

Money wasn't the worry. Un-fucking my head, on the other hand...

Slept like the fuckin' dead. My brain must've needed it after short-circuiting, full of whiskey, hate, confusion.

When I woke up, Bingo was rubbing his muzzle on my hand, draped over the side. "Shit," I swore, sitting up, scratching his head.

A spicy, garlicky pizza's smell hung thick in the air. I let my eyes focus, toward the little table next to the kitchen, where Summer had Alex in a new booster seat. One that couldn't have shown up here unless she'd gone out to get it.

I sprang up, ignoring the last pain banging at my temples. *Fuck. She hadn't fuckin' listened.*

"Thought you'd sleep through the night," she said, spooning some applesauce into Alex's mouth.

I pulled out a chair and sat down, resisting the urge to stuff pizza into my hungry, dry mouth. "Babe, you go out again alone while you're under my protection, and we've got a big goddamned problem. You hear me?"

"No, I don't, Jackson. Didn't know what to do either, when I needed things for our son and you were...well, out of commission."

Fuck her smart mouth. But fuck me for having no argument against it, because I'd been laid up, all thanks to my own stupid, impulsive ass.

"Won't happen again. Not after today."

"Mm-hmm." She batted her long lashes skeptically and smiled at the kid, blotting at his mouth. "It's nothing new, Jackson. Really. It's just been Alex and me for the last three years. Alone."

"You weren't stalked by fuckers who'd slit your throat at the first fuckin' chance," I growled, stopping myself at the last second from slamming my fist on the table. Didn't want to startle my son. "Put him down for a nap. We need to talk. Looks like there's some shit I've still gotta drill into your head, Summertime, because right now you're pretty damned clueless."

Bingo perked up in the corner, laying his ears flat against his head. Damned dog had a sixth sense for bad voodoo in the air.

"He usually doesn't lay down for another hour. I still have to give him a bath." She looked at me defiantly, her pupils expanding in the deep, green seas around them. "But since I got him a new play pen while I was out, I'll listen. Put him down early, just this once."

Without another word, she rose, walking into the bedroom. I heard her humming softly to the kid before she shut the door gently behind her, and walked back out with her arms folded.

"Seriously, Joker, why do you have to be such an ass?"

I wanted to lay the fuck into her. Shut her up with my lips on hers, press her so hard into the fuckin' wall I put a Summer-shaped silhouette through the damned drywall.

"Same reason you're wandering around, pretending like you ain't fucked when the Deads come around. Christ, Summer, even if you don't give a shit about getting yourself killed – you *won't* drag my kid into in!"

I stepped up, grabbed her, let her twist around in my arms 'til our faces were only inches apart. "Let me go!"

"Not 'til you shut up and listen. I'm trying to do right by you. I fucked up bad this morning, swigging all that booze. I'm man enough to admit it, and it's time to move the fuck on."

"You're a fucking idiot," she spat, slowly surrendering.

She knew I was too strong, and my grip told her I wouldn't let go. Not 'til I was good and ready.

"You think this shit's a game, don't you?" I growled, fighting to keep my eyes off her evil little lips.

"Jesus, no. I don't think that. Believe me, I *know* how

much danger we're in, ever since that fucking asshole kicked down the door to the place I'll never see again, and forced me to deal with you again. If it wasn't for the monsters, I'd have made certain you never got your hands on me or Alex!"

Fuck. That was a long, barbed spear rammed straight through my fuckin' chest.

My hand swept up her back, grabbed her hair, and pulled so hard her face jerked up. I held her just like that when my lips went down on hers.

Kissing her was the safe choice, the only other option I had. It was either kiss her, or slap her across the face, and I wasn't a big enough bastard to slap girls unless they were naked and begging for it.

Goddamn, Summer tasted good. Even when I fuckin' hated her, every miserable word pouring outta her mouth, her kiss burned like napalm on my lips.

She fought me for at least a solid minute, digging her teeth into my bottom lip.

This kiss had everything.

Pain. Lust. Heartbreak. All rolled together in a bitter dance of mouths.

I tasted blood before she stopped resisting, opening for my tongue. I slipped in, taking what was mine. What always fuckin' would be, love her or hate her.

Twined it so damned hard and intense with hers that she lost it a hot second later.

My fingers tore at her hair as she jerked away, her lungs sucking precious air. My other arm around her waist only tightened, holding her to my chest, a short thrust away from making her feel the hard-on straining in my jeans.

"Fuck you, Joker. Fuck you," she snarled, wiping my taste off her lips. "We are *not* having a repeat of last night. Not when you've spent the whole day drunk. Ain't letting you fool me again."

"That the only reason?"

A hateful laugh escaped her lips. "You're joking, right? I really can't tell anymore."

"I'm not. No more bullshit, babe. I already fuckin' apologized for this mornin'."

"Really?" she quirked an eyebrow. "You call that an apology?"

"Nah," I growled, snatching her hand with mine, holding her fingers damned tight. "I'm sorry, Summertime. Sorry I walked the fuck out without knowing you were knocked up. Sorry for kicking you to the curb when you were under the gun. Sorry for being so fuckin' oblivious to everything. The boozing this morning? That shit's minor, stacked against all this."

For a second, I thought she'd sling more shit my way, but her lips just trembled. Real soft and quiet.

"You know I'm telling you the God's truth, Summer. I ain't perfect, but I'm gonna do my damnedest to be a good dad, like one I never had. I'm gonna have the family I never thought I would since Freddy left this planet, mowed down in cold blood." I looked at her, a killer fire running into my eyes. "That shit's never happening to you while I'm alive and breathin'. Never to Alex. You listen to me, babe, about going out on your own. Or I swear to Christ, I *will* strip you naked, throw you down in my bed, and chain you up like a fuckin' dog. Then I'll be the only one who has to worry about feeding and diapering Alex."

"You're a pig!" she shrieked, her voice dying in a shrill little whisper.

I smiled, looking down through her tank top. She must've taken off her bra when she'd gotten home because it wasn't hiding shit.

"And your nipples are begging to be sucked, Summertime. How 'bout we forget all this shit? You accept my apology, tell me you're gonna listen 'til the Deads are buried? Tell me we'll find some way to navigate this bullshit, and give our kid everything he deserves?"

She shook her head, but it didn't take long for the fight in her to collapse. My hand pushed her into my chest, so hard I could feel those buds beneath her shirt pulsing against my skin.

If I reached between her legs, stuffed my hand down her jeans, I knew I'd find a sticky, wet mess.

Hadn't taken what I really wanted last night. Now, it was fuckin' calling to me, consequences be damned.

"Tell me, Summer," I growled, moving my face against hers again, licking the tiny cut forming in the middle of my lips from her bite. "Fuckin' tell me, babe."

Four more steps, and I'd backed her against the wall, watching her pupils widen in the dim night light. Her lips quirked one more time, hating me for being the bastard I was. Still failed to stop her smile.

"We'll try," she said softly. "Just as long as you stop being such a prick."

"Prick, huh? You'd think after all this touchy-feely shit, you'd have something else on your mind."

She looked like she wanted to slap me again. Instead, I went for her lips, pressing my mouth down on hers so hard she didn't even bite.

We kissed. We lusted. We clutched shoulders, so desperate for each other's bodies I thought we'd leave scorch marks on the damned wall.

My hands ripped her clothes off, one piece at a time. I pushed my jeans down with a growl, throwing off my coat, rolling the t-shirt underneath it away. My bare ass bumped into the edge of the pizza box, still on the table.

Fuck it, dinner could wait. I'd become possessed by another hunger, and it glowed like a nuclear core, a thousand times stronger than the need to eat.

My arm swept across the table, knocking everything to the floor. Summer looked at me in disbelief, stunned. Didn't leave her a second more than I needed to before I spun her around, pushed her hands against the table, and pushed her legs apart, mounting her from behind.

"Fuck!" It shot outta my mouth like a bullet when I slipped inside her, taking the pussy I hadn't had for three fuckin' years, the only one I'd wanted.

"Ohhh!" she moaned, tilting her hair back into my hand, perfect for tangling my fingers in it.

I fisted those dark, sleek locks like I'd missed them for a hundred fuckin' years. My hips pulled back, winding up, crashing into her again in long, slow, powerful strokes. She moaned, her legs shaking a little more with every beat, that perfect, round ass calling for my palm.

My free hand swept down, clapped her across one ass cheek with a resounding *smack*. "Scream, baby girl. Scream my fuckin' name, the one you missed all these years, almost as much as I missed your hot little cunt."

"Joker!"

I smacked her ass again.

"Jackson!" she moaned.

Goddamn, that set me off. My balls churned like fire, forcing my hips to move a whole lot faster, power fucking her good and proper.

Her tight, wet heat hadn't changed a bit since having a kid. Shit, she was tighter than most of the whores I'd been fucking for three years. I'd used condoms a plenty with those bitches, too, but never with this woman.

I never fuckin' would.

"Say it again," I growled, slapping my hand across her little ass. Caused her body to seize up, her face flying forward, only to be caught by her hair in my fist, all the better to slam her back on my cock.

Fuck, fuck, fuck.

"Joker. Jackson. Baby. God, yes!"

"Yeah, Summertime. Fuck, yeah."

Damn if I didn't mean it. She could've called me the King of England just then, and I still would've fucked her faster.

My fist tightened, pulling on those locks, pushing her against the table. My thrusts drove deeper, harder, pushing into her, straight to that belly I'd poured my seed into and knocked the fuck up years ago.

Couldn't stop my jaw from clenching like a motherfucker when I thought about it. Having a kid was the last thing I should've wanted.

Now all I wanted was right in front of me, and sleeping in the other room.

My brain went rampant with thoughts of breeding this pussy again. Nah, not today.

We'd wait and do it right, this time, but I wasn't fuckin' waiting long.

I'd take her. Mount her. Own her from the inside out, 'til Alex had a brother or sister to laugh and chase.

"Oh, oh, oh!" she stuttered, perfectly synched to her walls wrapping tighter with every stroke.

She was about to blow. Perfect timing for me to reach down, push between her legs, and thumb her clit like a madman.

Summer's body exploded, raging like a furnace, every muscle twitching underneath me. All her power went straight to her pussy, convulsing around my cock, desperate to suck every greedy drop from my balls.

I gave it a fuckin' chance. A few more blinding, rough strokes, grunting out my pleasure, and I slammed my hips into hers.

My dick swelled in the middle of her explosion, igniting that charge at the base of my shaft I couldn't hold back for a billion dollars. "Fuck, babe, take it!"

Roaring, I came, pouring it into her, marking my territory. This pussy got away from me once, but it never would again.

Fucking, pumping, growling like a maniac, I shot my load deep, snarling through the fire rising in my balls. So damned hot it ached.

Halfway through, I was still grinding, holding her against me, practically tearing out her hair. She was screaming, begging, burying her face against the wood. We'd just hashed things out more than words ever could, and we'd be doing it every fuckin' night from here on out.

My come flooded out the slick spaces where we fit together, dripping down her leg. I kept thrusting, my dick moving with a mind of its own, pushing it deeper, soaking it into her very skin.

"Fuck, that felt good," she whined. Her voice sounded like it was a mile away.

Hadn't realized how intense the blood was howling in my temples 'til I'd finished. "Yeah," I said, leaving my cock in her, refusing to pull out 'til my body made me.

Shit, the way it was going, I'd probably stay hard enough to fuck her all over again before I took it out. My fist pulled her hair, tilting her face for my lips.

We kissed again, a little softer this time. No less sweet.

Goddamn those lips. Damn, this fuckin' body.

She was a walking, talking, fucking tease, charming my cock like a witch, even when I'd just pumped her full of me. My tongue wagged against hers, owning her mouth, remembering how good it felt all over my cock and balls last night.

We'd fucked around twice in the last forty-eight hours.

Once, I'd walked away, too full of my own shit to deal with the consequences.

Wouldn't be happening a second time. Didn't care how much hell she sent my way.

"We should get cleaned up," she said, squinting at me with something besides frustration in her eyes for once.

Love? Appreciation? Whatever the hell it was, I liked it.

"No. We're fuckin' one more time, then I'll take you out myself. We're gonna need a few more things to set this place up."

"Why? I already picked up some extras today."

"My kid deserves more than having some cheap shit stuffed in my bedroom. He can sleep out here, in something cozier, while we take the bed like a man and woman should."

She grinned. "Jeez, you're really serious this time, aren't you? About this family thing?"

"Get ready to fuck. A lot, babe," I told her. "Get ready to wear my brand on your skin. We're burying the hatchet, and I'm taking you for my old lady, so no other stupid fucker ever tries to beat me to the punch. You know I'd kill him, whether he shares my patch or not."

"Is it bad that I like you when you're jealous?"

"Whatever makes you scream, Summertime," I said, smashing my lips down on hers.

Then I started to move my cock inside her again, bringing it fully back to life. We fucked slower the second time, taking a few more minutes to savor every bit of shock and awe. Didn't stop us from coming just as hard.

* * * *

I stayed up half the night, putting all the new kiddie shit together. Bingo watched from the side, the big dog's tongue hanging out. We'd rode into the big box store in Knoxville without a hitch, our first real shopping trip as a family. Alex looked around excitedly in the cart, laughing when we took him down the toy aisle, and zonked out the whole way home.

Fuck, what the hell was happening? Was this real life?

I'd gotten the boy a new play pen fit for sleeping, twice as comfy as the one she'd picked up. We'd donate the old one to somebody who needed it through the club's charity drives.

Sometime after midnight, Summer came padding in, fresh from lulling our boy back to sleep with a new story. She stopped next to me, scratching Bingo's ear, wearing nothing except that tank top and a pair of pink panties I wanted to rip off with my teeth.

"You should turn in soon. We can tuck him in, see how he likes the new bed. He won't put up much of a fuss either way, sleepy as he is."

"Yeah, we're gonna have an early morning," I said, giving her that smile. "Want to take Alex to see Grandpa. It'll perk the old man up to know he's lived to see his first great grandkid."

First of many, I secretly hoped. Freddy left me to do all the work, and I wouldn't let him down.

My eyes crawled hungrily over my girl, staring at those long, creamy legs I wanted wrapped around me. My gaze stopped at her belly, picturing it stretching with my seed again.

I'd see her knocked up at least three more times before I even thought about slowing down, by God.

"Wow. This is moving fast." Summer smiled nervously, tempting me to bite that lip all over again. "Are you going to tell him the truth?"

"Fuck yeah, I will. Everything except how the Deads are breathing down our backs. The old man doesn't need any more stress. Just something to be happy about."

He's paid his dues in hell and blood, I thought. Knew he'd probably put down at least a hundred vicious motherfuckers with all his years in the club. I'd always wanted to blow past his body count before I hit forty, and I'd be making good progress with the Deads coming toe-to-toe.

Why the fuck did it feel so hollow, now? Was I going soft? Letting the same slack Skin and Firefly allowed to take over when they decided to settle down with their girls?

Maybe. Shit, maybe it didn't even scare me.

I wrapped my hands around her waist. Laughing, she toppled to the floor, rolling around on it with me, while Bingo paced excitedly around us.

"You know, through all this shit, I never got a chance to tell you how bad I missed you. Hurt like fucking hell all these years, babe, one of the two chasms gouged out inside me since that brutal night."

Her hand swept across my cheek, feeling my stubble. Fingertips like ice and steam, tingling through my skin. Made my cock as hard and eager as if I hadn't had pussy for a solid week.

"I may have missed you too," she said, a playful note in her voice hiding the pain.

Didn't need to talk more with words. We needed skin to say everything else.

I held her down for another kiss, long and hot and sweet as ever.

Before I fucked her again, we had to get the kiddo down. I got up, gently plucking Alex from the old play pen, carrying him out here to the living room. He only stirred a couple times in my arms.

Kid didn't realize he'd just become front and center of my whole fuckin' world. Summer's fingers clenched my shoulders while I lowered him into the new crib, tucking a tiny blanket around him.

When he stopped moving, I craned my neck down, and gave him a quick peck on the forehead. These instincts were strange, but damn if they didn't feel right.

Turning around, I saw my girl again, her eyes softer than before. "It's like you're a natural, Jackson. None of his babysitters ever put him down so easy. Just me. And that goodnight kiss...God. Are you trying to break my heart again?"

Smiling, I hugged her close, slowly pushing my fingers through her long, black hair. "Fuck no. I'm done with that shit. Told you before, babe, this time is different. No more boozing 'til whole days slip by. No more fuckin' around. No more fistfights with assholes in bars just for the hell of it. I've got something more to look out for than just me and my club now."

Bingo brushed against my waist, letting out a little whine. We both looked down, and she laughed, kneeling to ruffle his fur.

"He can chill on the balcony tonight so we have some extra privacy. It's clear out there, nice breeze coming in." My hand jerked the screen door open.

The big dog stepped out onto the small wooden frame, the bed I'd laid out there a couple weeks ago waiting. He settled in, staring at the stars, his furry tail wagging lazily behind him.

Left the door open so he could come back in when he was good and ready. It was too good a summer night. Everybody fuckin' loved it, especially the dog.

Our kid did, too. Little Alex rolled in his sleep, smacked his lips, and the last tension lining his face smoothed.

"He looks so much like you," Summer said, still leaning on me.

"Like both of us," I agreed, grabbing her hand. Pulling it to my lips, I kissed her skin, flicking my tongue against the back of her hand for a single second.

Woman didn't need much reminder of what she'd be getting in about five more minutes. Too bad I enjoyed teasing her anyway, building the fire, the loving we'd missed for three goddamned years.

"Let's go to bed," she whispered, laying her head flat against my chest.

Whores, bitches, sluts had all said the same damned thing to me before dozens of times.

Usually got my dick up, but never made me feel more. That changed, standing next to the cool summer breeze and our kid.

For the first time in all my life, I looked forward to

passing out next to this girl. Shit, I wanted to wake up next to her, without having to worry about kicking her ass out first thing in the morning.

What. The. Fuck?

What is this feeling?

Her greedy little lips brushed against mine, all I needed to pick her up, throw her over my shoulder, and move.

There'd be plenty of time tomorrow to think this shit over. Tonight, we'd fuck for a few more hours, put a dent in making up for the thousand nights we'd lost.

Summer didn't realize it yet. But I was gonna fuck her every night she shared my bed.

Fuck her 'til she'd bring me off instead of just sassing. Fuck her 'til I drew my last breath.

Fuck her and fuck her and fuck her 'til the unthinkable happened, 'til I couldn't imagine my dick inside any other chick.

This was day one of my dick taking her pussy all the time, and only hers. There'd be at least ten thousand more days after it, too, mark my words.

IX: Engine Roar (Summer)

"She's back. You never bring a girl around, much less twice, Jackson. What's with the kid?" Old man Taylor looked at Joker, his eyes as friendly and suspicious as ever.

"Decided I'm gonna spend the rest of my life with this woman, Grandpa. You were right." Joker's huge arm went around my shoulder and pulled me close. I held Alex a little tighter in my lap, sitting in the chair next to him.

The three of us were gathered around another table in the commons area, Bingo laying at our feet. This shouldn't have felt so natural, so fast, like I belonged...but God help me, it did.

Grandpa Taylor beamed at both of us. "No shit? 'Bout time you finally decided to settle down, Jackson. A man can share the sheets with a thousand different women, but there's only one that'll ever matter. What's the story with the kid, again?"

I looked at him and blushed. Raw, intense heat came over my face.

Things were going perfectly. Too perfect.

I expected a disaster any second, some offhand slur or

gesture ruining the moment.

"Stand up, Summertime," Joker whispered, helping me up with a gentle hand. "Pass him Alex. It's time you met your great grandson."

The old man's eyes bugged out. Didn't stop him from holding his old hands out, wrapping them around Alex, and pulling him into his lap when I passed him over.

"Goddamn. *Great* grandson?" he repeated, staring into the little boy's matching hazel eyes. "How? When?"

They all had them, the Taylors. If there was any doubt in the back of his mind, Alex's eyes told his great grandpa the truth, shining with an honesty no one could deny.

"Shit. Don't tell me," the old man said, his voice growing softer. "Doesn't matter. I know it's true. This boy, Jackson...he looks like you. Like us."

"Damned straight," Joker growled. When his grandfather looked up, he was smiling. "We had a fling back in Seddon, 'bout three years ago. She came back and filled me in. We've smoothed things over, Grandpa. We're making them right. Never thought I'd have a family so damned fast, but here I am. Want you to be a part of it, same as always."

"Jesus, boy!" Grandpa Taylor smiled at the little boy in his arms.

No, correction – *Great Grandpa Taylor.*

Alex bobbed his head, unsure what to make of the old man holding him. "You don't have to ask. The rights and wrongs in the past don't matter worth a damn. Only thing that counts is the now, and I'm telling you, I wanna see this boy here every week. All the good weeks I got left to this earth."

"Not a problem, Mister Taylor," I said, grabbing the old man's arm and giving it a friendly squeeze. "Alex needs more strong, smart men in his life. Two Taylors are better than one."

Beneath me, Bingo stretched, wagging his tail. It was early afternoon. Orange sunlight poured through the blinds behind us, giving everything a dreamy, bright glow.

My heart probably grew several sizes in a few seconds. And for once, I wasn't afraid of it, scared that it'd all be taken away from me in the blink of an eye.

We were a *family*. We were man and woman, new blood and old. Just two rough bastards and a bitch trying to hang up their darkness, and a sweet, innocent babe who hadn't decided yet who he'd become.

I sat down next to Grandpa, grabbing Joker's hand. He laced his fingers through mine, squeezing to add his warmth, his reassurance, his joy.

Never gonna let you go, babe, he said with his touch. *Never.*

"How old is he?" Grandpa Taylor asked, his eyebrows furrowing.

"Just celebrated his second birthday a couple months ago," I said, reaching over with my free hand to ruffle the little boy's hair.

He looked at me, smiling, and then did the same to the old man. "Dina-dina-sore!" Alex jerked, reaching out with his tiny hands to touch the old man's weathered cheeks.

My mouth dropped open. I looked at Grandpa Taylor apologetically. "I'm sorry! I've been reading him a lot of dinosaur stories lately before bedtime. He doesn't really mean you."

"Forget it. Just forget it, hon'," the old man said, chuckling and hugging Alex tighter. "Kid's a damned natural. Didn't Joker tell you my road name was Steg? All those spikes we used to wear on our leather and helmets in the old days…"

Laughing, I relaxed, shaking my head. "No, no!"

"Who the fuck knew the kid had a psychic streak?" Joker said quietly, squeezing my hand tighter. "He's got your brains for sure, Grandpa. Watched him solve the shit outta his numbers game this morning."

"Damn! You don't know what that means, huh?" Grandpa Taylor looked at us, waiting for us to both lean in anxiously. "Already had a lot of checks to write to catch up on all the birthdays and Christmases I missed. Now, I'm gonna have throw money at him for learning like a good boy, too."

I laughed. My heart fluttered deep in my chest. Alex really couldn't ask for a better grandfather, and I couldn't ask for a better adopted family, something I thought I'd never have after mama died.

I wasn't blind.

The Deadhands were still out there, ready to ride in anytime and knock everything to hell. But today, I had hope.

I had life. More than I'd had for the past three years,

desperately scrapping by all alone, trying to do the best for my baby. And maybe, I finally had love.

Bingo walked over, pushing his big head into my lap. Reaching down, I scratched his head, watching as the dog's tongue rolled out lazily.

"There's one more thing I want to hear about," the old man said, shooting Joker a sharp look. "When's the wedding?"

Crap. My heart stopped beating in my chest.

Smiling, Joker looked at me, his eyes moving up and down my neck in that slow, fuck-hungry crawl that had become his trademark. "Soon. Sooner than anybody thinks, Grandpa. I'm gonna level with you – me and this lady are just getting acquainted again after years apart. Too many damned years. I promise you, sure as the vow I made for Freddy, you'll live to see me hitched."

His grandfather cleared his throat, smiling and shaking his head. "Guess I'm due for a heart attack next week. Gotta do something to move things along."

Did he really just say that? I broke down laughing, cutting through the awkward silence.

One thing was for sure – the Taylor men took shit from no one. They never gave a single inch. And, of course, they always, always fought until all the rules were bent down to a nub.

Grandpa Taylor bounced Alex on his lap, joking and smiling for another fifteen minutes. Then we made our way out, Joker taking the old man's wheelchair and pushing him back to his room. Before we left him alone, Alex scrambled up in my shoulders, and waved to his grandpa.

"Bye-bye!"

"Bye, kid," Grandpa nodded, a firm smile on his lips. "Until next time…"

"We'll be here next week," I promised, quietly praying we'd be able to live up to it.

Anything might happen in the next seven days. This might all fall apart, if Joker and I had another fallout, or maybe the club wars would come to our doorstep.

I was still thinking about it when he led me out, one hand in mine, the other on Bingo's leash. "Babe, what the fuck? You're walking like you're on nails."

"It's nothing," I said glumly. "Just thinking. I wish every day could be this nice."

"It will be," he said. There wasn't a shred of uncertainty in his voice. "Because I'm saying it will. Grandpa's been waiting for something like this since the night they got my brother. Haven't seen him that happy since…since, shit, I can't even remember. Maybe not since your uncle's place closed down."

I smiled. "That was a million years ago," I said softly, stepping outside into the evening light.

Alex had started to doze in my arms. On our way to the truck, we passed an elderly couple out for a stroll. Probably from the assisted living place attached.

"Not as long ago as you think," Joker said, leaning in so I could feel his hot breath on my neck. "We've got a million fuckin' more ahead, Summertime. Trust me. Let's make the most of it."

"We will," I promised. "Long as you're here, by my side, we will."

* * * *

It was a perfect day. The club hadn't called Joker in, and I didn't want to waste it. I begged him to drive to a park on the way back from the nursing home, a lovely little stop I'd seen on my way, at the foothills of the Smokies.

"Okay. What's with the fuckin' doe eyes now, babe? Don't tell me you're still choked up about meeting the old man?"

"I'm more choked up about our first real family outing," I said, sticking out my tongue. He steered the truck into the little parking space, next to a stone wall separating the grassy picnic area from the trails leading into the forest.

"Good thing I brought plenty of fuckin' tissue to dry your eyes and some water so you won't run dry," he growled, smirking the whole time.

"Aw, come on, don't be a dick. I just...need a moment." I did. Oh, God, I did.

He shut the truck off and we sat for just a moment, Bingo squeezed into the back seat behind him, Alex in his kiddie seat on the left. Joker looked at me, his eyes soft, almost understanding, grabbing my hand.

"Take all the time you need. Gonna have to let Bingo stretch sooner or later. Shit, I'm gonna need a bigger truck, next time the club share comes in."

I smiled. There'd be one more thing on my mind, ever

since we left the nursing home. Looking at him cautiously, I undid my seatbelt and popped the door, the question hanging on my lips.

I waited until we were all outside, Alex safely in my arms, and Bingo walking next to us. We headed for the picnic tables.

"Joker, what did you mean back there at the nursing home? When you told him about the promise you'd made to Freddy?"

"Blood vow," he said, the light going out of his eyes. "Finding you and my son changes a lot of shit, babe. But it doesn't change that. Nothing fuckin' can. The Deads would've been on the chopping block because they're wearing the wrong colors and they've treated civvies like you like shit for too long. Can't let go of what happened years ago. Absolutely fuckin' not."

I sat down on the cool bench next to him, squeezing his bicep. God, he was tense.

"I won't get in the middle of this. As long as you're safe, and you come back alive when the time comes...that's all that matters."

"Good," he growled, letting Bingo off his leash to run around. "Because that's all I'll accept. I'm doing this for our family and the club, Summertime. Living and dead. Nothing's gonna stop me."

I looked at the ground, sadness flooding my heart. He talked about riding into life and death like it was nothing, and there had to be a chance it would get him killed. The men who'd threatened me, threatened Alex, they didn't care about courage.

"Listen, when the club goes on lockdown, you focus on Alex. Nothing else. You keep him safe and happy. Do it for me, no matter where I wind up." He took my hand with both fingers, squeezed it until we locked eyes. "Promise me, babe. Fuckin' promise me."

"I will. I'll do whatever it takes to get through this. I'm not going to screw this up when we've finally got ourselves a second chance."

"Yeah, thank fuck for those," he said, releasing me.

He turned, reaching for a blanket he'd pulled out of his truck. He spread out next to a tree, a perfect spot for the big dog to rest. Also good for Alex to wander over when I set him down a minute later. We both watched as he toddled over to the dog, burying his face in his fur.

"They're so good together," I said, shaking my head in disbelief. "Is this all just a dream? Sometimes I wonder if I woke up from a nightmare and fell straight into something else."

Joker's hand landed on my thigh, caressing me. Slowly, teasingly, he opened his palm, gently pressing his fingers into my bare skin, underneath the skirt.

He leaned in. "Dream? Fuck, no. No man ever fucked you half as hard as I did last night. You ever start to doubt it, you just spread your legs for my dick again. I'll give you another reminder."

Oh. My. God.

Wet, fiery heat flooded my core. I tried to keep it together, but the humidity hanging in the air didn't help. High summer was here, soft and supple as a southern sigh, the air thicker here in the Smokies than in Seddon.

"Yeah, about that. I'm going to get on more than just Plan B soon. We can't afford another mistake just yet," I said, staring into his eyes.

His wild, hazel gems pinned mine down, as if he disagreed. "Whatever, babe. You do what you need to. I'm never gonna stop putting my come inside you. Get ready. We're working on a baby brother or sister for Alex, soon as we're hitched."

When?! I almost said it, but my tongue held me back, my teeth digging in so I wouldn't self-combust from the desire soaking me from the inside-out.

The bastard said nothing. He pushed his fingers through my hair, pulled my face close, and kissed me. Lit me on fire for the hundredth time.

His tongue swept over mine, piling new promises into the darkness and light. These were all depraved vows, licks and swirls and pinches, hinting at everything he'd do to me tonight.

Joker only broke away a minute later – or was it more than that? – when Bingo started barking. We both looked up, and I got another shock, this one far rudder.

We heard Bingo, but we didn't see him. The dog was gone. So was little Alex.

"Shit!" Joker bolted up, realizing the full gravity before I did, stepping toward the blanket like he'd just seen it burning.

God, no.

I ran right behind him, trying not to faint, wondering

how the hell we'd gotten so distracted they'd slipped away from us.

We ran on, heading toward the crop of trees, a little ways down the first trail. The park was completely deserted, except for us, which wasn't helpful.

Bingo barked like mad in the distance, somewhere in the trees. Joker looked over his shoulders, just once.

"No! Stay the fuck there, babe. Let me go." His eyes were a killer's again.

It took all my might to anchor my feet to the ground, unmoving. I poked my head through the thick brush, angrily pushing the branches aside, trying to see.

Oh, Christ. What were those shapes moving in the distance, deep in the woods?

I saw Joker's silhouette. Another shadow blurred past him, lower to the ground, probably Bingo's. The dog was going insane, crashing through the brush, chasing a tangle of other dark shapes moving up ahead.

"Motherfucker!" A man's voice rang out, surprised, but barely audible. Not Joker's.

My man dropped to his knees, pulled his gun, and –

"Holy shit," I whispered, right after his gun went off.

One of the shadows went down. The others were moving, moving, and I heard it then.

A motorcycle. No, make that several, roaring in the distance.

Something else wailed. High, young, and very scared.

Alex.

Jesus Christ. Alex!

Two shadows went tearing into the trees, deeper into the woods, where I couldn't see. I heard the bikes peeling out, and I followed the sound, forgetting everything he'd told me. I ran through the brush, desperate to catch up, but it was already too late, and I knew it.

We'd been ambushed. My baby boy was gone.

I plunged through the trees, stabbing down the tangled shortcut along the trail, until I couldn't hear anything except my own breath catching in my lungs. Hot tears blurred my vision. Ignoring the sharp branches and thorns scratching at my skin, I pressed on, ripping through everything I could.

If I could catch them, find the bikes, see what was going on, then maybe I'd have a license plate. Or a face.

Something, anything, fucking *anything* to save my son!

About a minute later, I collided with a huge, thick slab of chest. He grabbed me, pulled me into him, but not before the scream leaving my throat echoed across the whole park.

"Babe, babe, fuckin' stop! Baby!"

Joker. It took me forever to realize it was him. Even longer for me to stop scratching, biting, kicking.

I was a total mess. So was Bingo, who paced angrily around us, his fur a tangled mess, forest debris clinging to him. He'd tried to chase them down, the same as me.

"Where did they go? Did you see them? Jackson, did you hear the bikes?!"

"Heard it all. Killed one of them. I was fast. They were fuckin' faster. Saw the last of their goddamned shit drive away before I could get there. Three bikes. One truck." He swallowed, his big arms starting to shake. I looked at him, shuddering when I saw his eyes.

Pure, hellacious rage was eating him alive. I didn't have a clue how he held me, squeezed me so tight it wasn't easy to breathe.

"God. What else did you see? Is he..."

Gone? I couldn't bring myself to say it. Bingo rolled on the pavement, another small parking lot across the park, where the demons had snuck in when we hadn't been looking.

Joker just looked at me and nodded, his jaw clenched so tight I could see the bulge in his temples. There must've been a hurricane exploding inside him. It had to hurt.

Maybe as bad as the savage hell swallowing me up, stabbing its knife in my back, driving it deep until the world became a detached, maddening blur.

"Don't even fuckin' say it," he growled, his phone in one hand. "Walk with me. Stay close. I ain't fuckin' losing the second half of the only thing that ever fuckin' mattered in one fuckin' day."

I walked behind him, halfheartedly putting Bingo back on his leash, tugging him along as the dog followed lazily at my feet. We hit the trail, walking back to where we'd come.

When I saw the empty blanket next to the tree and the picnic table, I fucking lost it. Just froze up, buried my face in my hands, and cried.

Our son was going to die, innocent as the day he was born.

Joker's voice echoed around me like an engine roaring.

He screamed. Swore. Begged his brothers for help, for backup, *right this fucking instant.*

What did it matter? If the club showed up in the next five seconds, it was still too late.

We were too late. I fell down in the blanket, numb to everything, Bingo whining and pawing at my side.

"Summer? Babe? What the fuckin' fuck?!"

Joker threw the phone down, grabbed me, and shook me with all his might. I couldn't feel it.

I couldn't feel…anything.

Regret wrapped around my throat like a snake, choked the life out of me. Deep inside my chest, something splintered, gave way.

That hopeful, fragile ball swinging in my heart all day went flying off, hit the ground, and shattered into a trillion deadly pieces.

I started laughing.

A woman never really imagines what it feels like to lose her mind until it's too fucking late.

Joker couldn't bring me back. He grabbed me, shook me, thundered in my face.

I'd been so stupid it made me sick to death. I'd sacrificed our son for a lie, an illusion, and now it was too late to take it all back.

Our happiness had cost us everything.

X: Going Solo (Joker)

Once, when I was a stupid piece of shit going on my first real run as a prospect, we all stopped in this little bar on the Virginia border. This place was dirty, right down to the grime on the floors, the cheap booze, and the dirty bitches offering their holes to us for the night.

Piece shit his pants for a fuckin' week afterward, wondering if he'd picked up the clap, or something nastier from the whores. My biggest sin was taking a long, discolored smoke from the fucker managing the bar, grinning at me with his dirty teeth.

Never knew what the fuck the asshole laced it with.

Whatever it was, it sent me to fuckin' Saturn and back, ripped me outta my body and threw me down on the ground so fuckin' hard I woke up screaming, turning over tables, making a goddamned fool outta myself.

Dust had to punch me out cold before I woke up again, the pain sobering me up. He was just the Veep then, leaning over me with his old man, Early, our Prez in those days.

"Don't move, you goddamned psycho sonofabitch," Early growled, his thick gray beard matching his eyes.

"Prez! Fuck, I –"

"Shut up. I'm talking. You want your bottom rocker, you'd better wisen up about a few things, boy. This club's got no damned room for loose cannons, fools, or fuckin' jokers."

I looked at him coldly, and nodded. Later, we were still milling around the bar, waiting for these other fucks coming down from Jersey to launder some money, far from home.

Assholes were a big crime syndicate in Atlantic City, some proxy group tied to the Russian mob. We were counting their cash, separating our fee from the shit we were banking, when this big, bald fucker crept up on Dust.

I got between him and the devil's switchblade with about a second to spare.

That sleek, metal sonofabitch slid straight into my side, narrowly missing my guts. Didn't feel the burn 'til after I had my nine out, aimed at his head, and pulled the trigger.

I blew the bastard's brains out. The brothers put holes in more of them before we realized they'd come here to fuck us over. A few more fucks limped away, begging for mercy. None of 'em would answer what the hell they were trying to pull, so they got their brains shot out too.

Piece pulled a marker outta his pocket on Dust's order, cursing underneath his breath. Every single bill he checked was counterfeit.

Early fuckin' lost it. Reached into our truck for gas, poured it all over the black bag of cash, and lit it the fuck up. We warmed ourselves in the rainy forest that night, stoking the flames with the shit they'd tried to feed us, before we burned their bodies.

Before it was over, the old Prez ripped off half his t-shirt, tied it around my waist, stopping the bleeding. "I'm sixty two years old, but I'm man enough to admit when I'm wrong about shit. Dusty, you tell him." Early looked at his son, strange amusement flashing in his eyes.

Dust looked at me, the same cold, dark stare I'd see for the next seven years. Maybe for the rest of my life.

"This club needs a joker after all, brother. Some fucker who's crazy enough to move, not think, even when he's been stabbed. Joker. That's what we're calling you from here on out."

I rode home with the rest of the crew the next day, numb to the core. The whole thing had been nothing but a fuckin' accident, all due to a drug laced cig that fucked up my head and my nerves so bad I couldn't feel the pain in my guts.

The name stuck.

* * * *

"Joker." Dust said my name about a split second before his big hand fell against my shoulder. "It's time, brother."

I looked up, hating him for making me rip my hand away from Summer's. She lay on the little cot in our makeshift infirmary, dazed and asleep from the shit Laynie had given her, but still tossing and turning every few minutes.

Bingo slept at her feet, dead to the world. Best part about being a dog was that you never had to suffer through this shit.

"Go. I'll be right here, the whole time, in case she needs anything."

Prez led me into our meeting room. All the brothers were already there, gathered around, waiting. Every man looked at me, sympathy or sadness carved into his face.

"Where's the fuckin' video?" I sat down in my usual spot, running my fingers over all the cuts I'd left in the wood over the years.

Normally, my blade would've been out, stabbing through my fuckin' fingers, relieving the blackness rising up inside me like tar. I'd lost too much today for that to do a damned thing, though.

I'd had it all and lost it in one goddamned week.

Fuck.

"It's here," Skin said nervously, pulling out his phone. He looked at the Prez and then at Sixty, both of them on each side of me. Quietly making sure they were ready to hold me down when I lost my shit, before I turned the whole clubhouse upside down.

I'd only seen pictures of the sick, pockmarked motherfucker who showed up on the screen a couple times before. His lips twitched, smug and punchable, making my knuckles burn. Fuck, I wanted to break his jaw, and then keep going 'til the goddamned thing was just a mess swinging on his face.

"Hi, assholes. It's your old friend, Hatch. Listen, I've got something that belongs to you." He stood up, stepped aside, and I saw him.

Alex. Sitting glumly in a booster seat, an ugly looking bitch with neon purple hair at his side, grinning like the wicked witch. Probably some nasty fuckin' slut they'd recruited to watch over him while they decided what the fuck to do.

"Let me tell ya, this little shit's got nine lives or something. Came close to gutting him before, having a sniper put a hole through his little head. Right in front of his ma. Whatever I had to do when I wanted that fuckin' bitch to crawl up your asses and pull out some gold." He paused, and my fists flexed 'til it burned up to my shoulder, watching that shit-eating smirk die on his face. "Well, we all know how that worked out. She bailed on me. I've lost two of my men. If we weren't in open fucking war before, we sure as shit are now!"

He spun around, shook the camera, screaming into it. I caught a blur of the bitch holding my kid, pulling him to her chest, covering his ears. "Hatch, please..."

"Here's how it's going down, kids. You want this brat to keep breathing – and I know you pussies do – you'll drain your fuckin' accounts. Eight hundred big. A million if you've got it, and you want more insurance I won't pluck a hair outta his tiny little head. Dumped on my doorstep, outside Seddon, where I've set up camp, in forty eight hours or less. You tell the Grizzlies and the Devils to fuck right off, stay in their own territory. Better, you tell 'em our business is the way to go, give us free access through Tennessee, and maybe we won't mow you fuckers down."

A slow burning rage moved through every man in the room. All eyes were glued to Skin's phone while the piece of shit ragged on.

"No negotiations. No other choices. You fuck me over, the brat dies. You fuck me over, we ride up to Knoxville the second after we cut his fuckin' throat, slam our boot up your asses, and kill every last one of you. We burn your clubhouse. Tear apart your shitty fuckin' strip club, drag every bitch we can find back to Georgia in chains. Old lady, whore, who the fuck ever. This ain't a conversation, boys. It's a demand, motherfuckers, and it will be fucking met. Because if it ain't…"

The shithead trailed off, smiling. Slowly, he turned toward my son, and pointed his knife, guiding one long cut through the air. Up and down.

The bitch holding Alex gave him a sour look before the screen went black.

"That's all we've got," Skin said quietly. "Intel says they're somewhere around Seddon, just like the bastard said. Don't know how many. Could be half a crew if this is just a raiding party. Could be a whole fuckin' army if he brought in men from the other chapters."

"When do we go?" I growled, looking at the Prez.

"We have to wait for the Grizzlies. Blackjack says his boys are about fifteen hours out. I've told him everything, and they're hauling ass to get here, coming through the Midwest right now. We can't do shit 'til we've got numbers. He's luring us into a trap. He knows damned well we won't comply."

"Yeah," Firefly said, trying to pin me down with his cold blue eyes. "He ain't wrong. We're going over everything before we rush in blind, making damned sure we can creep into Georgia without them finding out. We break into two groups, hit 'em from two directions, they won't see it coming. They're used to us being small, moving together. They don't know about the deal with the Grizzlies. We've got reinforcements. Just need to wait for 'em."

He talked calmly. Smoothly. A commander's words intended to diffuse the anger turning my blood molten, keep me from doing something stupid.

Fuck, stupid? That was wasting one more second here waiting, sitting while those fuckin' jackals did God only knew what to my kid.

"Reinforcements?" I said coldly, straining my throat. "No waiting. The damned Grizzlies ain't greenhorns, they can fuckin' catch up to us."

"Brother, please," Dust said, the tension on his place bleeding out, begging for calm. "I know you're torn up. Know you're losing your mind, listening to us pinpoint strategy while they've got your kid and put your girl in a fuckin' coma. You've got to wait."

Wait? Wait?!

Was this motherfucker serious?

For three goddamned fuckin' years, he'd told me to sit on my ass. Wait.

Be a good, patient little boy while he schemed to bring down my brother's killers, the same ruthless assholes who had my son hostage, who'd put my old lady in a stupor.

Fuck him. Fuck me.

Hell, I hadn't even officially claimed her yet, and if this went sideways, I never fuckin' would!

The growl tearing my throat apart started like an earthquake. I was on my feet before either of the brothers at my side could jump me, Sixty moving slow as usual, a smoke hanging outta his bearded mouth.

"Bro –"he started, laying a hand on my shoulder. I threw him off with one violent shake, stepping up to Dust.

"I've waited years, Prez. *Years,* just like you fuckin' said. Lived by your promise that we'd get our chance to tear their guts out for what they did to my brother. Piece was dead and gone before I could do shit about it. Ain't the same with my kid, and I'm not sitting on my fuckin' hands!"

Dust's eyes widened. His salt and pepper stubble twitched, turning his look of surprise into a fatal glare. My words slipped a dagger into his back, spilling the beans in front of the brothers.

Ask me if I fuckin' cared. Nothing, nothing, nothing else mattered right now except having my family back.

Sixty, Skin, and Firefly shared a look. Lion and Tin hung back, halfway outta their chairs. I'd stopped them all from creeping up and throwing me on the floor with nothing but my words.

"Cap'n? What the fuck's he talking about? Motorcycle accident got Piece…right?" Anger distorted Firefly's voice.

Very slowly, Dust pulled his pipe outta his mouth, coldly turned his eyes away from me, and looked at the rest of the boys. "No. There's more to that shit I've kept to myself 'til now. Just between me and Joker."

Practically heard about a dozen jaws hitting the floor. The prospects lined up against the wall looked at each other nervously.

We had about one more second of brutal silence before all hell broke lose.

"You cocksucking, lyin' motherfucker!" Skin lost it first, flying outta his chair, pointing a stern finger at the Prez like a dagger. "You're gonna tell us what happened, but first we oughta vote on whether or not you keep the fuckin' gavel for this bullshit!"

Half the boys in the room nodded. I just stood there, fists almost trembling at my sides. Couldn't decide whether I was going to march the fuck out or break Dust's jaw over this shit.

Dust looked at all the brothers, one by one, a calm like ice running through him.

"Careful, boy. Before you start calling for any changes around here, ya'll better realize I did it to save everybody's asses. We're barely in a position to fuck with the Deads now, and we sure as hell weren't three goddamned years ago. When we lose one of our own, we've got a blood oath. Every damned brother in this room would've been obliged to risk his life on it. You all would've died, going off before we were good and ready. And so, I sat on it, asked the Veep to do the same, biding our time, 'til we could pay those motherfuckers back without losing the whole charter."

"You fuckin' lied." Firefly wasn't convinced. His fist came up, falling against the table like a sledgehammer. "You fuckin' lied to each and every one of us about a dead brother, just like you bullshitted me to my face about boning my goddamned sis!"

Shitstorm status? Hurricane.

Dust and Firefly stared each other down, taking everybody's eyes off me.

The big Enforcer echoed the dark, pissed off energy shredding my guts. I couldn't take it standing here a second longer. I had to fuckin' go.

Turning, I started marching for the door, but only made it halfway there before it popped open. One of the young, lean prospects we'd taken to calling Buck stood there with a smoke in his mouth, his eyes rolling around like marbles, wondering what the fuck he'd walked into.

"Guys, I'm sorry as hell to interrupt. But Prez, I thought you oughta know, the Grizzlies are here."

"Fuck," Dust said.

Last line of bullshit I heard before I pushed past him, walked the fuck out, and kicked the door shut behind me. They were still screaming as I made my way to the little room in the back, where Summer was laid up.

Or maybe not so laid up anymore. When I came in, I found her sitting on the bed, staring sadly into a steaming cup of tea.

She looked up. Our eyes locked, and it was like a fuckin' dagger going into my chest.

All the hurt. All the loss. Everything I felt for our missing kid, except a hundred times worse.

And it was all my fault that I'd let that shit invade her, shut her down, kill her like a fuckin' cancer.

"Babe," I said, walking up and putting my arms around her.

She didn't hug me back. My heavy ass heart crashed

through my ribs and sank straight to my guts. I wanted to fuckin' puke.

"What? What do you want?" she whispered, barely moving her lips.

"Came to tell you I'm taking off. I'm going down to Georgia and bringing Alex home, or I'm gonna die trying. I ain't waiting for the rest of the boys. Won't lose another goddamned second while he's with those bastards."

"I heard about the video," she said. "Heard it from Meg, who overheard it from her old man, Skin."

My jaw tensed. I pulled back, staring into her eyes, wondering if I'd ever see that warmth again in her soft, green pools.

"Don't bother thinking about it. The fucker holding him, he's gonna die, same with all his brothers. I'll do shit that'll turn your stomach. They'll pay, with every drop of blood they got, baby."

"So, what, then? You came for a goodbye kiss? A medal? To see me drop down, hugging your knees, begging you not to go? Thanking you?"

What the fuck is she trying to say? I looked at her, rage and confusion whirling in my skull.

"Get the fuck out, Jackson!" she snarled, pushing hard against my chest. "You won't bring him back. It's all my fault. I should've taken Alex and *ran* at the first chance, taken him far, far away from all this, before you pulled me back in and ruined my life. You took the only fucking thing I ever cared about!"

No, no, and fuck no.

I stood there like a statue, taking all her shit. The regrets, the abuse, the ugly fuckin' crying. Didn't even flinch when she started screaming at me to *go, go, and never come back.* I didn't move when she dumped out her tea, looked at me with more hate than a woman's eyes should hold, and whipped the mug past my head.

Shit glanced my ear, flew behind me, and smashed against the wall. She crumpled over on the bed, bawling her eyes out, losing her fuckin' mind.

It was brutal. Wrong. Volcanic.

Never barked back at her, not once. Because I knew what it felt like to lose my damned mind.

I fucking understood.

All the shit I'd gone through with Piece was eating her now. Worse, because it ate me too, knowing they had our kid.

She sank her claws and teeth into me because there was nobody else she could.

Killing Hatch, destroying the Deads, and bringing our kid home – that was up to me. I'd do it, or I'd die. Alone.

Didn't need her approval, or the goddamned club's.

Before I walked the fuck away, I hovered over her, throwing my arms around her one more time. She was too lost in her hot, painful tears to fight me anymore.

"You rest. You can think twice about some of the bullshit you just said if I come back alive." Releasing her, I walked, stopping by the door for one more confession. "Bye, Summer. Go ahead and hate me all you want. I loved you, I love you now, and I always fuckin' will – love you as much as I do that kid, the second I laid eyes on him."

She stared quietly, tearing running down her cheeks.

Time to go. I headed into the clubhouse, where I could still hear the brothers screaming at each other in the meeting room.

Several big men in Grizzlies cuts were milling around near the bar. Two or three full patch brothers, plus a gaggle of prospects, one with a glass eye. There were crates of weapons they'd brought in stacked around their feet. The men held their beers while they all eyed the scrum going on behind the wall.

"VP? Shit, you're the only man we've seen in charge," a tall, powerful looking man with a crew cut said, lightning bolts on his head. "What the fuck's going on in there? Sounds like they're gonna kill each other!"

"Asphalt, no. Not our damned business," another one said, a massive bastard named Roman, wearing their Enforcer patch. He could've given Firefly a run for his money in size and strength. "Hey, Joker, where the fuck you going?"

I walked right past, not even stopping, 'til I was at the other end of the bar. Then I reached up, caught the loose stitch on my V. PRESIDENT patch, and tore. Hard.

"Talk to somebody else if you wanna know. I ain't in charge of shit here anymore." I let it drop to the floor while they all stared at me, trying to figure out what the fuck they'd stepped in. "They'll be done soon in there, one way or another."

I left it at that. A couple of the men called after me, but

I was gone, this time for real.

The numbness took over. The evil, killer darkness I'd caged since that kid came into my life, since I'd come within a couple inches of making Summertime mine.

God willing, I still fuckin' would. I wasn't giving up, no matter how shitty the odds.

I fit every gun, grenade, and bayonet I could in my saddlebag before I took off. Then it was nothing except me and the Harley, the road beneath us, its sweet vibrations pouring more rough grief through my bones so I didn't have to.

The mission counted. Nothing else did.

Had to focus. Had to get the fuck outta town, blow down to Seddon, and figure out where the hell they'd set up camp, waiting for our demands.

I got about a hundred miles south of Knoxville, deep in the wilderness, before the motherfuckers came crawling outta the woodwork.

They must've had a prospect tailing me when I passed through one of those little mountain towns, with barely a soul in sight. It was night, and the visibility was shit, thick fog rolling across the road when I passed through the dips in every valley.

I barely hit my brakes when I saw the spikes laying across the road. My bike turned, screeching to a halt, and I fought like a madman to keep it from tipping over.

Three Deads punched their engines and raced forward, trying to surround me, keeping me from leaving the fuckin' state line.

My hand pulled a flash grenade off my belt. I pinched my eyes shut while the bastards around me went blind, buying me a few precious seconds to jump the fuck off, head for the trees, carrying my biggest semi-auto.

There wasn't any full proof way to keep my eyes from going halfway blind when that shit went off. I was still seeing dark green when I crouched down, taking aim at every mean, dark shape I could, firing and screaming like a fuckin' lunatic.

I must've dropped three of them, or maybe four, before the fire hit my shoulder. The round cut through bone, burning like it was ripping my goddamned arm off. Fought it all the way, straining every muscle through the blood pouring down my side, shooting at the assholes crouching on the road 'til the bitter end.

Had Piece lost this much blood before he died? I had about ten more seconds to wonder what the fuck went through his mind before they slashed his throat, or came in with a machete, separating his head in one clean blow.

Fuck, fuck. I had to keep going.

Keep shooting. Keep killing. Keep fighting.

Even though my fuckin' arm, for all intents and purposes, was gone.

If it was still attached to my body, I couldn't fuckin' feel it. Screaming, I fell back, firing wildly at the sky.

Boots crunched on the brush around me, cursing me like bloody murder. Closer, closer.

The gun fell against my chest. Reaching for my knife with my good hand, I swung for the leg closest to me, howling into the night, trying to kill, kill, kill.

For Summer.

For Alex.

For the brotherhood, blown to shit because Dust's lies had finally gone off like dynamite.

All gone. All fuckin' gone forever if I didn't force myself up, swing again, and execute the motherfucker trying to stomp my head in.

Another kick. Miss.

I swung the knife again, planted it in his leg, and heard a satisfying howl of pain.

Fucker went down. But there were too many others. Too goddamned many – these bastards always had numbers.

The shit-kicker smashing against my skull came from behind. A twig snapped, and I was too damned slow before I dropped the other asshole, pulling out my blade.

Never knew if the blood loss got me first, or the toe of his boot stabbing into my head.

Perfect, cold blackness put me down.

* * * *

"Three men. Three good men ate fuckin' dirt because of you, motherfucker." A sick, angry voice taunted me in the dark.

My eyes were open, but I couldn't see shit. I'd gone blind.

In the corner, somebody cried. A tiny, helpless voice I

recognized, scared for his life.

Alex. My son.

I couldn't see a fuckin' thing, but I crawled on my hands and knees toward the sound, across what felt like a cool concrete floor, covered in dirt.

"He he, look at this bastard, going around in circles like he's chasing his tail!"

"Shut up, Skelly. Shut the fuck up."

Finally recognized that other voice. Hatch, the abuser, the killer, the demon who'd put my girl through the grinder and had my son out in front of me, like a carrot.

"Alex, Alex, don't be afraid. Don't let them fuckin' scare you," I growled, laying in front of what I hoped to God was him.

"Father and son," Hatch said softly, pausing for what had to be a puff. I could smell smoke swirling around me, sinister as a ghost. "I'd say it made me feel some shit if it didn't look so goddamned weak. Jewels, get the little bastard out of here. His fuckin' daddy can't even see him, so he ain't gonna be any use to us."

"Right away," a woman said. Probably the bitch with the neon purple hair I'd seen on the video.

I held in my fury, listening to my son cry. Couldn't see her pick him up, but I knew she did, cooing softly to him the whole damned time as they left the room.

Somewhere, a door closed. They were gone. Leaving me alone with who the fuck knew how many evil bastards. A heavy boot slammed down on my bruised ribs a second later.

I heard a gun cock, dangerously close, up against my temple. My teeth pressed together 'til I tasted blood, and I thought they'd fuckin' crack to pieces in my mouth.

"You fucked up, just like the bitch you left on her own," Hatch said, breathing hot death in my ear. "All my boys are gonna get a piece of you, Joker. Fingers, asshole, ribs, sockets, I don't fuckin' care. Yeah, you heard me. Sockets."

That last one, he repeated, and I finally knew who'd killed my brother. My whole body shook, wondering what the fuck I'd done to make God bring me face-to-face with his killer, without letting me fuckin' see the motherfucker.

"Don't look at me like that, you ungrateful sack of shit. We could've done it all right in front of your fuckin' kid. We've got rules here, asshole, same as you and all the sorry fucks wearing those popguns on your leathers. You sing, we'll make sure the kid doesn't have to suffer much longer. He'll go out clean, assuming your Prez doesn't show up to pay the fuck up. Then we'll let him walk." He pushes his gun harder into my head, digging the barrel into my temple. "I'm honest, Joker. I'm easy as fuck to deal with. So, let's try to get this shit off right before I give the go ahead to knock your fuckin' teeth out. Just wanna know one thing – where the fuck's your Veep patch gone?"

Heart pounding like mad, I tilted my head, 'til that gun was right between my eyes. "Go ahead and shoot me, fuckwit. You already know I ain't telling you shit."

XI: Stupid, Stupid, Stupid (Summer)

When I woke up and crawled out of my hole, none of the men were speaking. Not with words, anyway.

But their movements said too much. Everyone buzzed around like drones who'd just had their hive caved in by a hungry bear.

This was serious. This was war. Men walked around with long, dangerous guns unlike anything I'd ever seen outside the movies. Their faces were all long, deadly serious, as if they were all quietly making peace before riding into the death.

I watched Meg, the elegant brunette who'd been keeping me company on lockdown, suck face with Skin. He smiled into her kiss, held her close, the long, jagged scar on his cheek catching the light.

Firefly kissed his pregnant wife. Cora, the blonde I hadn't spoken to very much. She sobbed when the big, angry powder keg she called her man swept her up in his arms, laid his lips on hers, and didn't stop until one of the

Grizzlies bikers tapped him on the shoulder.

Numbly, I watched in wonder, walking toward the garages with a blanket draped over my shoulders. The huge group of men got on their bikes and fired their engines all at once, with one notable piece of the club missing.

Joker. He'd gone off somewhere on his own, riding solo into death, just like he'd promised me. He'd kissed me goodbye, told me he loved me, loved Alex, and I'd treated him like the biggest bitch in the world.

God. God fucking damn it.

"Back inside, mama." One of the newer prospects named Tray stopped me from going any further, his shiny bald head gleaming. "Only three of us here to watch the old ladies, and we're gonna do our jobs to the dotted fucking line."

I'm not really an old lady. Stopping just short of saying it, I turned with a sigh, and went inside.

The clubhouse was insanely quiet with the men gone. Meg, Cora, and several strippers from their club sat at the bar. The dancers all pouted, probably disgusted that they'd been thrown into the club's protection for the evening, when they could've been out on the floor, earning.

"Hey, girl," Meg said softly.

I took a seat next to her without saying anything, reaching across the counter for a fresh beer. The men had barely touched a lot of the bottles and cans left behind.

Meg watched me pop the brew open and take a long drink. It was nice to have something harder with tea, something to warm me. Not that it had a prayer of melting the glacier welling up inside me since my little boy disappeared in that park.

"Drink up while you can!" Cora said cheerfully, smiling, lifting a glass of some amber liquid. "I'm stuck with apple juice until after this baby comes out."

Meg shot her a tense look. "She's going through some crap. I'd say she needs it. None of the brothers have heard from Joker since he stormed out a few hours ago..."

My fingers tensed against the can, hard enough to leave several metallic dimples. Like I needed any reminder.

Over in the corner, a couple strippers squeaked, laughing at some stupid joke between them. God, it was dead and different here without the men around. Especially without mine.

"I've already been through it," I said to Cora quietly. "One kid, I mean. Haven't been doing a lot of drinking since my uncle's bar shut down years ago, before I got pregnant. He'd been teaching me to make drinks before it all went to shit."

Meg sat up, cocking her head, taking a swig off her mixed drink. "Ah, you know the Heel could use a relief bartender sometime in the next month or two? We definitely need one before the holidays roll in, and the tips are great. Men don't think twice about throwing extra at their drinks when they're already dropping bundles on the girls."

I drained the can halfway before I answered, letting the fizzy alcohol wind through my stomach. "Not planning on staying here a day longer than I really have to. I mean, the way things are going, doubt I'll have much reason to."

The old ladies looked at me, their smiles disappearing. If it was suddenly awkward enough to choke a mule, well, I'd made it that way, and I didn't fucking care.

Why couldn't I have kept my mouth shut before he went away? I wished so badly I could've taken it all back.

"Well, the offer stands if you change your mind," Meg said matter-of-factly, flicking her brown locks over her shoulder.

"I'm sorry, Summer," Cora said, leaning toward me from behind her. "I shouldn't have rubbed it in. The baby, I mean. I wasn't thinking. You must be worried sick about him..."

Didn't know if she meant Alex or Joker. I wasn't going to ask.

"Don't worry about it," I snapped, even though part of me wanted her worry. "It's out of my hands now. Same as mama dying one day at a time, same as losing our house, same as Uncle Robby's bar going down. I'm used to taking punches. Never being able to hit back."

"There's always a way to fight," Meg said, staring me down. "I was a prisoner once, before Skin saved me. Did more disgusting things than I ever want to think about. Cora here next to me, her daddy took his life. The club helped her big time, saved her from some really awful men, just like the ones all the boys are out there fighting, right now."

"It can't be that simple," I said, trying not to let my anger take hold.

"It is. First thing's first, you've got to be honest with yourself."

I snorted, polishing off my beer in another gulp. "What the hell does that mean?"

Meg hesitated, turning on her stool, until we were completely level. "Means I see a woman in front of me telling herself a lot of lies. Refusing to forgive. Hell, refusing to let herself even cry." Meg took a pull from her drink while my mouth dropped open, ready to lay into her, but I held my tongue. "It doesn't do you a lick of good to hold it all in. You're hurting. You think you hate him. You're afraid you're never going to see your son again, or his father, and there won't be a chance to sort all this out. I get it. I've been there."

"You don't know shit," I lied. Who the hell did she think she was, and where had she gotten the ability to read a stranger's mind?

"You're wrong about that. We both do," Cora said, eyeballing me with the same stark pity in her big blue eyes.

"I'm not asking for miracles," Meg said, reaching for my hand. "All I'm asking you to do is be true to yourself. We both know you can't do that unless you quit fighting it, bottling it up. Let yourself breathe."

Damn her. Even the whores across the bar were watching us now, whispering to each other. I knew I looked like I was about to explode, and give his clubhouse one more drag out fight to soil its walls forever.

"I was a total asshole before he left," I said slowly, facing them like my own private jury. "I blamed him. Told Joker it was all his fault for losing Alex, for dragging me into this, for breaking my fucking heart when I thought I'd just gotten it back in one piece."

"And did he scream at you?"

I shook my head. The bitter lump lodged in my throat wouldn't let me breathe anymore, but I tried to hold it. Tried so fucking hard.

"Then he'll forgive you. He knows you didn't mean it," Cora said softly. "Babe, you can't beat yourself up. Only thing left to do is hang with us through the rest of this, waiting for him to come back. Then you'll talk it out."

"And he *will* come home. With your son. They always do, Summer." Meg grabbed my hand forcefully, refusing to let go, and squeezed. "These men are tough as diamond."

Tough.

Strong.

Brave.

So many words, fit just right for Joker.

So much for holding it in.

Hot, monstrous tears boiling inside me since Joker walked out broke through. I cried in front of them and the whores, looking like a total mess.

But they weren't wrong. The tears saved me, like pushing poison from a wound.

"The worst part...the worst fucking part...I never got to tell him I loved him." I just stammered now, collapsed into Meg's arms, surrendering to this stranger.

Maybe she was more familiar than I thought. Maybe they both were.

The two women at my side had done their share of suffering. Even if I didn't know their life stories, I could see it in their eyes.

Too bad they'd gotten good out of it, though. A lot of good, judging by the patches they wore on their matching leather jackets, PROPERTY OF SKIN and PROPERTY OF FIREFLY. *So much* fulfillment, as Cora's swollen belly showed.

Truth, love, and passion with these men who loved like storms, and stormed out like they loved life itself more than any person should.

I hated it. Hated myself for tearing it to pieces, burying what might've been my last chance to experience just a small part of what they'd had with the men who'd made them theirs.

That evil asshole, Hatch, he'd taken my son. But he'd taken my man, too, and I'd fucking let him without so much as a protest hidden in a tender kiss.

"Summer – stop." Meg dug her fingernails into my arms, the only thing that stopped me from trashing so hard I banged my head against the hard counter. "Hurting yourself won't bring him back. Just let the pain out. Fucking all of it."

Something brushed against my leg. Looking down through the tears, I saw Bingo, his head tilted in human-like concern.

"You're right," I said, sniffing, and sliding off the stool. "I need to feed him. Take him for a walk around the building. It's the least I can do when Joker isn't here to do it himself."

I left the two women with their understanding nods, tugging gently on his collar until we were halfway down the hall. Then he moved on his own.

The big dog didn't need any urging to walk with me.

He'd been like Joker's shadow, the only true companion he'd had in all those wicked years before I'd shown up on his doorstep.

Now, he was mine. All I had left, with both my man and the son he'd given me gone.

Gone.

Outside, on the patio overlooking the shooting range, another burly prospect watched me the entire time. He told me not to leave the concrete, or he'd carry me back inside himself with the dog in tow.

Standing there, overlooking the Smoky Mountain night was good enough. A high moon hung overhead, yellow and otherworldly. I crouched down next to Bingo, scratching his muzzle, touching his thick, gray forehead to mine.

"You miss him, boy. Well, so do I. I'm not afraid to tell anyone the truth. I've told too many lies for too long."

Wagging his tail, he pulled me up, with my fingers still tucked underneath his collar. We walked the perimeter together.

The big dog followed my lead as I cried, ignoring the prospect, who stared out into the humming forest like a sentinel. I prayed, hoping that maybe this gentle giant would help send them a little higher.

Dear Lord, please bring them home safe. Please.
Bring me my little boy. Bring me my man.

I promise, on my life, on my soul, they'll never leave me again.

I'll never push them away.

I'll never lie to them, to myself, to you.

Amen.

If He willed it, I'd have my family, and nothing would ever take them away from me again.

XII: Last Cut (Joker)

My sight came back after the third beating.

Shit must've knocked something loose in my head, or maybe they'd just laid off my face long enough to make my eyes work again. Their punches and kicks sure as shit focused on other parts, slamming into my joints, my ribs, my spine every time I rolled.

They beat me fuckin' stupid, and then some.

My throat tasted like rust from coughing blood. Every time some new pain jolted me awake, I saw their faces every time.

Summer. Alex. Freddy.

Fuck, that last one, I knew I was hallucinating. I knew I was dying.

My brother's dead, eyeless face peeled back in a nasty grin. "Welcome home, brother. Didn't think you'd see me so fuckin' soon, did ya?"

Freddy's dead face become somebody else. It wasn't his ghost tormenting me. I looked, let my eyes adjust, and the real bastard slowly materialized.

"Piece of shit's silent as a stump. Nothin'.," Hatch said,

brandishing something that took my eyes another minute to see.

His bastards were all around me in a circle. Must've been half his fuckin' crew, maybe more. Never seen a gang of such dirty, rotten, drugged out bastards. The wiry motherfucker he called Skelly couldn't stop snorting crystal up his nose long enough to give me a proper beating, thank fuck.

"I'm guessing you ain't gonna talk, rat fuck. We've been at this for hours, and I'm getting fuckin' tired. Mama Peacemaker here, she's getting hungry. So's Betty G. Too bad her big, mean bitch of a cousin's got a hunger ten times worse." He ran his finger along the edge of a big, sharp machete.

Shit, I could see it now, gleaming in the dull light. Damned thing was rusted, stained, maybe from blood he'd never bothered to wipe away.

"Get fucked," I growled, my tongue so swollen it slurred my damned words worse than being plastered drunk.

Fuck it. Didn't care how hard it was to talk.

I'd keep cursing his evil ass 'til the end, all of them, even if it came out like mush.

Hatch paused, hovering over me for a moment, brandishing the blade. He shook his head, the rough lines on his face catching the light.

"You know that shit they say about the more things change, the more they say the same? I'm looking at it. Right fuckin' now." Slowly, he crouched down, balancing on his knees. "This is fuckin' funny. Familiar. I've seen this face before. Joker, you realize you're giving me the same broken look your bro did before my boys held him down and ripped his eyes out? He screamed like a stuck pig. Betty G and Mama Peacemaker drank deep that night."

He held the machete up to my face. Fuck me, I began to struggle, instinctively trying to pull my skin away from the sharp, hot death pressed against my cheek.

Two other bastards caught me, held me, grabbing at my head. Hatch reached into his pocket, pulled out a switchblade in his other hand, and popped it open. Betty G.

This was fucking it. His evil mismatched eyes said it all.

He'd toy with me for awhile. Torture me. Take me apart piece by piece.

I'd die like a fuckin' man, though. I'd die without him hearing me scream, thinking about my girl, my kid, and praying to god the brothers caught these motherfuckers in time to save Alex and get him home.

"Hmm. Shit," Hatch mused to himself, looking at me and smacking his lips. "You know, motherfucker, I've been around for more than six fuckin' decades and I still don't know if twins sound the same when they're dying. Thought I'd seen it all, Joker. Not that. Maybe you can give me something better than another hit or the keys to taking your boys apart. You can teach me something new, taking you apart."

"You won't take shit," I growled, looking the demon dead in his eyes. "You thought you'd get my family. Truth is, you ain't getting a fuckin' thing, and we both know it.

Go ahead and take my hands. Take my eyes, take my nuts, pry my damned heart outta my chest. You'll never take the only fuckin' thing that matters, even after I'm shoveled in my grave."

Bastard didn't like that. For a long second, he looked at me, like a volcano winding up to explode.

His hands moved. Then the switchblade was square against my cheek, pressing down, flaying my skin to the bone.

I closed my eyes. Expected the motherfucker to cut clean through my face, saw my head in half, take me out quick, dirty, and clean because I'd pissed him off so bad.

That kaleidoscope from hell started flashing through my eyes, dozens of faces I'd killed, all staring at me in one blinding split second. I'd ended a lot of fuckin' lives, always bastards who deserved it, but the karma train rolled home in the end.

Please, I thought, praying to whatever the fuck was in charge now. *Just let me see my family one more time.*

Their faces came.

Summer, the innocent. Green eyes, long dark hair, legs and tits and ass that set me on fire. Beautiful as the first night I kissed her, smiling and looking at me, holding our kid.

Alex, the blank slate. My son. Laughing, running his little hands against my stubble, like he knew he could grow up and be anything as long as he took the spoonful of applesauce I held out to his mouth.

Freddy. Piece. My face and his were one. He'd been my

fellow hellraiser, the other half of me. He looked up and smiled, saving a seat for me in hell.

Grandpa. He'd done the best he could with us, bringing us up in the only family he'd known, the club.

He'd raised us better than that fuckin' junkie our old man had been, dying young when he'd choked on his own vomit. He'd brought us up better than that whore who'd shat us out, and run off with a hitchhiker, never to be seen again.

He'd done his damnedest, and I'd never forget it. I'd be waiting for him with Piece on the other side, so help me God.

But a noise like the world ending upended everything.

Hatch stopped on my cheekbone, his ears perked up, his mouth slowly falling open when he heard the sound. "Go, go, go you stupid fuckin' idiots! That's gunfire, goddamn it!"

He dropped his machete and spun around, reaching for his gun while his men went flying outta the room. The boys were already inside their clubhouse.

I watched two men jump out, only to get mowed down by long, brutal rounds.

An explosion. More bullets, some coming straight through the thin walls. Damned good thing I stayed on the floor, slowly reaching for the blade with my good arm.

A dark shape climbed over the dead men, just as Hatch began shooting. "Fuck. Fuck, fuck, fuck, fuck, FUCK!"

He sounded like a cornered animal.

When a man's cornered, he does the stupidest shit. Like

forgetting what's behind him.

I saw my chance and jumped. Hurt every damned muscle in my body, but I caught him around the neck, screaming while I dragged him to the ground.

He kept firing the whole time, 'til I knocked the gun outta his hand. Small fuckin' miracle I hadn't caught a bullet.

Even bigger miracle once I had the evil asshole on top of me, fighting my fucked up arm harder than I fought him.

Die, you twisted fuck. Die!

He kicked, moaned, brayed like a bull going down.

I had to keep squeezing. Had to knock him the fuck out, or he'd wriggle away. Used the only weapon I had.

Just started going fuckin' *loco*, bashing my head into his from behind, hammering the shit 'til he was too dazed to keep going.

Our heads were both a bloody mess, soaked in hot, red grease by the time the boys came running in.

"Holy fucking shit!" a strange voice said, keeping his gun on us.

At first, I thought it was one of the Deads because the colors weren't Pistols. But the Grizzlies were our friends on this op, and they'd shown.

"Don't shoot." That was all I could manage before I rolled weakened Hatch with all my strength, laying on top of him, holding him down.

"You shittin' me? You're a crazy motherfucker, Pistol!" The man crouched next to me, and I saw the lightning bolts on his temples out of the corners of my eyes.

"Don't. Shoot," I growled again. "Just watch. This asshole's mine. Killed my fuckin' brother."

Shit, how many ribs had they broken? I could barely even speak.

Where the fuck were my boys?

Didn't need to ask a second later, when several more men filed into the room.

"Veep!" Firefly's familiar voice hit my ears before I felt his big hands on my back. He pulled me up, against my protests, but I kept my boot on Hatch's back the whole time, watching him twitch.

Skin and Crawl added their hands to my shoulders, holding me up. That was when the Prez walked in, angry and steely eyed, drunk on the smell of blood and gunpowder, thick in every breath.

"They're smoked," a big man said next to him, the Grizzlies MC Enforcer, Roman. He had something else in his arms.

"Fuck. Fuck – Alex!"

"Calm the hell down," the big man growled, holding my son against his chest so he couldn't see the nightmare around him. "I've got two of my own. We'll get him outta here, soon as Dust gives the word. Their bitch with the purple hair kept him safe. Let her run off."

"Go," Prez said, motioning to the two Grizzlies at his side. "Get the kid in the truck and don't let him out of your sight. Lock this place down. Nobody else leaves 'til I say, not even one more whore."

Dust stepped forward, looking over my battered body. "Joker…"

He put his boot down next to mine, making Hatch squirm twice as hard from the pressure on his spine. "This him? The Deads' leader?"

I nodded. Behind me, Skinny boy, Crawl, and Firefly all had their eyes on Dust, waiting for the only thing he could say to make shit right.

"Not much to look at. Shit, your shoulder's all fucked up. Can you walk?"

"I'll work with it," I said coldly.

"Let him down," he said to my brothers.

My muscles and bones ached as they let me stand on my own two feet again. I dropped down, banging my knees one more time, gripping the machete in my good hand.

"Listen, I owe you an apology for holding you back so long, boy. For lying to the whole damned club. Blood won't take it back. But it can make it right. You left something behind at the clubhouse." Dust reached into his pocket, pulled a little scrap of fabric out.

I stared. Saw it was my V. PRESIDENT patch. "Okay. It'll be back where it belongs after we've burned this trash, Prez."

A slow, brutal smile pulled at Dust's lips. He reached into his other pocket, took out his pipe, and gave it a light.

"Go ahead, brother. Take as much time as you need. This fuckhead won't tell us shit we can't get from his files, so there's no use interrogating. Do it for Piece. Do it for us. Mostly, do it for yourself."

And I did.

My closest brothers watched as I slowly, brutally,

mercilessly fucked up the rabid animal under me for the better part of the next hour.

I used Betty G and Mama Peacemaker. Gave both evil fuckin' blades the last taste of demon blood they'd ever sip, straight from their master. Then I snapped the motherfuckers on the floor with two bending, savage kicks.

When it was done, and his blood was on my hands, I collapsed.

Lion walked in with a bucket. Everybody helped wipe me down because I was too fuckin' exhausted to do it myself.

Prez took the bloody scrap of Hatch's cut I'd kept as a trophy. "We'll bring Don by the clubhouse next week so he can see it for himself. Old man deserves to know the deed's done."

I nodded. Freddy's ghost finally seemed pacified, but it wasn't the peace I'd been expecting.

Murder never satisfied me like this. Before, I'd always wanted more of it, to keep killing when I'd already cut a bastard's throat, or mowed him down with bullets.

This time, I didn't even want to kick the chunks of the dead President I'd carved up around the room.

I wanted to go home.

I wanted to hold my kid.

And I wanted to put my lips on Summer's, good and slow, without either one of us ever wanting to pull away.

* * * *

The next thirty hours were just a fuckin' blur.

I had a vague sensation of my brothers carrying me to the truck, putting a better dressing around my fucked up shoulder, and throwing pills down my mouth like candy.

Alex was in the kiddie seat next to me in the back. I reached out, holding his little hand, watching him sleep.

I blacked out sometime in the first few miles.

When I woke up, I was flat on my back, Dust's ma, Laynie, standing over me.

She had her long gray hair pulled back in a bun. She checked the IV plugged into my arm before turning to the Prez, muttering a few words.

"He's stable, Dusty, but I'm worried about infection. If he takes a turn for the worse, we have to bring him in."

"Infection? Bullshit. He's a tough sonofabitch. No fuckin' germs are putting him under, ma."

Laynie turned to me, noticing I'd woken up. "Oh, Jesus. Don't move. You've lost a lot of blood, Joker. Lots of bones in casts. Don't freak out."

Easy for her to say. For a second, I tried flexing my limbs, but everything moved like it was stuck in concrete. The drugs, the daze, the overwhelming blows I'd taken the last couple days struck like a truck colliding into my ass before any panic could set in.

I blacked out.

When I came to, it was like somebody lit a furnace under my ass.

No, wait. More like my entire back.

When I opened my eyes again, the hurt all over me

turned to fire. I sweated through the worst fuckin' fever of my life.

Summer sat next to me, squeezing my hand something fierce, tears in her eyes. "Goddamn it, stay with me, Jackson. I've been waiting all day for you to wake up."

"Sorry, babe. I'm so fuckin' sorry…"

"Don't." Her little fingers covered my lips. I could barely feel them through the delirium. "Don't apologize. Please. I'm the one saying sorry. I tried to run from you, Joker. Ran like hell when I should've known it was way too late. Truth is, I didn't want to be hurt. I couldn't handle it again, after I'd loved and lost, knowing Alex might be gone, too. But you weren't the one hurting me. I screwed up – never should've blamed you for what that bastard did."

"He's dead now, baby girl. Motherfuckin' dead."

Her eyes widened, just two big, green, placid oceans. "Yeah, he is. You saved us. You saved Alex."

"Whatever. Did what I fuckin' had to. I ain't no hero. I stopped playing at that shit years ago."

"Stop," she said sharply, leaning down, looking over to somebody else and mumbling a few words. "Can I kiss him?"

If it was Laynie, I would've screamed *say fuckin' yes*, if only I could've gotten my voice an octave above leaves blowing through the trees.

Thank fuck, I didn't need to.

She had her little lips on mine, hot and wild as ever, making me feel alive despite half of me being dead. Eaten up with fever and infection.

"You're mine, Joker. You're my hero. My love. You always were, and I wish I hadn't doubted it for so long. Never again," she sighed, shaking. "Whatever happens, we'll always have family. I love you, and everything you've given me. You're my whole word, and you always will be. You, me, Alex, and Grandpa. Even Bingo."

Hearing that shit made me smile. Only thing I could do before the hot, fiery darkness reached up, squeezed my throat, and knocked me the fuck out again.

* * * *

Fifteen Days Later

I sat up in bed, propped up, watching as Laynie worked off one of my casts. Summer was by the window, playing with her hair, Alex bouncing happily in her arms.

Bingo brushed up against my leg. I was smiling too much to give a shit about the pain.

"Here, take my hand," Laynie said, holding it out. "I want you to try standing. Your shoulder's a lot worse than your feet are, like we discussed, so you should be able to walk."

That last part, she didn't sound too sure. Fuck it, I had to try.

When I first stood up, it was like I had burning napalm running down my thighs, my knees, all the way to my feet. Summer's eyes were huge, focused on me. I could practically hear her lungs holding in breath.

"Come on," she whispered under her breath. "You can do it."

I made it out about a minute, maybe two, before I had to sit my ass down. Laynie lowered me onto the bed, a grin on her face.

"Much better than I'd hoped! Yes sir, I think you'll be back on your feet, with some help, in another couple weeks. Until then, I'm sending you home with this."

I took one look at the walker and groaned. "You gotta be shittin' me."

Never fuckin' thought I'd have this in common with Grandpa, I thought.

Damned well better be a little while.

Over in the corner, Summer laughed. Alex stretched out his hand, waving to me as I grabbed the bars, helped myself up, and took my first brutal steps.

"Just take it easy, Joker," Laynie whispered. "Exercise your muscles, every day, but don't overdo it. Patience. Ya'll need loads of it here."

"Patience, patience, my fuckin' ass." I snorted.

When I looked up, feeling the sweat beading on my brow, Summer stood in front of me. "You're doing good, baby. Let me help. It's the least I can do."

I hated looking weak, especially in front of my own damned woman. But fuck, I didn't refuse taking her hand, helping her steady me on this damned contraption.

Not the manliest shit in the world, but it brought us together.

It did something. Soothed the hurt we'd suffered over

Alex getting kidnapped, dried all the tears she'd cried when I was laid up a week ago, half dead from fever.

Bingo stood by the door, watching me. When I moved a few more inches, he tilted his head up, barking several times, like he was trying to pump a brother up.

"Take him slow," Laynie told Summer. "Dust wants to see him out back. Here, let me walk behind you."

The old nurse grabbed Alex, carrying him along with us, while Summertime opened the door. We slowly trundled down the hall, passing the empty bar, heading for the first church session I'd had in fuckin' forever.

Halfway there, Alex yawned in Laynie's arms, and then belted out a sound that stopped us in our tracks.

"Da-da-da!" he giggled, clapping his little hands.

My shoulder burned like a complete motherfucker as I whipped my head around. Damn if it wasn't worth it.

The kid watched me like I'd just flown down from the moon and handed him a chocolate bar. He admired me. Fuck, he *knew* who I was, finally, his own flesh. His old man.

"Oh my God," Summer gushed, throwing her arms around my neck, kissing me on the cheek. "It's about time! I've been waiting for him to say it forever."

My lips quirked, sly as ever. "And we're celebrating with a peck on the cheek? Come on, girl, just because I have a walker doesn't mean I'm eighty fuckin' years old. Give it up."

Laughing, she leaned in. I pushed my fingers through her hair, holding myself up with the one good arm. I'd crawl over rusty nails to taste these lips.

Really fuckin' taste them.

I drank her deep, kissing her like I hadn't for weeks, because I'd been too fucked up. My lips were hungry, making up for lost time. Even my dick came outta its coma, straining in my pants.

Fuck, my lust didn't know my own limits. I didn't care.

"Shit, bro, there you are!" Sixty interrupted the perfect moment a second later. "Everybody's waiting for you! Need a hand?"

"Nah. I'll take it from here," I said, watching him approach, Lion at his side. Two scruffy bastards, the opposite of the sweet, suckable face I remembered how bad I wanted to ravage.

"Later, babe. We'll catch up later," I promised, looking back over my shoulder.

I saw Laynie pass the kid to his ma. They stood there the whole time while the brothers helped me along, underneath the neon red beer sign, smiling like I'd just handed her the world.

If only she knew what I was planning to drop on her later, as soon as I got my full strength back, or close enough to it.

Woman didn't have a clue. She wasn't the one who should've been there, looking at me with those, loving puppy dog eyes.

She'd given me everything. Her and that kid. *Family.*

Soon, I'd be giving it back.

* * * *

Grandpa sat in his wheelchair next to Dust, our guest of honor, who hadn't been to the clubhouse in at least a solid year. They were all gathered around the old fire pit, all the boys, full patch only.

"Christ, Joker. They really busted you up bad," the old man said, shaking his head. "That why I'm here?"

"No, Grandpa. It's fine. You're here 'cause some other fuckers got what they deserved. Prez, show him."

Dust nodded to Firefly, who stood up from a big rock. He'd been sitting on the torn scraps we'd pulled off Hatch in the end, right before we poured gasoline all over their clubhouse and lit it the fuck up.

"Take it," Firefly said, nodding respectfully to Grandpa.

His old hands shook when he took the scraps. He needed about another minute to realize what the fuck he was holding, turning it over, studying it.

"Shit. No, fuck, no. You boys bullshittin' me?" He looked up, staring at me, and then moved his eyes along the brothers, one by one.

"No bullshit," Dust said, reaching over to squeeze his hands. "These came straight off Piece's killer. Joker heard the fuckin' devil admit it himself."

Grandpa lost it. He slumped back in his wheelchair, clutching the dead man's patches, staring through the tangled branches reaching over the clubhouse to the sky.

If he were younger, maybe he would've screamed.

Fuck. I walked over, forcing myself to through the pain,

shaking my head at the brothers who were halfway off their seats, ready to help me.

Didn't fuckin' need it for this. I had the strength.

This was a moment for the brotherhood, for my family, written in blood. I crouched down on the empty seat next to him, threw my arm around his shoulder, squeezing him as tight as I could.

"God. Fuck. Damn." Grandpa shook when he said each word, overwhelmed. "Finally. I can go to my fucking grave in peace, seeing this."

"No fuckin' way, old man," I growled, waiting 'til he looked at me, seeing the tears in his old eyes. "You've got at least a few more good years, being a great grandpa, before we let you bite the bullet."

His wrinkled face smiled. "You're a good boy, Jackson. All you boys."

He looked up, taking my hand for a second, before I let him go back to clutching the bloodied trophies he was holding. "Dusty, you've done right by this club. Right by me. You did what you said, even if it was a long goddamned detour."

"No. Don't deserve none of that praise. Truth is," Dust said, standing up, pulling his pipe from his lips. "Every man here made this happen. It should've happened sooner, if we'd been stronger, and I fuckin' lied so it didn't."

Everybody went silent. Yeah, I'd forgiven his lying ass for holding me back on my choke chain for years. But the rest of the brothers? Who the fuck knew.

They'd gotten their shit together well enough to come

storming in with the Grizzlies, kicking Deads' ass. Didn't mean the wound was closed. Half the boys around me looked like they were seething, waiting for an apology that hadn't come.

Dust cocked his head, looking around. "Everybody here, you delayed the vote on whether or not you wanted me to put down the gavel so we could deal with Hatch and his assholes. That was the right choice. Now, ain't my place to say what's right and wrong anymore. It's up to you. I owe you boys that vote."

Grandpa looked at him slowly, and the two men locked eyes.

"You strike me down," Dust said, a tremble in his voice. "That's your damned right by the club charter. I'll step down in peace and pass the Prez patch to Joker, 'til you decide whoever the fuck you want running this club permanently. That's the other reason you're here, Don. You've got yourself a vote as long as you're alive and breathing. You rode with my old man, Skin's old man, and all the brothers who ain't here anymore to make a choice one way or another. You weigh in with the rest of us."

Grandpa leaned in his chair, the scrap of Hatch's cut dropping to the ground. He looked at me. "Joker votes first. It's only right."

All eyes were on me. I stood up, grinding my teeth through the pain, steadying myself on that fucked up walker.

"Brothers, I know what Dust did. His shit cut all of us, but it cut me the fuckin' deepest. He lied, sure. Fuck, though, he kept us alive." I paused, feeling the tension roil the air. "You demote him, I'll take his patch for ten days. No more. I don't want the fuckin' gavel. Going through the shit I did – all the beatings, the torture, watching that piece of shit taunt me with my own kid – it flung my head around 'til I came face-to-face with God. He told me exactly how I oughta live the rest of my life, and I'd be a damned fool to say no. I'm doing my duty to this club, to my brothers, but I ain't taking on any more. Soon as I'm healed up, I'm going home every second I'm not here. I'm gonna give my woman and my son the world."

Slowly, the brothers began nodding. They understood.

No matter how much shit went flying between us, sometimes, we all had each other in our hearts.

Always. *Fuckin' always.*

Dust was about to start the vote, looking at Firefly first, but I stopped him in his tracks.

"We're not finished yet. Every brother gets to speak before this shit goes down, and I'm putting in my word. I *want* Dust keeping the gavel." A couple men snorted, and others balled their fists. "He's a motherfucker for lying about my brother, but he's been a fuckin' hero every time the bullet meets the gun. He just cut us a deal with clubs a helluva a lot bigger than us, ten states away, when they wouldn't have given us a fuckin' second of their time a couple weeks ago.

I turned, staring at Firefly, his blue eyes raging the most. "Whatever the he did, or didn't do, that counts for something. Something big. There's nobody else I'd want at the helm when the blood flies, and we've got more coming. Sooner or later, it always comes. There's always fuckin' more, but gutting the Deads in Georgia like we just did, looks like there'll be a little less to worry about for the first time in forever."

I sat back down. Fuck, that felt amazing, especially when the fire in my legs had been about to put me under.

"We'll start with you, Veep, because we already know your vote. All in favor of turning me out, handing over the President patch, say 'aye.'"

"Nay," I said, without a second of hesitation.

"Nay." Grandpa voted the same. He looked at me and bowed his head, more respect shining in his eyes than he'd shown me since the night they butchered Piece.

Two more Nays came quick. Sixty, moving onto Skin, who both voted the same way.

Club charter said it took seventy percent to elect a President or turn him out.

"Aye." First one came from Lion, who'd taken a fuckin' beating a few months back, almost as bad as mine at the hands of the Torches MC. "We need fresh blood, somebody who'll give it to us straight."

He stared at the Prez, anger in his eyes. Turned my damned stomach, but I respected his balls, him and Tin both for flexing nuts when they were the newest boys here.

His closest brother, Tin, followed with another Aye. If the tension was like a vice before, it felt like we'd dropped ten thousand feet beneath the ocean, the pressure caving in our skulls.

The vote moved to Crawl, staring at us through his long dark hair, a hint of Hispanic in his skin. His old man had been Brazilian or Argentinian or some shit.

"Aye." His vote was like a fuckin' lightning bolt, the first senior brother to turn against the Prez.

My fuckin' heart sunk. I started, clenching my teeth, making the fresh pain in my jaw drown out everything else healing in my body.

A dozen eyes burned. Appreciation, anger, and respect, all of it aimed his way.

"You're a good man, Dust, and a good brother. You meant well. But you've just lost my trust," he said, smooth and measured. Motherfucker was gonna take my place sooner or later as the eerily calm one.

Fuck. I did the tally in my head.

Three ayes. Four nays. And it was moving to Firefly, who still had an axe to grind with the Prez over the fling with his sis.

Fuck me again. My jaw got tighter, tighter, realizing I'd have a temporary gavel I never fuckin' wanted hanging over me, as real as this bum leg and all the lovin' I had for my family.

Firefly didn't say shit. He looked at the Prez, his face as angry and electric as ever.

"Firefly?" Dust said, when the staring contest lasted too long. "What's your vote?"

"Nay."

Holy shit.

Heads dropped. Men cursed in shock and relief, sometimes both at once.

Grandpa had been holding the gavel while this shit went down. He passed it back to Dust, who took it on one hand, giving it a slow spin like he'd picked it up for the first time.

He walked down the center line, stopped at the big brick oven next to the fire pit, and slammed it down on the concrete so hard the hammer went flying off its handle. It bounced loudly on the pavement, rolling to a stop next to my walker.

Bingo jumped up, wandered over, and started sniffing away at it, his fat tongue hanging out.

"Brothers, thank you all for every vote. I fuckin' mean it. Those of you who decided to give me a second chance – won't let you down. Everybody who wanted me gone – you'll think twice in a few more months. Won't let anybody down, even the ones who hate me. I promise. This club's in my blood. I'll die before I ever fuck it over."

He turned around, taking a good, hard look at each and every one of us. I spoke first.

"We done here, or what?"

"Yeah. We'll do church again in a few days, soon as I've got the next shipping details from Blackjack. We owe the Grizzlies more than money for sending their guys out here, having 'em move on the fly. We'll send a few kegs of the best Tennessee whiskey we can get our hands on out their way."

Every brother nodded. I'd personally thanked that big, mean motherfucker, Roman, who'd loaded Alex and me in the truck. Said he'd been through some shit with his kid too, and everything happening was real familiar.

Slowly, the brothers filed out. I took my sweet time trailing Grandpa out to wait for his ride from the home, letting Skin and Firefly help me along.

Summertime came running up next to us, scratching Bingo while holding Alex in her arms. "Looks like we're about ready."

I looked at her, smiled, and nodded. "Yeah, babe. Go warm up the truck. Just a few more minutes here."

Perfect timing. The van rolled by about a minute later, and we all waved to Grandpa as they loaded him in, and took off.

We'd have a happier visit next time, when I brought the family around to see him. He hadn't even bothered to keep the torn up strips of Hatch's leather we'd offered, and who the fuck could blame him?

Enough blood. Enough bullshit. I wanted my wife, my old lady, my kid. Fuck, I wanted to start working on a little brother or sister for Alex, soon as my body let me.

"Rest up, brother," Skin said, slapping me gently on the back. "I've got tax shit to crunch the rest of the day."

Firefly hung with me 'til Summer came around, winding the truck against the curb. Before she parked it and stepped out to help me in, I turned to him, looking at him sideways.

"Why the fuck did you vote for Dust? You hate his ass more than the rest of us, that shit going on between him and your sis."

"'Cause I agreed with everything you said, brother." He stood up straight, looking me dead in the eye. "This club needs leadership. I'm still aiming to knock his shit in if he doesn't stop fuckin' around with Hannah. Still, we've got too much on our plate to get petty. I ain't letting personal grudges come between me and the club. We're family, Veep, same as Cora and my kid about to be born."

Family. That word was starting to haunt me.

I looked at him and nodded. "Yeah, you've got a point."

I'd only begun to figure out what it meant. Had a feeling there were a hundred meanings left to find, too.

One of them stared me right in the face as Summer opened my door and helped me in.

This was everything. All of it. In here.

Long as I had her, my son, my dog, and my brothers, I'd be fuckin' dandy.

Unraveling the mysteries of the universe could wait.

* * * *

Several Weeks Later

I'd been at the chop shop all day by myself, and now I was coming home. My shoulder still ached when I worked the tools, but I was able to work again.

That meant something.

Almost as much as climbing on my bike for the fifth time since the showdown with the Deads. It hurt like hell going more than a few miles.

Damn if it wasn't worth it, though. I'd lost the walker awhile ago, and borrowed one of Grandpa's old canes about a week longer.

I'd never been happier to give anything up, when I finally kicked them both to the curb.

Never would've believed I'd take moving on my own two feet for granted, or jumping on my Harley without a second thought.

After this brutal fuckery, I never would again.

I rode, free from all the demons.

Freddy's ghost didn't haunt me no more, except when I saw him in my dreams. His face was back. So were his eyes, and his smile.

I dreamed about the good times instead of the bad. Dreamed about us wrestling, laughing, beating up on each other in the mud and the grass with grandpa watching from the porch, just like when we were kids.

The Deads were...well, pretty fuckin' dead. And they'd stay that way.

Intel said the motherfuckers left behind in Georgia and Florida after we'd killed their Prez were fighting like headless snakes. They'd be too busy killing each other across the deep south to think about retaliation anytime soon.

Grandpa, he'd never been so fuckin' happy. Not since before they closed down Robby's place in Seddon. Not since Freddy was still breathin'.

Every Sunday, he was up early, sitting in his chair waiting for us, ready to take a summer stroll around the pond behind the home with me, Summer, Alex, and Bingo at his side.

We never let the kid outta our sight. Ever.

Today, I was free. Balmy mid-summer wind tore across

my face like nobody's business, sweeping down from the Smokies; haze, humidity, and all.

Today was the day. The shit I'd been working on for the last week sat in my pocket. It was missing one more piece, the most expensive one, but I couldn't fuckin' wait.

Not since my girl got herself branded last week.

PROPERTY OF JOKER, the big, dark tattoo across her shoulder read. Firefly did the ink with the same care and attention he'd used on his own girl, Cora, her belly getting bigger by the day as her due date crept up.

Seeing that shit only made me want to fuck my girl harder. Longer. Spill my balls inside her every chance I got, and throw those fuckin' pills she popped every morning to keep from getting knocked up in the fire pit with a light.

No, goddammit.

Had to keep a lid on my lust, just a little while longer. I'd already been fuckin' her for the past week when Laynie said I shouldn't, telling me it could still do damage.

It'd been torture staying away from that pussy while I was laid up. Almost as bad as feeling what I had in my pocket, ready to burn a hole right through it, if I didn't hand it over the second she walked through the door.

A short ride later, I walked into my place. Cora sat in front of the TV with Bingo and Alex, all three of them watching some kid's show with a pirate singing about booty or some shit.

"Seems about right," I said, standing by the door. Couldn't help but feel a little damn appreciation for the bastards who used to rule the seas, the same way the clubs ran the roads.

Alex jumped up right away, toddling toward me, a sunny smile on his little face. Bingo raced ahead of him, and I got down on my knees as the big dog crashed into me, licking my face.

"You're home early!" Cora said, standing, her baby bulge like a small basketball. "Firefly won't come by for another twenty minutes to get me."

"Figured you could use some extra down time since you're getting closer to the big day. You're doing us a solid, watching him like this after your shift."

"Oh, please." She stuck out her tongue and waved her hand. "My pleasure. I need all the practice I can get. Just hope my own turns out half as sweet as Alex."

My son put a big fat exclamation point on it by jumping as high as his little knees would allow, hanging around my neck like a damned monkey. I hauled him up, carrying him on my shoulders, grinning while Bingo raced around us.

Yeah, this was the life. Just needed to put one more thing where it belonged.

"You heard from Summer?" I asked her, walking over and taking my spot in the chair across from the sofa. Shifted the kid down into my lap, all the better for him to grab at the dog.

"She's about five minutes out! Texted me a little while before you walked through the door. I think she meant to beat you here to start dinner." Cora smirked. "She's picking up fast at the Heel. Kinda feels like torture watching her mix the drinks, knowing it'll be a few more months before I can try them!"

"Yeah, she's a quick learner. Always has been."

"Yup. This club's really becoming a family thing, isn't it? We've got our business, our spouses, our kids. Maybe in a few more years I won't have to see all those drunken skanks wandering around for the single guys."

"There'll always be bitches just for fuckin'," I said, turning up my nose. "Damned glad I don't need that pussy anymore to get off."

Fuck, that was an understatement. The club had families in the old days, but it was...messy.

More than a few of the old crew fucked around on their girls, men like Early. They got hooked on booze or took to shit they should've been smart enough not to touch. Dust cleaned house since we'd lost his old man.

Early had been good for keeping the dream alive, but he'd been too damned lax. Thankfully, the norm was slowly returning. None of the boys who'd taken an old lady showed any signs of fuckin' on the side, and I'd sure as hell never go down that road neither.

Strange pussy didn't matter since Summertime gave me hers. Every morning, every night, and I still couldn't get enough.

I held onto Alex while the pirate jabbered on TV, slashing his plastic sword. Kid dozed in my arms, slipping off just before we all heard the lock jingle. Cora's phone buzzed at the same time.

"That's Firefly!" she said, springing to her feet. "Bye bye, Joker."

I nodded, listening as she went for the door, stopping

next to my girl for a few seconds. The girls swapped a hug on the way out, giddy about some gossip at the Heel about the strippers. Soon as Cora was out the door, heading for her old man, I turned the chair around.

Even after all these months, she looked damned beautiful.

It was surreal. The sweet, twisted kind of weird I liked.

"Busy day?" I asked, standing up with the kid.

She walked over, put her arms around us both, and gave Alex a little kiss on the cheek. "Yeah. Summer crowds. I'm starting to see the rush Meg warned me about."

"You'll be fine. Summertime's your fuckin' name, lady."

Smiling, she rolled her eyes. She leaned in for a kiss, but I stopped her lips, moving away.

"Hold on. He just started dozing off, and I want to get him down for a nap so we can talk."

"Talk?"

I turned my back so she wouldn't see the smile pulling at my lips. Once the kid was down, I walked back to her, leading her out to the balcony.

Bingo tried to follow, but I shut the screen on him this time. He'd get his chance to soak up the summer air later.

For now, we needed some damned privacy. Just her and me.

"Well?" she said, sounding nervous. "What is it?"

Finally. "You're talking to Meg everyday. I know she's told you about the wedding coming up, her and Skin's. Just a few weeks away now."

"Uh, yeah. She's pretty excited." Her eyes glowed,

confusion shining full bore.

"Let's make it a double." I reached into my pocket, took her hand, and dropped to one knee, pulling it out. "Marry me, babe."

Her mouth dropped. Didn't have a box for the hard silver ring I'd forged in the club's workshop, its edges perfectly smooth, polished with platinum.

Didn't fuckin' need one for shoving it into her hand, everything out in the open, do or die.

"It doesn't have a gem in it yet. That's coming later. I've been too fucked up lately to find the perfect one, but I'm going shopping tomorrow." I pointed to the space where I'd have the jeweler wedge it in. A nice, big space for a big goddamned diamond. "We missed three years we could've been living together, lovin' each other, raising our kid. I ain't missing anything a day longer, the whole package, soon as you tell me you're gonna be my wife. Fuck perfect. You and me, Summertime, that's enough. Second you tell me you're ready to be Summer Taylor, more than my old lady, everything else can wait. We've got all the time in the world to figure it out – together."

"Joker...Jackson...of course I will!"

She dropped right into my arms. Pressed her tight. Laughing, kissing, I took her mouth, greedily rolling her over on the balcony, pushing the ring into her palm so hard it must've left its imprint on her skin.

Fuck. Completely fuckin' beautiful.

We could've tangled lips for an eternity, without a witness in the world except Bingo laying next to the screen, and the wide summer fading down behind the Smokies.

"I don't care about the diamond," she moaned, when I finally peeled my lips off hers. "I love you, love you, love you, baby…"

I smiled, grabbing the ring outta her palm, and pushed it on her finger. "Looks goddamned good there. Now, say it one more time. Need to hear it again, babe."

"I love you, Jackson."

"Love you, too, baby girl. Love you through the next hundred storms, 'til hell calls me home."

My hip and my busted up shoulder still pulsed fire. But I wouldn't let myself feel anything except my lips roaming all over her that afternoon, greedy as ever.

XIII: Down That Aisle (Summer)

Six Weeks Later

Joker told me the club hadn't been so full and carefree since the bash they had celebrating Cora and Firefly. I hadn't been around for that, but Lord if the ruckus here didn't toss me headfirst into a biker wedding.

I stood at the makeshift altar, outside in the huge open valley at the foot of the Smokies. Dust's family owned land around here going back years. He put it to good use when the time came for shindigs like these.

Whatever else I still had to learn about MC life, I had a feeling nothing – and I mean *nothing* – compared to this.

The words coming out of the oddball preacher man's mouth washed over me. Meg stood next to Skin. Her decked in lily white, a short dress that clung close to her body. Him, with a cut he'd cleaned up so much it glowed in the sunlight, a new coat of polish on his boots that must've wiped away all the blood and violence they'd waded through.

"Do you, Parker Bradley, take this woman…"

I let myself look at Joker. We were right behind the happy couple, waiting, next in line. He turned his head, barely holding in a smile.

Fuck, you look beautiful. Every single hungry glance he gave said it. We were beyond words – one more way this wedding was anything but traditional.

"Yeah, I do. Shit." Skin covered his face, as soon as the words were out of his mouth. "I've been waiting to say those words since the second I saw you, babe, down on your knees in front of me, begging for help."

Off to the side, Grandpa sat in his chair, with Alex on his lap. He'd taken his place with the rest of the crew, two Taylors mixed into the club, two generations going back to the same source.

Without the club, I wouldn't be here. Without Joker, I wouldn't have the club, my son, or my sanity.

The little boy probably didn't understand what was happening, but he knew it had to be big. He just started at us, wide eyed, shifting ever-so-slightly in his great grandfather's lap.

"And do you, Megan Willow Wilder, take this man to be –"

"That'll do," she cut in, sassy as ever. "Of course I do!"

Preacher man smiled. He seriously looked like an ordinary church man, and I quietly wondered what he'd done to wind up so hitched to the club for these weddings.

Joker decided just then to grab my hand. His fingers pushed through mine, and I heard a low, feral growl vibrate through his throat as he gave me *that* look.

Shit. Forget about preacher man.

Suddenly, I couldn't wonder about anything except how I was going to make it through this ceremony without freezing up, thinking about all the ways he'd rip off my clothes, press me down on the bed, or maybe just the forest floor, and fuck me until I screamed.

Love mingled with lust, romping in his eyes. I beamed back, refusing to bite my lip.

Anything to pretend I still had a little control here. *Yeah, right.*

"All right, all right already!" preacher man stumbled over his last words, giving in to the raw desires seething through the crowd. "By the power invested in me by the Deadly Pistols MC and the state of Tennessee, you may now kiss the –"

Heaven itself wouldn't have been able to hear the word *bride.* Deafening biker applause and cheers drowned out everything. Small as it was, they all made up for it, and so did the enthusiastic girls from the Ruby Heel and the scant few relatives from Meg's side who'd decided to show up.

They kissed – and boy, *what a kiss.*

Joker's eyes grew hotter on my skin every second. I knew he was thinking hard, wondering how he'd outdo the explosive passion Skin poured on his woman.

In a couple more seconds, I'd find out.

His hand pulled me forward. The row in the crowd died down just enough for preacher man to start over, reaching up to fix his spectacles.

"Dearly beloved, brothers of the Deadly Pistols, we're

gathered here today..."

I looked at Joker, falling deep into his bright hazel eyes. Maybe deeper than ever before.

There was beauty. There was love. There was pain. There was life.

The preacher's words washed over me. That fire on my skin became a roar underneath it, warming my blood, turning everything molten.

When he looked at me, his eyes pinned me down. But sometimes his eyes broke away, traveling down to my feet, and slowly, achingly rising.

The beautiful bastard stripped me bare with his eyes.

And up here, in front of him, God, and all the brothers, I felt completely naked. Vulnerable.

But vulnerable, and loved. Did I really need any more confirmation I'd made the right choice, becoming an outlaw's bride?

"Do you, Jackson Taylor, take this woman...in sickness and in health...'til death do you part?"

"Yeah, but I ain't gonna say what you're waiting for. I've got my own vows."

Huh? My mouth fell open. I looked on in total surprise, only coming out of it when he grabbed my hand with both of us, and shook them gently.

"Baby, lovin' you taught me there's heaven and hell in this life. More important, it showed me some things are meant to be. Call it fate." He paused, squeezing my little hand tighter. "I thought I lost everything for good the night my brother died. All those rotten years, I had. Lost myself, lost my brothers, lost my family. Lost you. First time you stepped back in my life, I told myself I didn't need that shit. Thought I could never have it all, because it'd all been taken away for good."

He paused – more than a little dramatically, damn him.

My heart began to pound, so hard I was sure he could feel my pulse. The thick, white dress I'd picked out started to swelter in the high Tennessee sun, but I sweated through it, hanging on every word, awestruck by the emotion spilling from his voice.

"Baby, you showed me what a damned fool I was. You, and that adorable boy we created. You took me to paradise and straight down to Hades. We burned together. Hurt together. Dragged ourselves over the barbed wire of darker times 'til I thought we'd bleed out." Pausing, he grabbed my hand, and brought it to his lips.

Great. So much for promising myself I wouldn't cry.

"We didn't. Every time my bones and skin broke, I thought about you, babe. Only you, and the kid we created. We ain't shattering, Summertime. Not now. Not ever. Making this official just throws a fresh coat of polish on what we've had this summer – what we were always meant to. I love you, babe, from my next damned breath to my last. Love you and this family we've got so much it feels like saying 'I do' is nothing but an afterthought, so I've saved it for last. Yeah, woman, I fuckin' do."

Waterworks? Broke open. Tears flooding, pouring down my face in warm, glossy streams.

I had to kiss him. And I damned sure wasn't going to

wait for the preacher man to give me permission.

His arms were waiting when I flung myself into them a second later. We kissed like the whole sky opening up and blinding everything.

Kissed like love.

Kissed like death.

Kissed like we'd been through everything, full circle, and we'd do it all again. Over and over and over until our lives were over, or else our love was done.

And I knew what would come first.

As long as I lived, as long as I breathed, my heart would *always* belong this to crazy, gorgeous, incredible man.

"Babe," he whispered softly. "Look up. We've gotta finish to make it official."

He kissed me again, more softly this time, and I finally noticed the insane cheers exploding around us.

"Yeah, yeah, yeah, fuck yeah!" at least a dozen brothers and prospects shouted in unison.

Bingo stood up next to Grandpa and howled, temporarily going werewolf, instead of just wolf hound.

"Okay, okay," I said, wiping the tears from my eyes. "Let's do this. I'm ready."

"Summer Olivers," Preacher man said, a thin smile on his face. "Do you take this man to be your lawfully wedded husband, to have and to hold, for better and for worse..."

Come heaven.

Come hell.

Come the end of everything and the start of it again.

Preacher man finished, while my mind imagined the last

few lines, my heart singing loud. Joker, and the entire world had their eyes on me.

Smiling, I finally said it, forcing it out through raw emotion twisting my tongue. "I do."

"Then, by the power invested in me by the Deadly Pistols MC and the state of Tennessee…"

I never heard the rest. We kissed so hard it was like a tornado swept through my body, rattled my bones, and left me moaning into his mouth.

Luckily, a new wild roar in the crowd covered up the last part. But there was no hiding the way he picked me up, swung me around in his big, strong arms, and dug his hands into my ass, pulling me in.

I didn't even care about hiding it, and neither did my brand new husband.

* * * *

"There's history in these grounds, boys and girls," Dust said, a couple hours later, after we'd stuffed ourselves on drinks and the finest barbecue in Dixie. "You know my great, great granddaddy drilled his regiment in the Civil War here? Come out here with a metal detector, and you'll find all kinds of shit. Stuff that makes you think…"

We were gathered in a circle with all the brothers, me leaning drunkenly on Joker's shoulder, while his Prez gave us a history lesson.

God, these men were full of surprises. I'd have never guessed the cold, fierce Dust was such a history buff, but he kept going, even when half the guys were laughing to themselves, their eyes glazing over.

It seemed like he was the only one here without a date. I'd heard rumblings about the drama between him and Firefly's sister, Hannah. Meg said she was supposed to be his date tonight, but the girl was missing, leaving him the only man in the club who wasn't paired up with an old lady or one of the strippers from the Heel.

Firefly stood next to us, brooding the entire time. Cora kept leaning in sweetly, whispering in her man's ear. Eventually, he relented, relaxing just enough to smile at her, and wrap a possessive hand around the bump growing in her belly.

I'd missed that with Joker when I was pregnant. But I had a feeling it wouldn't be long before he gave me another baby. Next time, we'd experience everything together.

Jesus.

Everything.

He turned to me slowly, and we shared another intense look. Probably the thousandth that night.

Joker leaned in, ignoring the nitty-gritty war stories Dust described, whispering in my ear. "That dress is coming off, babe. Less than an hour. Then you're gonna get pounded so fuckin' hard you'll think you married a damned jackhammer."

Holy shit. I smiled, kissed him, trying to stop more filthy promises from spilling out of his mouth.

My body couldn't take it. My nipples were like stones underneath my bra, begging to be teased.

Truly, every inch of me wanted out of this dress. It

wanted to be naked, sweaty, and wrapped around him while he reminded me what ecstasy really meant.

A couple men over, Grandpa Taylor yawned, rubbing his eyes. Tinman had taken over holding Alex, giving him sips from a juice box when he reached out his little hands.

"Shit. The old man's getting tired," Joker said, pulling away from me reluctantly. He stepped up, guiding me along by the hand. "Lion, Tin, get him back to the home. We'll take the kid from here."

"You got it, Veep."

Tin passed Alex into my arms, while Joker watched Lion take the handles to his grandfather's chair. The old man seemed to perk up when he rolled by us, tugging on the brother's sleeve.

"Wait." They came to a full stop. "Jackson, I gotta say, I never thought I'd see you happy again after that night the evil bullshit went down. All these years I've had on this Earth, boy, and I've never been happier I was wrong."

"Me, too, grandpa," Joker growled, leaning in to give the old man a warm hug.

I watched a smile on my face, rocking Alex as he whined for more juice. "There, there, little man. Someday you'll be old enough to appreciate all of this."

"Come on," Joker said, turning his attention back to us. "I think it's time we get this honeymoon on the road."

The brothers began to split as soon as the old man left us. We made our way through the last of the party, stopping my Skin, Meg, and her parents on our way out. They looked so happy.

Her rich, mild mannered family looked like they'd finally made peace with their daughter marrying a biker. Or at least they put on one hell of a show.

It didn't matter to me. Nothing was going to ruin this night, not even a few of the people around us stuffing their feelings down their throats.

Joker called to Bingo, who came running after us. All four of us headed up the small, rocky hill to his truck, loaded and ready to take us deep into the Smokies. We had a nice cabin reserved the next week, right next to a mountain spring.

A cabin with two rooms. We'd need the extra wall like air and water for what he planned to do to me.

I was fixing Alex in his kiddie seat, Bingo wedged in next to him, when I felt my man's palm glide against my ass.

I jumped, my teeth digging into my lip, savoring the delicious tingle.

"What's that for?" I asked, turning around, running my hands up over his shoulders. His stubble hadn't ever felt this good, or maybe I'd just never been so horny in my entire life.

"Last part of the vows I couldn't say out in the open."

Smirking, I folded my arms, looking him up and down. "Yeah? You're telling me Jackson Taylor has limits to what he'll do in public?"

"Whatever. Sure, babe, if you wanna put it like that. Smacking your sweet ass is only the first word of them vows. Once I start, I don't fuckin' stop, and you know it. You're about to find out what I'm all about when I talk about forever."

Growling, he reached around, pushed his fingers through my hair, and kissed me. I leaned against the truck, moaning, wishing I could rip this stupid wedding dress off right here.

It served its purpose earlier in the evening. But now it was just annoying, a wall between me, him, and that bulge he pushed hard between my legs.

Shit. I wanted to take him, all of him, and soon.

"Christ. You're really serious, aren't you?"

He looked at me, his eyes narrow. "Babe, you know it. Get in the fuckin' truck."

* * * *

Beautiful didn't begin to describe the cabin. It was decked out in rustic splendor with a full bar, a bear skin rug on the floor, and a grill on a tall deck reaching for the woods, overlooking a Smoky Mountain stream below.

All ours for the next week.

We put Alex down for a nap and let Bingo out into the fenced in area to catch the sweet breeze.

I leaned down to kiss the sleeping little boy, still marveling at the son we'd created. Joker came up behind me, pressed his big, thick hands around my waist, and squeezed.

Then my attention belonged to somebody else, and so did I.

"Come on, babe. Can't wait any fuckin' longer."

Smiling, I turned. His lips caught mine without waiting another second.

Instant pleasure. Explosive, sizzling, raw, and electric.

Somewhere in the middle of that kiss, I ran out of words to describe it. It overwhelmed me, and so did his hands, running up and down my body.

Growling, Joker pulled me in, hiking me up over his shoulder while I wrapped my hands around his neck.

We went straight to the bedroom. Before he threw me down on the bed, he grabbed my thigh, sinking his fingers in while our lips collided in yet another hungry kiss.

Fuck, this man. This body. This handsome, broken bastard I'd achingly put back together, piece by piece.

He probably didn't know it, but he'd done the same for me. Months ago, I'd lost everything. He'd given it back, more than I ever dared to imagine.

For now, he gave me something else. I hit the mattress hard, thanking my lucky stars it was comfortable.

"Careful, careful! This dress is just a rental and —"

Rrrrrrrip. When I turned my head, one strap was hanging, and the other came off. His crazy hands sank underneath the fabric and sheared me like a bear ripping curtains.

He looked up with a wicked smirk on his face. "Babe, I'm sitting pretty with the club getting richer and those fuckin' medical bills paid. I'd lay down a million right now to get you naked."

How the hell could I argue with that? The raw, greedy tingle in my pussy wouldn't let me think about it.

I kicked my legs, lifting my butt up in the air when he moved lower, taking away the tatters of my poor wedding dress. At least it would live on in the photographs, a thousand angles captured by the prospects.

"We shouldn't be too loud. Alex just went down a couple minutes ago and we've only got one wall between us. Joker, I –"

His hand went over my mouth. Slowly, he snaked his head up across my cleavage, pouring hot breath as he went, before his lips stopped next to my ear.

"Everything coming outta your mouth's mine tonight, baby girl. Nobody else's. You worry too fuckin' much. It's our wedding night."

As soon as his hand eased up, his lips were on me again. This time, I surrendered.

He was right. He was gorgeous. And Jesus, he tasted good.

My hands went around his neck, my fingernails gingerly catching the edge of his cut. He kissed me harder, growling into my mouth, overpowering the moan seeping out of me.

Pressing one hand between my legs, his fingers lifted underneath the waistband to my panties. He cupped my mound, squeezed, and I nearly lost it on the spot.

"Oh, God! Jackson!" I sputtered.

"Fuck, yeah. Give it up for me, Missus Taylor."

Holy shit. Missus Taylor.

Hearing him whisper my new last name through sheer lust lit my brain on fire.

The next couple minutes were a blur as he kissed me, teased my clit with his thumb, so long and hard I couldn't help but grind against it.

"Fuck my fingers. You get this tongue when I know you really want it."

"Yes," I moaned. "Please!"

"Not good enough, Summertime. Make. Me. Believe." His dense, hazel eyes drilled through mine. "I can't hear you, girl. I'm deaf, or you ain't begging hard enough."

Oh, hell.

I twisted against him, biting my lip when he pushed my hips back, every time I tried to buck back against him a little tighter. Snarling, he grabbed my hands, twisted them above my head, and pinned them down.

The delicious torture must've went on for at least a solid minute before I started to tremble, moaning all the way.

His lips covered mine. His tongue pushed through, taking mine, taking me over.

PROPERTY OF JOKER, my new tattoo said. I finally felt it, all the way down to my very soul, just kissing, teasing, and surrendering to the beast on top of me.

When he'd finally had enough, he stood up, lifting away my panties with a final jerk of his hand. "Stand up," he growled, taking my hands and placing them on him.

He moved my fingers, helping me undress him. Withering need coursed through me. I had to press my thighs together while he held me by the wrist, smiling as I helped him out of his cut, his shirt, and then his jeans.

Boxers went down. His cock sprang out in my hand. Angry, pulsing, and alive.

Two could play at this teasing game. I wrapped my fingers around it, barely edging the tip of his cock with my tongue.

"Fuck, yeah, yeah," he growled, looking down when he felt me stop. "What the fuck?"

"Make me believe you want it," I said, smiling sweetly. I kissed the head for good measure, my lips passing right across the stud in his swollen tip.

"Suck it, babe. I want my fuckin' wedding present, and I want it *now*. Not gonna ask again."

"No?" I said, keeping my lips away this time, blowing hot air across his swollen shaft. "Not even one more time?"

It twitched in my hand, tempting me so much, but still I held back. I loved it when he got mad.

Loved it, because it was a one way ticket to getting fucked twice as hard.

He lasted about five brutal seconds. Then Joker grabbed my hair, fisted it, and shoved my face down on his cock. I opened wide, taking every inch of him, pulling him along my tongue.

I moaned. I sucked. I worked his cock like my life depended on it, or at least my next orgasm.

His next few growls were pure satisfaction. His fingers tugged a little tighter as his pleasure built, twining my hair together in tiny knots.

Perfect, really. It mirrored everything I felt inside.

Every ache and need and want wrapped up in this man. My badass, my husband, my savior.

"Fucking shit," he swore, jamming my mouth down harder on his dick.

I sucked him better still, tasting the salty pre-come oozing out along my tongue. It always brought me a strange satisfaction, wherever it ended up inside me.

I doubted he'd let me take it down my throat, though. And I was right.

"No, no, fuck no," he said, jerking my face off him by the hair. "Stand up, Summertime. You know the rule."

"Do I?" I asked, taking his hands. He violently jerked me up, spun me around, and pushed me past the bed.

He didn't say anything until I was against the wall, his swollen cock against my ass cheeks, kissing at my neck. "Yeah, you fuckin' do," he growled, nipping at my sensitive skin. "Your mouth, your ass, your tits don't get my come 'til you're knocked up again. I'm spilling every drop I got in that hot little cunt, poundin' it straight to your womb. Alex needs a little bro, a little sis, maybe fuckin' triplets."

Fuck! I moaned loudly, enough to get his hand across my lips.

He moved it down when I'd stopped making noise, cupping my breast, sinking to his knees. His free hand pulled my pussy open from behind, stretching its lips, making way for his hungry tongue.

Oh, Joker. Oh, Jackson. Oh, shit, shit, shit.

My knees began trembling as soon as he started to lick. His tongue fucked me, straight up, edging along the most sensitive spots he'd be taking with his cock next.

He held me up, just enough so I could rest on his face, closing my eyes. I reached out behind me, clawing for his shoulders, losing it while I fell into total bliss.

He growled through his licks, pulling my clit into his mouth, strumming it with his tongue like never before.

Countdown.

Ignition.

Launch.

I went off like a rocket. *He* brought me off, so hot and intense and cataclysmic that I'd never come like that in my life.

I barely held in my screams. Joker wrapped his arms around my waist, holding me against his mouth, savaging me with ecstasy through the next few mind blowing minutes.

When it was over, I was still shaking, dripping on the floor. He licked and kissed softly at my inner thigh, rising up, bringing more kisses up my back.

When he was standing again, his hands tightened around my waist. Touching his hot, slick lips against my ear, he leaned in and whispered.

"I'm gonna fuck you now, babe. Gonna take your body the same fuckin' way I did that summer night, without even knowing it. Except this time we know exactly what we're working for," he growled, reaching for my clit again, and digging his knuckle in against it.

"Yes, please, please," I moaned. "Fuck me, Jackson. Give me another baby."

His throat rumbled more thunder as he brought the tip of his cock against my opening, rubbing it, but not yet slipping in.

"I'm fucking you ten times harder than the first time I knocked you up," he said, pausing to flatten harder kisses against my throat, pulling at my hair. "We're fuckin', night and day, and we ain't stopping 'til I see you stretch with my seed. We're fuckin', hard and slow, hot and cold, like demons and like lovers. Whatever the fuck it takes to make you mine again, inside and out. *Mine forever.*"

No more talk. I couldn't take another word, pushing my ass back against him, moaning and pleading all at once.

He must've lost it too. Lost his patience, straight in the stormy need to bury his cock in me.

Finally, he pushed into me, gliding up, deep inside my unprotected pussy.

I'd been off the pill for about two weeks before the big day.

We'd talked about it, and decided I should do this sooner, rather than later, before I got too far in work at the bar.

He'd given me a new life, here in Tennessee. He'd given me a ring. I'd give him a baby in return, deepening our bond, giving our son a new sibling to play with.

Family. That was everything now. He talked about it every week, and showed it whenever we visited his grandpa in the nursing home.

Today, he made me feel it in a different way. His hips pulled back slowly, like a gun cocking, before they crashed against mine again.

He filled me. Fucked me. Sped into me like a man feeding a furnace to stave off the cold, anything to build our future, stroke by growling stroke.

My pussy burned, ached, tightening around his cock. My whole body knew what was coming, nipples hard as diamonds.

I squealed two or three times before his hand clapped across my mouth. My teeth sank into his finger, hard and wild, before losing it in my first climax full of my husband's cock.

He fucked me harder, straight through the shuddering, the moaning, his free hand flicking furiously at my clit. My pussy tightened around his cock so hard I wasn't sure how he didn't lose it.

Every muscle in my body wanted to squeeze him, milk him, take him so fucking deep we lost ourselves in that wet, fiery, animal pleasure.

I was panting by the time I came out of it, sucking in desperate breaths. I'd need the oxygen, too, because he wasn't done.

Not even close.

Growling louder, he pushed me against the wall. Joker's hips moved, fucking me faster and harder than before.

Everything synchronized. Our thrusts, our pulses, even the sound of our ragged breath. We hadn't bothered to turn on the fan since we stepped inside, and it was shaping up to be a hot summer night.

Sweat poured off him in rivulets. My pores oozed more down my back. Our fluids mixed inside and out. I was a dripping mess with tangled hair, a far cry from the blushing bride I'd been just a few hours earlier, and damn if I cared.

Nothing else mattered except feeling him erupt this time, flooding me to the hilt.

"Come, you bastard," I said, arching my back, slamming my ass back against his body. "Come inside me, please!"

Yes, I even begged. Shamelessly.

This wasn't just some stranger, or even a rough bastard who'd swept my heart away. This was my husband, the man I'd sworn the rest of my life to.

I'd become his everything, and he'd become mine.

His wife. His mate. His pussy. His whore.

His.

Irrevocably. Completely. Until the end of time.

"Fuck," Joker growled, thrusting harder still. "Here it comes, woman – here it fuckin' comes! Take it."

And I did.

He pinned me against the wall, sucking the soft spot between my neck and my shoulder. His cock stabbed into me, swelled, and exploded.

Hot, thick ropes of sperm swept into me. Our bodies jerked and thrashed, coming together, so intense it was blinding.

My pussy sucked greedily at his cock, taking it deep, absorbing everything he'd given.

Every muscle in his body twitched against my skin. He tightened, turned to stone, pouring himself into me, forcing my spasms to mimic his.

We came together in every sense of the word.

We came breathless. Beautiful.

When the storm in my body relented, I flattened my hands against the wall, purring as he kissed me tenderly across the spot he'd bit. I'd probably have a hickey on steroids there tomorrow, but I actually liked it.

My head turned. We kissed again, softer than before.

Joker swept in so close his eye lashes brushed against mine, connecting foreheads.

"I love you," I whispered, feeling him slip out of me. My legs automatically pushed together, the better to hold his seed in me. "God, Jackson, I really do. I never thought I could love anyone this much."

"Bullshit," he said, taking my chin in his fingers. Gently, he tilted my face. "Look at me, babe."

I did. Our eyes caught the new moonlight coming in from the windows. He held my gaze while he stepped away, pulling the two robes hanging next to us off their hooks.

"You knew, all those years ago. We both did. I knew there was a helluva lot more than just another fuck the second I put my lips on yours the first time, underneath those stars. Remember?"

I smiled. Of course I did.

I surrendered, let him take me back to what felt like a million years ago after everything we'd been through.

But I remembered it like yesterday. Very slowly, I nodded.

He wasn't wrong.

The way my heart beat for him – that hadn't changed. God help me, I loved him, through all the hate, the sadness, the agony, and the loneliness.

Knowing he'd come back someday was all I had to hang on during the early years with Alex. I'd just *known,* in some crazy sixth sense I couldn't describe.

I'd known in the bad times, too. I'd kept the faith we'd wind up here when Hatch was threatening to kill me with my son, when all I'd wanted was for him to keep breathing, busted up in that bed, after he'd destroyed the men threatening us.

"You're right," I said, turning so he could tuck the purple robe in over my arms.

"Fuck yeah, babe, always am." He grinned, throwing on his own robe. It matched, except it was bigger, and completely black.

He took my hand, and we walked out onto that deck, eyeing the sunset as Bingo snoozed at the bottom of the gated steps below. The big dog looked up, barked once, and happily wagged his tail.

I laughed. Joke took my hand, raised it to his mouth, kissing me again.

His mouth moved slowly. Tenderly. I almost thought I'd stepped back in time and married a country gentleman, rather than an outlaw biker.

"You're so sweet today," I said, cocking my head. "What's gotten into you?"

He lowered my hand, turned it, and thumbed that heavy ring on my finger. He wasn't kidding about the diamond – the one he'd gotten was *huge.*

"You. This," he said quietly, stepping closer, into another embrace. "You're my wife, babe. Mine tonight, mine tomorrow, mine for fuckin' ever. Don't tell me you're complaining about a little honey. It's never been about nothing besides dirty, wild fuckin' between us, even though that's all I think about when I see your sweet ass naked. We've got more. We've got everything. We always did,

Summertime, and we always will. Mark my fuckin' words."

He turned me around, pressed in behind me, and wrapped a possessive arm around my waist. "Okay, Joker, I will. You tempt me, and I'll hold you to it."

"Shit, yeah, you will. You're a spitfire, woman. That's half the reason I married you, half the reason I'm whispering shit I'd never say to anybody else, in between puttin' another kid in you." Smiling, he pushed the top of my robe aside, kissing at my neck.

Out here, in the cool summer night, it tingled when his stubble brushed my skin. Hell, everything did.

"Yeah? Just half of it? What's the rest?" I asked, flashing him a mischievous smile.

"You make my heart pound straight into my dick like nobody else. Like nobody fuckin' ever. That's all you, baby, all I'm gonna fuck 'til I go back to the wind as ashes. All I want my mouth and hands and cock all over. All I'll ever need from now to kingdom come."

"Mmm," I purred, running my fingers through his short, dark hair while he kissed at my neck again. "Show me some more of that forever in case Alex interrupts us for a bedtime story, hubby."

"Yeah, I will," he growled, spinning me around and tearing down my robe, leaving us both naked in the soft night. "I'll show you, Summertime. Pound you so damned hard it'll leave your ears ringing. You'll be lucky to hear me say anything about lovin' you, but you'll know, baby girl. You'll know."

I did.

He did, too.

We lived our wedding night knowing every sweet, soft angle of our love. Just like every night that came after.

Every night we had together as man and woman, outlaw and wife.

Thanks!

Want more Nicole Snow? Sign up for my newsletter to hear about new releases, subscriber only goodies, and other fun stuff!

JOIN THE NICOLE SNOW NEWSLETTER! - http://eepurl.com/HwFW1

Thank you so much for buying this book. I hope my romances will brighten your mornings and darken your evenings with total pleasure. Sensuality makes everything more vivid, doesn't it?

If you liked this book, please consider leaving a review and checking out my other erotic romance tales.

Got a comment on my work? Email me at nicolesnowerotica@gmail.com. I love hearing from my fans!

Kisses,
Nicole Snow

More Erotic Romance
by Nicole Snow

FIGHT FOR HER HEART

BIG BAD DARE: TATTOOS AND SUBMISSION

MERCILESS LOVE: A DARK ROMANCE

LOVE SCARS: BAD BOY'S BRIDE

RECKLESSLY HIS: A BAD BOY MAFIA ROMANCE

STEPBROTHER CHARMING: A BILLIONAIRE BAD
BOY ROMANCE

STEPBROTHER UNSEALED: A BAD BOY
MILITARY ROMANCE

Outlaw Love/Prairie Devils MC Books

OUTLAW KIND OF LOVE

NOMAD KIND OF LOVE

SAVAGE KIND OF LOVE

WICKED KIND OF LOVE

BITTER KIND OF LOVE

Grizzlies MC Books

OUTLAW'S KISS

OUTLAW'S OBSESSION

OUTLAW'S BRIDE

OUTLAW'S VOW

Deadly Pistols MC Books

NEVER LOVE AN OUTLAW

NEVER KISS AN OUTLAW

NEVER HAVE AN OUTLAW'S BABY

SEXY SAMPLES: OUTLAW'S KISS

I: Cursed Bones (Missy)

"It won't be long now," the nurse said, checking dad's IV bag. "Breathing getting shallower…pulse is slowing…don't worry, girls. He won't feel a thing. That's what the morphine's for."

I had to squeeze his hand to make sure he wasn't dead yet. Jesus, he was so cold. I swore there was a ten degree difference between dad's fingers in one hand, and my little sister's in the other. I blinked back tears, trying to be brave for Jackie, who watched helplessly, trembling and shaking at my side.

We'd already said our goodbyes. We'd been doing that for the last hour, right before he slipped into unconsciousness for what I guessed was the last time.

I turned to my sister. "It'll be okay. He's going to a better place. No more suffering. The cancer, all the pain…it dies with him. Dad's finally getting better."

"Missy…" Jackie squeaked, ripping her hand away from me and covering her face.

The nurse gave me a sympathetic look. It took so much effort to push down the lump in my throat without cracking up. I choked on my grief, holding it in, cold and sharp as death looming large.

I threw an arm around my sister, pulling her close. Lying like this was a bitch.

I wasn't really sure what I believed anymore, but I had to say something. Jackie was the one who needed all my support now. Dad's long, painful dying days were about to be over.

Not that it made anything easy. But I was grown up, and I could handle it. Losing him at twenty-one was hard, but if I was fourteen, like the small trembling girl next to me?

"Melissa." Thin, weak fingers tightened on my wrist with surprising strength.

I jumped, drawing my arm off Jackie, looking at the sick man in the bed. His eyes were wide open and his lips were moving. The sickly sheen on his forehead glowed, one last light before it burned out forever.

"Daddy? What is it?" I leaned in close, wondering if I'd imagined him saying my name.

"Forgive me," he hissed. "I...I fucked up bad. But I did it for a good reason. I just wish I could've done it different, baby..."

His eyelids fluttered. I squeezed his fingers as tight as I could, moving closer to his gray lips. What the hell was he saying? Was this about Mom again?

She'd been gone for ten years in a car accident, waiting for him on the other side. "Daddy? Hey!"

I grabbed his bony shoulder and gently shook him. He was still there, fighting the black wave pulling him lower, insistent and overpowering.

"It's the only way...I couldn't do it with hard work. Honest work. That never paid shit." He blinked, running his tongue over his lips. "Just look in the basement, baby.

There's a palate…roofing tiles. Everything I ever wanted to leave my girls is there. It was worth it…I promised her I'd do anything for you and Jackie…and I did. I did it, Carol. Our girls are set. I'm ready to burn if I need to…"

Hearing him say mom's name, and then talk about burning? I blinked back tears and shook my head.

What the hell was this? Some kinda death fever making him talk nonsense?

Dad started to slump into the mattress, a harsh rattle in his throat, the tiny splash of color left in his face becoming pale ash. I backed away as the machines howled. The nurse looked at me and nodded. She rushed to his free side, intently watching his heartbeat jerk on the monitor.

The machine released an earsplitting wail as the line went flat.

Jackie completely lost it. I grabbed her tight, holding onto her, turning away until the mechanical screaming stopped. I wanted to cover my ears, but I wanted hers closed more.

I held my little sister and rocked her to my chest. We didn't move until the nurse finally touched my shoulder, nudging us into the waiting room outside.

We sat and waited for all the official business of death to finish up. My brain couldn't stop going back to his last words, the best distraction I had to keep my sanity.

What was he talking about? His last words sounded so strange, so sure. So repentant, and that truly frightened me.

I didn't dare get my hopes up, as much as I wanted to believe we wouldn't lose everything and end up living in the car next week. The medical bills snatched up the last few pennies left over from his pension and disability – the same fate waiting for our house as soon as his funeral was done.

Delirious, I thought. *His dying wish was for us, hoping and praying we'd be okay. He went out selflessly, just like a good father should.*

That was it. Had to be.

He was dying, after all…pumped full of drugs, driven crazy in his last moments. But I couldn't let go of what he said about the basement.

We'd have to scour the house anyway before the state kicked us out. If there was anything more to his words besides crazy talk, we'd find out soon enough, right?

I looked at Jackie, biting my lip. I tried not to hope off a dead man's words. But damn it, I did.

If he'd tucked away some spare cash or some silver to pawn, I wouldn't turn it down. Anything would help us live another day without facing the gaping void left by his brutal end.

My sister was tipped back in her chair, one tissue pressed tight to her eyes. I reached for her hand and squeezed, careful not to set her off all over again.

"We're going to figure this out," I promised. "Don't worry about anything except mourning him, Jackie. You're not going anywhere. I'm going to do my damnedest to find us a place and pay the bills while you stay in school."

She straightened up, clearing her throat, shooting me a nasty look. "Stop talking to me like I'm a stupid kid!"

I blinked. Jackie leaned in, showing me her bloodshot

eyes. "I'm not as old as you, sis, but I'm not retarded. We're out of money. I get that. I know you won't find a job in this shitty town with half a degree and no experience…we'll end up homeless, and then the state'll get involved. They'll take me away from you, stick me with some freaky foster parents. But I won't forget you, Missy. I'll be okay. I'll survive."

Rage shot through me. Rage against the world, myself, maybe even dad's ghost for putting us in this fucked up position.

I clenched my jaw. "That's *not* going to happen, Jackie. Don't even go there. I won't let –"

"Whatever. It's not like it matters. I just hope there's a way for us to keep in touch when the hammer falls." She was quiet for a couple minutes before she finally looked up, her eyes redder than before. "I heard what he said while I was crying. Daddy didn't have crap after he got sick and left the force – nothing but those measly checks. He didn't earn a dime while he was sick. He died the same way he lived, Missy – sorry, and completely full of shit."

Anger howled through me. I wanted to grab her, shake her, tell her to get a fucking grip and stop obsessing on disaster. But I knew she didn't mean it.

Lashing out wouldn't do any good. Rage was all part of grief, wasn't it? I kept waiting for mine to bubble to the surface, toxic as the crap they'd pumped into our father to prolong his life by a few weeks towards the end.

I settled back in my chair and closed my eyes. I'd find some way to keep my promise to Jackie, whether there was a lucky break waiting for us in the basement or just more junk, more wreckage from our lives.

Daddy wasn't ready to be a single father when Mom got killed, but he'd managed. He did the best he could before he had to deal with the shit hand dealt to him by this merciless life. I closed my eyes, vowing I'd do the same.

No demons waiting for us on the road ahead would stop me. Making sure neither of us died with dad was my new religion, and I swore I'd never, ever lose my faith.

* * * *

A week passed. A lonely, bitter week in late winter with a meager funeral. Daddy's estranged brother sent us some money to have him cremated and buried with a bare bones headstone.

I wouldn't ask Uncle Ken for a nickel more, even if he'd been man enough to show his face at the funeral. Thankfully, it wasn't something to worry about. He kept his distance several states away, the same 'ostrich asshole' daddy always said he was since they'd fallen out over my grandparent's miniscule inheritance.

All it did was confirm the whole family was fucked. I had no one now except Jackie, and it was her and I against the world, the last of the Thomas girls against the curse turning our lives to pure hell over the last decade.

A short trip to the attorney's office told me what I already knew about dad's assets. What little he had was going into state hands. Medicare was determined to claw back a tiny fraction of what they'd spent on his care. And because I was now Jackie's legal guardian, his pension and disability was as good as buried with him.

The older lawyer asked me if I'd made arrangements with extended family, almost as an afterthought. Of course I had, I lied. I made sure to straighten up and smile real big when I said it.

I was a responsible adult. I could make money sprout from weeds. What did the truth matter in a world that wasn't wired to give us an ounce of help?

Whatever shit was waiting for us up ahead needed to be fed, nourished with lies if I wanted to keep it from burying us. I was ready for that, ready to throw on as many fake smiles and twisted truths as I needed to keep Jackie safe and happy.

Whatever wiggle room we'd had for innocent mistakes slammed shut the instant daddy's heart stopped in the sharp white room.

I was so busy dealing with sadness and red tape that I'd nearly forgotten about his last words. Finishing up his affairs and making sure Jackie still got some sleep and decent food in her belly took all week, stealing away the meager energy I had left.

It was late one night after she'd gone to bed when I finally remembered. It hit me while I was watching a bad spy movie on late night TV, halfway paying attention to the story as my stomach twisted in knots, steeling itself for the frantic job hunt I had to start tomorrow.

I got up from my chair and padded over to the basement door. Dust teased my nose, dead little flecks suspended in the dim light. The basement stank like mildew, tinged with rubbing alcohol and all the spare medicine we'd stored down here while dad suffered at home.

I held my breath descending the stairs, knowing it would only get worse when I finally had to inhale. Our small basement was dark and creepy as any. I looked around, trying not to fixate on his old work bench. Seeing the old husks of half-finished RC planes he used to build in better times would definitely bring tears.

Roofing tiles, he'd said. Okay, but where?

It took more than a minute just scanning back and forth before I noticed the big blue tarp. It was wedged in the narrow slit between the furnace and the hot water tank.

My heart ticked faster. So, he wasn't totally delusional on his death bed. There really were roofing tiles there – and what else?

It was even stranger because the thing hadn't been here when I was down in the basement last week – and daddy had been in hospice for three weeks. He couldn't have crawled back and hidden the unknown package here. Jackie definitely couldn't have done it and kept her mouth shut.

That left one disturbing possibility – someone had broken into our house and left it here.

Ice ran through my veins. I shook off wild thoughts about intruders, kneeling down next to the blue plastic and running my hands over it.

Yup, it felt like a roofing palate. Not that I'd handled many to know, but whatever was beneath it was jagged, sandy, and square.

Screw it. Let's see what's really in here, I thought.

Clenching my teeth, I dragged the stack out. It was lighter than I expected, and it didn't take long to find the ropey ties holding it together. One pull and it came off easy. A thick slab of shingles slid out and thudded on the beaten concrete, kicking up more dust lodged in the utilities.

I covered my mouth and coughed. Disappointment settled in my stomach, heavy as the construction crap in front of me. I prepared myself for a big fat nothing hidden in the cracks.

"Damn it," I whispered, shaking my head. My hands dove for the shingles and started to tug, desperate to get this shit over with and say goodbye to the last hope humming in my stomach.

The shingles didn't come up easy. Planting my feet on both sides and tugging didn't pull the stack apart like I expected. Grunting, I pulled harder, taking my rage and frustration out on this joke at my feet.

There was a ripping sound much different than I expected. I tumbled backward and hit the dryer, looking at the square block in my hands. When I turned it over, I saw the back was a mess of glue and cardboard.

Hope beat in my chest again, however faint. This was no ordinary stack of shingles. My arms were shaking as I dropped the flap and walked back to the pile, looking down at the torn cardboard center hidden by the layer I'd peeled off. Someone went through some serious trouble camouflaging the box underneath.

I walked to dad's old bench for a box cutter, too stunned

with the weird discovery to dwell on his mementos. The blade went in and tore through in a neat slice. I quickly carved out an opening, totally unprepared for the thick leafy pile that came falling out.

My jaw dropped along with the box cutter. I hit the ground, resting my knees on the piles of cash, and tore into the rest of the box.

Hundreds – no, thousands – came out in huge piles. I tore through the package and turned it upside down, showering myself in more cash than I'd seen in my life, hundreds bound together in crisp rolls with red rubber bands.

Had to cover my mouth to stifle the insane laughter tearing at my lungs. I couldn't let Jackie hear me and come running downstairs. If I was all alone, I would've laughed like a psycho, mad with the unexpected light streaking to life in our darkness.

Jesus, I barely knew how to handle the mystery fortune myself, let alone involve my little sis. I collapsed on the floor, feeling hot tears running down my cheeks. The stupid grin pulling at my face lingered.

Somehow, someway, he'd done it. Daddy had really done it.

He'd left us everything we'd need to survive. Hell, all we'd need to *thrive*. Feeling the cool million crunching underneath my jeans like leaves proved it.

"Shit!" I swore, realizing I was rolling around in the money like a demented celebrity.

Panicking, I kicked my legs, careful to check every nook

around me for anything I'd kicked away in shock. When I saw it was all there, I grabbed an old laundry basket and started piling the stacks in it. I pulled one out and took off the rubber band. Rifling my fingers through several fistfuls of cash told me everything was separated in neat bundles of twenty-five hundred dollars.

I piled them in, feverishly counting. I had to stop around the half million mark. There was at least double that on the floor. Eventually, I'd settle down and inventory it to the dime, but for now I was looking at somewhere between one to two million, easy.

It was magnitudes greater than anything this family had seen in its best years, before everything went to shit. I smoothed my fingers over my face, loving the unmistakable money scent clinging to my hands.

No shock – sweet freedom smelled exactly like cold hard cash.

An hour later, I'd stuffed it into an old black suitcase, something discreet I could keep with me. My stomach gurgled. One burden lifted, and another one landed on my shoulders.

I wasn't stupid. I'd heard plenty about what daddy did for the Redding PD's investigations to know spending too much mystery money at once brought serious consequences. Wherever this money came from, it sure as hell wasn't clean.

I'd have to keep one eye glued to the cash for...months? Years?

Shit. Grim responsibility burned in my brain, and it

made my bones hurt like they were locked in quicksand. Dirty money wasn't easy to spend.

I'd have to risk a few bigger chunks up front on groceries, a tune-up for our ancient Ford LTD, and then a down payment on a new place for Jackie and I.

It wouldn't buy us a luxury condo – not if we wanted to save ourselves a Federal investigation. But this cash was plenty to make a greedy landlord's eyes light up and take a few months' worth of rent without any uncomfortable questions. It was more than enough to give us food plus a roof over our heads while I figured out the rest.

Survival was still the name of the game, even if it had gotten unexpectedly easier.

Once our needs were secure, then I could figure out the rest. Maybe I'd find a way to finagle my way back into school so I could finish the accounting program I'd been forced to drop when dad's cancer went terminal.

It felt like hours passed while I finished filling up the suitcase and triple checked the basement for runaway money. When I was finally satisfied I'd secured everything, I grabbed the suitcases and marched upstairs, turning out the light behind me. I switched off the TV and headed straight for bed.

I sighed, knowing I was in for a long, restless night, even with the miracle cash safe beneath my bed. Or maybe because of it.

I couldn't tell if my heart or my head was more drained. They'd both been absolutely ripped out and shot to the moon these past two weeks.

I closed my eyes and tried to sleep. Tomorrow, I'd be hunting for a brand new place instead of a job while Jackie caught up on schoolwork. That happy fact alone should've made it easier to sleep.

But nothing about this was simple or joyful. It wasn't a lottery win.

Dwelling on the gaping canyon left in our lives by both our dead parents was a constant brutal temptation, especially when it was dark, cold, and quiet. So was avoiding the question that kept boiling in my head – how had he gotten it?

What the *fuck* had daddy done to make this much money from nothing? Life insurance payouts and stock dividends didn't get dropped off in mysterious packages downstairs.

He'd asked for forgiveness before his body gave out. My lips trembled and I pinched my eyes shut, praying he hadn't done something terrible – not directly, anyway. He was too sick for too long to kill anyone. He'd been off the force for a few years too.

I lost minutes – maybe hours – thinking about how he'd earned the dirty little secret underneath my bed. Whatever he'd done, it was bad. But at the end of the day, how much did I care?

And no matter how much blood the cash was soaked in, we needed it. I wasn't about to latch onto fantasy ethics and flush his dying legacy down the toilet. Blood money or not, we *needed* it. No fucking way was I going to burn the one thing that would keep us fed, clothed, sheltered, and sane.

Jackie never had to know where our miracle came from. Neither did I. Maybe years from now I'd have time for soul searching, time to worry about what kind of sick sins I'd branded onto my conscience by profiting off this freak inheritance.

Fretting about murder and corruption right now wouldn't keep the state from taking Jackie away when we were homeless. I had to keep my mouth shut and my mind more closed than ever. I had to treat it like a lottery win I could never tell anyone about.

Besides, it was all just temporary. I'd use the fortune to pay the rent and put food in our fridge until I finished school and got myself a job. Then I'd slowly feed the rest into something useful for Jackie's college – something that wouldn't get us busted.

It must've been after three o'clock when I finally fell asleep. If only I had a crystal ball, or stayed awake just an hour or two longer.

I would've seen the hurricane coming, the pitch black storm that always comes in when a girl takes the hand the devil's offered.

* * * *

An earsplitting scream woke me first, but it was really the door slamming a second later that convinced me I wasn't dreaming.

Jackie!

I threw my blanket off and sat up, reaching for my

phone on the nightstand. My hand slid across the smooth wood, and adrenaline dumped in my blood when I realized there was nothing there.

Too dark. I didn't realize the stranger was standing right over me until I tried to bolt up, slamming into his vice-like grip instead. Before I could even scream, his hand was over my mouth. Scratchy stubble prickled my cheek as his lips parted against my ear.

"Don't. You fucking scream, I'll have to put a bullet in your spine." Cold metal pushed up beneath my shirt, a gun barrel, proof he wasn't making an empty threat.

Not that I'd have doubted it. His tight, sinister embrace stayed locked around my waist as he turned me around and nudged his legs against mine, forcing me to move toward the hall.

"Just go where I tell you, and this'll all be over nice and quick. Nobody has to get hurt."

I listened. When we got to the basement door, he flung it open and lightened his grip, knowing it was a one way trip downstairs with no hope for escape.

Jackie was already down there against the wall, and so were four more large, brutal men like the one who'd held me. I blinked when I got to the foot of the stairs and took in the bizarre scene. They all wore matching leather vests with GRIZZLIES MC, CALIFORNIA emblazoned up their sides and on their backs.

I'd seen bikers traveling the roads for years, but never anything like these guys. Their jackets looked a lot like the ones veterans wore when they went out riding, but the symbols were all different. Bloody, strange, and very dangerous looking.

The men themselves matched the snarling bears on their leather. Four of them were younger, tattooed, spanning the spectrum from lean and wiry to pure muscle. The guy who'd walked me down the stairs moved where I could see him. He might've been the youngest, but I wasn't really sure.

Scary didn't begin to describe him. He looked at me with his arms folded, piercing green eyes going right through my soul, set in a stern cold face. He exuded a strength and severity that only came naturally – a born badass. A predator completely fixed on me.

An older man with long gray hair seemed to be in charge. He looked at the man holding my sister, another hard faced man with barbed wire ropes tattooed across his face. Jackie's eyes were bulging, shimmering like wide, frantic pools, pulling me in.

I'm sorry, I hissed in my head, breaking eye contact. One more second and I might've lost it. The only thing worse than being down here at their mercy was showing them I was already weak, broken, helpless.

They had my little sister, my whole world, everything I'd sworn to protect. No, this wasn't the time to freak out and cry. I had to keep it together if we were going to get out of this alive.

"Well? Any sign of the haul upstairs, or do we need to make these bitches sing?" Gray hair reached into his pocket, retrieving a cigarette and a lighter, as casually as if he was at work on a smoke break.

Shit, for all I knew, he probably was.

"Nothing up there, Blackjack." The man who'd taken me downstairs stepped forward, leaving the basement echoing with his smoky voice, older and more commanding than I'd expected. It hadn't just been the rough whisper flowing into my ear.

"Fuck," the psycho holding Jackie growled. "I like it the fun way, but I'm not a fan when these bitches scream. Makes my ears ring for days. Can't we gag these cunts first?"

Nobody answered him. The older man narrowed his eyes, looking at his goon, taking a long pull on the cigarette. My head was spinning, making it feel like the ground had softened up, ready to suck me under and bury me alive.

Oh, God. I knew this had to be about the mystery money the moment those rough hands went around me, but I hadn't really thought we were about to die until he said that.

Gray hair turned to face me, scowling. "You heard the man, love. We can do this the easy way or the hard way. I, for one, don't like spilling blood when there's no good reason, but some of the brothers feel differently. Now, we know your loot's not where it was supposed to be – found this shit all torn up myself."

Blowing his smoke, he pointed at the mess on the ground. I could've choked myself for being too stupid to clean up the mess earlier.

"You've got it somewhere. It couldn't have gotten far," he said, striding forward. "Look we both know me and my boys are gonna find it. Only question left is – are you gonna make this scavenger hunt easy-peasy-punkin-squeezy? Or are you gonna make all our fucking ears ring while we choke it out of you?"

I didn't answer. My eyes floated above his shoulder, fixing on the man across from me, stoic green eyes.

"Well?" The older asshole was getting impatient.

Strange. If Green Eyes wasn't so busy hanging out with these creeps and taking hostages, he would've been handsome. No, downright sexy was a better word.

My weeping, broken brain was still fixed on the stupid idea when Gray Hair grunted, pulled the light out of his mouth, and reached for my throat...

Look for *Outlaw's Kiss* at your favorite retailer!